through
indigo's
eyes

through indigo's eyes

TARA TAYLOR &
LORNA SCHULTZ NICHOLSON

VISIONS

HAY HOUSE, INC.
Carlsbad, California • New York City
London • Sydney • Johannesburg
Vancouver • Hong Kong • New Delhi

Library of Congress Control Number: 2012939086

Tradepaper ISBN: 978-1-4019-3528-3
Digital ISBN: 978-1-4019-3529-0

15 14 13 12   4 3 2 1
1st edition, July 2012
Printed in the United States of America

Part One

Chapter One

September 1997

My mind went blank.

I could see nothing but white.

No, please, no. Not again.

The guitar pick I held in my hand dropped to the floor, and I couldn't move to pick it up. My body was frozen. My father's old guitar, sitting in my lap, felt heavy and cold, like someone had suddenly placed a block of ice in my lap.

That is, until the spinning began. It usually happened right after my mind went blank and the cold set in. It was almost as if I were on a Ferris wheel at the fair and I couldn't get off, even though I wanted to.

I don't want to see. I don't want this. What if it's bad?

Spinning. Spinning. I kept spinning.

I squeezed my eyes shut until I was sure my face was creased like my favorite shirt when it had been in the drier for too long. I tried to breathe deeply, down into my stomach, to make it not happen. But there was no halting it or even

1

slowing it down, and the swirling sucked me into a deep vortex, a tunnel. I had no control.

Sliding.

Down a long tube.

Until, suddenly, I stopped. This was it—the place I didn't want to be, the place I had tried to avoid. Through no wish of my own, I was forced to look through a telescopic lens into a fishbowl—only I wasn't seeing fish.

No. I'm not seeing pretty fish at all.

I was having a vision.

Two people were in my lens: a boy and a girl. Burke Brown, the star hockey player in my high school, who was dating my best friend, Lacey. I couldn't tell who the girl was. Not Lacey. Burke grinned as he wrapped his arms around her. The girl's back was to me, though she looked familiar, and I knew she was someone from our class. She wore a tight, black, short skirt and an equally tight, turquoise T-shirt, both of which accentuated her curves.

Burke tilted his face down, and the girl stood on her tiptoes, reaching up and putting her arms around his neck, her T-shirt pulling away from her skirt to show bare skin and a small butterfly tattoo etched into the curve of her back. Their lips met; they kissed, long and hard, the heat between them igniting the air, creating sizzling sparks that I could actually see above their heads. The noise of the sparks crackled. I was watching and listening in 3-D.

I felt like a voyeur. This wasn't for me to see.

Only I am seeing it.

I wanted to turn away, but I had nowhere to turn. From past experience, I knew my visions had 360-degree powers.

The kiss ended, and the girl slowly pivoted and gazed in my direction with droopy, sexy eyelids, lipstick smeared across her face. *Oh, gawd.* It couldn't be. But it was.

Amber McKinnon.

Lacey's worst enemy.

The vision dissolved. I was back to blank for a second. Then, like the snap of a finger, I was once again in my purple-painted bedroom with the black furniture, my guitar nestled comfortably on my lap. The cold was gone. The white was gone. But the vision was carved in my brain. I buried my head in my hands as my body trembled and shook. A massive headache launched itself in my frontal lobe, and I pressed my fingers to my forehead, rubbing frantically, trying to make it go away.

At least you didn't see anyone die.

"Shut up!" I had this mean female inner voice that talked to me all the time. And then I had this soothing man's voice that also came to me. They were totally opposite and made me think I was going crazy.

"I never see people die, stupid. I only see *hints*."

I threw a pillow across the room, hitting my vintage Jim Morrison poster, the magenta and white psychedelic one where he looked as if he had wings growing out of his back. I loved the Doors, even though I knew no one else my age listened to them. Morrison's poetry just spoke to me, and sometimes it calmed me.

"Meow." Cedar, my black cat, sat up, licked her paws, and stretched as only a cat can, with her back arched and her tail spiked. Then she looked at me with wary eyes.

"I'm sorry," I whispered, scratching her behind the ears. "I didn't mean to scare you. Don't leave me alone, okay?"

As if she understood, Cedar gracefully walked in a circle before she lowered her body and curled into a ball, purring loudly. I petted her soft back. I wished I could forget things as easily as Cedar could and let my emotions fade in one purr. I slipped the guitar over my head and stuck it under my bed. Alone in my bedroom, I liked to strum out songs that I tried to write. The ones I made up to make me feel . . . make me feel what? Part of the world.

Or outside the world?

Face it, Indie, you will always be on the outside.

"Don't," I whispered. "Don't talk to me. I just want to be a normal seventeen-year-old. I want this all to go away so I can have a boyfriend."

Indie, this is not a bad thing.

This time the voice was the soft whisper of the kind man. I had no idea who he was or why he spoke to me, but he always tried to soothe me. He was nice. But today I didn't feel like being nice back.

"Yes. It. Is. It's awful."

Sometimes one must accept—

"Go away! You leave me alone, too."

I put my hands to my ears and rocked back and forth, my bed creaking underneath me. "Lalalala."

I kept rocking. I was always going to be on the outside because I had visions, visions that came true. And I'd been having them since I was little. When they first started, I was naïve enough to think that everyone around me also saw and heard things. I didn't know that other people weren't like me. Like that time with my friend Anna.

❖ ❖ ❖

I had been nine, and I was with Anna at church. We were dressed in pretty dresses, and we sat on the hard wooden church pews, our legs dangling below us, not quite touching the kneeling bench. I glanced around at all the people and the rainbow of colors above their heads as the minister talked on and on. I was supposed to be listening, but all I could see were the bright colors and . . . the pink and red hamster cage in my room. Suddenly my stomach felt sick. Was something wrong with my hamster, Teresa? Sadness swept over me and covered me like a heavy, scratchy blanket. My mom and I had gone to the pet store and bought the pretty cage to match my Strawberry Shortcake covers. And I'd picked Teresa because I liked that she was gray and brown, instead of just brown. I fidgeted until the minister stopped talking and we were excused. On the way out of church, I whispered to Anna, "Something is wrong with Teresa."

When we got home, I ran to my room and stopped as soon as I saw her lying frozen stiff in her cage.

Anna screamed. Then she turned to me and asked, "What did you do to her?"

4

"Nothing." My voice was quiet. Looking back, I now realize how calm my voice sounded. Unlike Anna, I didn't seem surprised at all.

"You're scary! I want to go home."

My eyes pricked with tears. Did she really think I was scary? Why did she think that?

✧ ✧ ✧

I stopped rocking and looked at the ceiling. "Why *am* I like this?" I was no longer a kid, but the same things still happened to me.

"Why did I have to see Burke with Amber? Why?" I yelled. Then I looked down and spoke softly. "I'd rather see a dead hamster."

I flopped back on my bed and stared at the ceiling again. *Was* Burke messing around on Lacey? *Please, be wrong.*

But I knew the vision would be true.

If only *this* vision wouldn't come true. Just this once, could I get lucky and not have it come true?

I got up, went to my dresser, and pulled out a sketch pad. I flipped it open to the page where I had doodled *Lacey Hughes and Burke Brown* together in black scrolling letters inside a big flaming red heart. Little peach-colored cherubs and sparkling silver and gold stars made with a special glitter pen surrounded the drawing. This handiwork had been done at the start of grade nine.

When Lacey and I started high school, each of us picked a guy to like, and she had picked Burke. We had sat cross-legged on the floor of her bedroom, with paper, scissors, colored markers, pencil crayons, and glitter sticks scattered happily and haphazardly around us, like we were back in elementary school. That was the last time we had done crafts, as we called it, and we promised not to tell anyone because we had just started our high school journey and needed to act mature. We'd giggled as we sketched the hearts, dreaming of the day when we would have boyfriends. Lacey and I had been friends since kindergarten. We were five; she had brunette hair, and

5

mine was blonde. She was tall; I was short. She was outgoing, and I was what teachers called "shy."

"Burke!" I exclaimed that day. "Lacey, he's the hottest guy in school."

"Might as well dream big," she'd replied, as she haughtily lifted her chin, having drawn a heart around his name.

Then she grinned, and suddenly my brain had felt like a computer downloading information. My eyes glazed over, my mind went blank, and I blurted out, "Red. You'll wear a red shirt the day he asks you out."

"Oh my god," she'd squealed. "It's going to come true! You've seen it." Then she'd smiled and wiggled her eyebrows up and down. "Red checked shirt? Red turtleneck? Or maybe . . . red sexy tank?" She did a little dance with her shoulders.

I heard the word *tank* in my head. I grinned. "Red tank, 'cause it'll be spring."

Then I had jumped up, and pretending to hold a microphone in my hand, I started belting out, "There goes *her* baby! And his name is Burke!"

Lacey rolled onto her side, laughing hysterically. "You crack me up."

I kept singing and dancing around the room. Lacey kept laughing.

Then she jumped up, made her fist into a microphone, and started to sing along with me. After a few minutes of off-key screeching, we both fell onto her bed in a fit of giggles. Lacey was my only friend who knew about my visions, and she accepted them as a part of me. I loved her for that.

As we lay on her bed, side by side, our shoulders touching, staring at her stucco ceiling, she asked, "Is he really going to ask me out?"

"Yup," I said with conviction. "He sure is."

Blond, muscular, and a stud hockey player, Burke was every girl's dream. He played center on his hockey team, and his photo was always somewhere on the *Ottawa Citizen*'s sports page after one of his games. He walked with a swagger, wore a hockey jacket, and was the star of his OHL Major Junior Team. In my city, and especially in my high school, hockey boys got perks. Dressed in his gear, leaning on his stick, looking serious and tough, his photo was also displayed in every Royal Bank in the city.

In the spring of grade 11, he finally asked Lacey out. Sure enough, that day she'd worn a red sexy tank top. It had taken Lacey almost two school years of dressing like everyone else, wearing the same makeup, doing her hair just right, and attending the "in" parties to get Burke to notice her. She'd also honed her skills as the star setter on the volleyball team. The combination of style and athletics made her one of the most popular girls in the school, and now they were a total power couple.

Today, many months later and after a full summer of romance, what was I to do with this vision? Tell her and ruin everything? She was in love with Burke and would be devastated. Maybe I was wrong about him and Amber. It was just a thought. . . .

You must learn to trust. It was the kind man's voice again.

"Stop talking to me!"

My throat dried up. I tried to swallow but tasted only dry dust. I covered my ears to the voice that haunted me, even though it was always nice to me no matter how I yelled at it.

"Okay, I'm sorry. I know you're trying to be nice. But please, I'm begging, leave me alone."

There was a knock on my door. "Hey, little sister, who you talking to in there?"

It was Brian! And he was mocking me again.

"See?" I hissed to the air. "Leave me alone." Then I said loudly, "Cedar."

"Yeah. Right you are. Cuckoo crazy girl."

Sometimes Brian barged in and made a joke about me talking to myself, but today I heard his footsteps heading down the hall to his room. He loved standing outside my door, listening to me talk to no one. He thought it was funny. Ha ha. So funny. Brian was older than me by two years and had finished high school. He was working now, at a popular hamburger joint called Licks. He was thinking about his future in the restaurant business, but to save money he still lived at home. Although we both had blond hair and blue eyes, our personalities couldn't have been more different. Loud—and what I would call obnoxious—Brian had friends from all different groups. He had jock friends, musician friends, and geek friends, and just . . . tons of friends. Everyone loved him because he was the life of the party. Girls loved him, too. There was always a new girlfriend at the house.

I exhaled, forcing the air out so that my lips vibrated. Then I ran my hands through my hair and listened to make sure that Brian was indeed gone. I heard his bedroom door slam and sighed. I'm sure he hated my issues as much as I did. Behind closed doors, every family has their "stuff," and ours was and still is me.

I slowly turned the page of this book that Lacey and I had madeto see another heart.

I would never reach *my* dream if I couldn't stop the visions. This heart had been colored with purple marker, not the traditional red associated with love, and the names were written in green block letters. Angels dressed in gray and black circled the heart, and there were no glitter stars. The two drawings were polar opposites: one dark, one light.

I traced my finger along the word *John*.

Then I let my finger slowly cruise along my own name. That day in grade nine, I hadn't chosen John. I'd chosen Dale Anderson just to pick someone, to feel part of the high school experience. Then last year, John was transferred to our school.

I closed my eyes. I'd been reliving the first time I saw him over and over and over since it happened. I couldn't help myself.

✢ ✢ ✢

I'd been sitting in English class, at the back of the room, of course. It was "hockey jersey day" at school, and most of the kids were wearing some sort of loud hockey jersey with a huge logo on the front and the number and name of their favorite hero on the back. It all felt so conformist, and I hated it. I refused to play the part and wear a stupid jersey. As I sat there brooding, slouching, and doodling, a waft of fresh soap and some type of musky, masculine woody aftershave combined with the familiar smell of cigarette smoke hit my nostrils. My body tensed and my stomach flipped and my breathing picked up speed and then . . . *he* passed by my desk. I tried hard not to stare.

Who was *he*?

I'd never seen him before. He had to be new to our school. I swear my heart stopped beating for a second. He wore jeans and a nondescript gray hoodie and . . . no jersey. His flip-flops slapped the floor, and his frayed jeans dragged along the tiles. Nobody wore flip-flops to school. Talk about not conforming. He sat in the desk kitty-corner to me.

Who was this guy?

My throat dried up, and sweat started beading on my upper lip. I slid deeper into my seat and lowered my head, letting my hair hang in front of my eyes, just so I could catch a glimpse of him without him knowing I was staring. Right away I was drawn to his strong, chiseled looks, his square jaw, straight posture, and wide shoulders. No way did he look like a jock, though. He was lean, almost skinny, but he had this strong, long look. And he had unruly thick, dark, curly hair that was so incredibly cool because it was wild and unkempt and yet still all in the right place. I continued doodling, my pen ripping right through my paper because I pressed so hard. Why was I still staring at him? This was crazy and totally stupid. But he was intriguing, because I just *knew* he wasn't a conformist. He was different, like me, perhaps. The teacher started talking, droning on and on, and I didn't hear one word until a question was posed to the class about the book we were supposed to be reading and *he* put up his hand.

I sat up in my desk, holding my breath, waiting to hear his voice, wondering what it would sound like, what he was going to say. His low, smooth, almost syrupy voice spoke words that were clear and concise, and he reeled off an answer that shocked me, because he sounded like he was a professor and not a student. The teacher nodded his head. "Excellent answer. And your name is?"

"John. John Smith."

"Excellent answer, Mr. Smith."

I'd never heard a student talk so intelligently before, and I'd definitely never met anyone who was as mystifying. Right then and there, I decided I was going to do everything I could to get to know him. I had to.

Later that week, Lacey and I were together in my room, and I said, "I want to change my guy in our book."

"Ah, so Dale is a dud. Figured as much."

I nodded. Unable to speak.

"So, who do you want?"

"John Smith."

Lacey looked at me wide-eyed and laughed. Then she said, "Indie, he's trouble. You know he got kicked out of his last school."

"I don't care." And I didn't. Not even one little bit.

"He hardly talks to anyone. No one knows who he is. Plus, he's got the worst name *ever*. I mean, honestly, *John Smith*? It sounds like John Doe. Bor-ing."

"He's not boring, Lacey." I hugged my knees to my chest. "Not even close. His name may be plain, but he's so mysterious. He's aloof, and it's like something I just can't describe surrounds him and makes him deep and dark, and . . . I want to *know* him." The last part of my sentence came out in a breathy whisper.

"He's a bad boy, Indie."

"But you just said that you don't even know him." I rested my chin on my knees and smiled. "And *that's* why I like him." Then I grabbed a black marker, scratched out *Dale,* and wrote in huge letters the word *John*.

❖ ❖ ❖

Fast-forward to more than a year later, and I still hadn't really talked to him. Sure we'd said hi and all that kind of stuff, but we'd never talked, just the two of us, alone.

I snapped the book shut, not wanting to turn the next page to read the pathetic poetry I'd written about John since that day, and shoved it in the bottom drawer of my desk. I grabbed some headphones, put them on, and turned on my portable CD player. I plopped back on my bed, and as I listened to the music, I stared at my white stucco ceiling. Did John like classic rock, too? It wasn't mainstream. I wondered what music he liked. Heavy metal? Grunge?

"Okay, so at least I didn't see anyone or anything die today," I said out loud. "And I hope I never do. Not even another animal."

"Indie," said my mom from behind my bedroom door.

I quickly pulled my headphones off and put them on the nightstand. "I'm okay," I replied "I'm just talking to Cedar."

We lived in a three-bedroom, one-washroom bungalow in the South Keys area of Ottawa, a typical middle-class neighborhood, and my parents' bedroom was just down the hall from mine. Sometimes I blame my parents for the fact that I'm an outsider. They must have known I was going to be weird when I was born—otherwise, why would they have named me Indigo? Yes, my real name is Indigo Russell. I'm named after a color. And the color is something in between blue and violet so in my book, it isn't even a true color. What parents name their kid after a color?

"Can I come in?" she asked.

"I'm in bed. Got a test in the morning."

"I think Sheena and Sasha want to sleep with you."

I sat up. "Let them in."

Mom opened the door, and our golden Lab, Sheena, and our black Lab, Sasha, came bounding into the room. Cedar snubbed her nose at them as if to say, "Ha ha, you get the floor," and sank further into my bed.

After I made a fuss over the dogs, they plopped down at the foot of my bed. Once my mom had shut my door and I heard her footsteps padding down the hallway, I curled under my covers, leaving a tiny opening for my nose. Just a peephole so I could breathe. Warm mist circulated around my nose, heating my face but not my body. I didn't want any white or gray or black visitors in my room, floating around, interrupting my sleep . . . making me quiver.

Sometimes, dead people appeared in my room uninvited. Just like my visions appeared in my mind. The only dead visitor I liked was my grandfather, who I called Papa. He died when I was seven, but he often came to visit me when I needed him. I curled into a tighter ball, hugging my knees.

I heard Sasha sigh and shudder before closing her eyes. Sheena snorted and stilled as well, and Cedar didn't move from her curled position in the crook of my legs. My animals gave me comfort, protection from the other spirits who liked to lurk. I curled into the tiniest ball possible, wrapping my arms around my body and closing my eyes to the world around me.

Then I said my prayer:

Matthew, Mark, Luke, and John,
Bless the bed I lie upon.
Four corners to my bed,
Four angels around my head,
One to sing,
One to pray,
And two to watch until the day.

Chapter Two

"Indigo Russell," my mom yelled, "get a move on. You're going to miss the bus."

"Yeah, yeah," I grumbled. I sat up and looked around. I'd had no visitors from the other side, and for that I was grateful. Sasha, Sheena, and Cedar were gone. Brian must have let them out so they could take their middle-of-the-night stroll to his bedroom. Although Brian and I were as different as night and day, we had one thing in common: we both loved our pets.

Eight minutes later, I gave myself one last glance in the mirror. "Freak," I said. "Weirdo. Stupid idiot."

Then I slammed my bedroom door and trudged to the kitchen.

"I have a twelve-hour shift today," Mom said. She was wearing her nurse's uniform—blue scrubs and white sneakers—and drinking her morning coffee. "There's chili in the fridge for dinner." She glanced at her watch and dumped the remains of her coffee into the sink. Then she looked directly at me. "Is that a new blouse?"

She had recently cut her light brown hair short, and it looked great. I wished I looked more like her; even in her scrubs, she looked so thin and pretty. All my friends thought I had the best mom.

But she could sniff out a problem from a mile off.

"No," I replied. "And it's called a T-shirt."

She smiled, ignoring my snippy attitude. "It looks nice on you."

I eyed her. She had that compassionate look in her eyes that said, "I'm sorry I birthed an abnormal child, and I sense something disturbing has just happened to you, so I'm saying something nice to distract you and make you feel good about yourself."

My mother was always worried about me, like, 24–7. I hated that she had to stress about me and my problems all the time. Looking at her now, I felt sad. She was worried about me again. She intuitively knew something was wrong. I couldn't tell her I'd had another vision, because that would worry her even more. As a teenage girl, I was supposed to hate my mom, like so many of my friends, but I didn't at all. And here she was again, trying to make me feel good about myself.

"Thanks for the vote on the top," I said softly.

❖ ❖ ❖

With orange juice sloshing around in my stomach, making me nauseated, I headed outside to walk to my bus stop on Bank Street, which is this really long street in Ottawa and one of the main streets that connect different parts of the city. Indian summer had hit; the air was warm, and the sky was a beautiful shade of sapphire blue. My jean jacket flapped open as I sauntered, not in any real rush to get to school. Maple trees lined my street, and because of their maturity, their branches almost touched in the middle, making me feel as though I were walking through a big tunnel poked with holes to let the sun shine through. The little beads of sun shimmered on the sidewalk, and I almost felt cocooned. I strolled by the ranch-style and bungalow homes that made up my neighborhood; most were blue, green, or tan with perfect white trim and white gutters that were cleaned every year. Of course, in typical Ottawa style, there were also red-bricked homes mixed in with the stucco and aluminum-sided ones. Brick houses are standard in Ottawa, because it is one of the oldest cities in Canada, and the coldest.

I think my neighborhood was built sometime in the '70s; I knew our house was around 20 years old, because my parents always complained about the upgrades they needed. Last summer they had put on a new roof, which meant I would have to wait forever to get a car—even a used car.

A few petunias and red geraniums still bloomed in front yard gardens and in clay pots, but some were starting to wilt and die off. One good frost, and they'd all be dead—that usually occurred sometime in early October, a few weeks away yet, although sometimes it hit earlier. My parents, along with most neighbors on the street, had spent the weekend in their yards, tidying up flower beds, pruning bushes to clean up for when the cold weather hit. Most of the rosebushes had been covered in burlap already, in preparation for winter, and I missed the wonderful summer aroma of the roses. Green garbage bags full of clippings sat in driveways.

The leaves had started to turn color already, and some had fallen to the ground because of a nasty wind. I used to love raking the leaves into piles and jumping on them. I looked at my watch and, although reluctant, picked up my pace. Those fun days were done. Sometimes I wished I could go back to when I didn't know that I was weird. I had kind of figured out something was wrong with me after my papa died, when I realized that not everyone saw dead people.

Funeral homes were strange places for me and made me really freak out. My parents had taken me for my first time to see my papa. Why was I thinking about him this morning?

❖ ❖ ❖

Lots of my family and Mommy and Daddy's friends were milling around a really quiet room, and there were framed pictures of Papa on a table. Everyone was staring at him and crying and wiping their eyes with white tissues from boxes that sat all around the room. I wanted to see him, too, so I stepped up to the long box and looked inside at the man who lay in

15

blue, shiny fabric that was the color of the sky on a warm summer day. His mouth didn't move and he didn't smile at me and his eyes were closed and his skin seemed old and wrinkly. But he didn't seem as sad as everyone else in the room. And I wasn't sad, because he wasn't sad. His hands were clasped together over his tummy, and I reached out to touch his skin. Poor Papa. His hands were so cold they felt like mine did when I went outside in the snow without my mittens.

That night I crawled under my Strawberry Shortcake comforter and had just closed my eyes when I heard Papa's voice calling my name. I sat up. He stood at the end of my bed. He didn't look as old and wrinkly as he had that afternoon, and he smiled at me, like he was happy. I smiled back. I knew he wasn't sad.

"Tell Mommy and Daddy that I'm happy. And tell them not to be sad. I'm okay. I'm where I should be."

The next morning, I skipped into the kitchen. "Papa said to tell you he was happy."

"Indie, what on earth are you talking about?" Daddy said sounding irritated.

"Papa came to see me last night."

"I'm sure you didn't see him, Indie," said Daddy. "You must have been dreaming."

I frowned. Why would he say that?

Everyone always thought I was dreaming: parents, school teachers, Sunday school teachers. But even back then, I had known I wasn't.

I shook my head. Geez, I so wished it had been a dream. Then I wouldn't have had to hide this stuff from all the kids in my high school and pretend I was normal when really I was a teenager who *still* saw dead people and had *visions*. Like the one with Amber and Burke.

✤ ✤ ✤

Ridgemont High wasn't within walking distance, so I had to catch the OC Transpo, or as I preferred to call it, the red and white limo. Although we lived in a nice middle-class neighborhood and there was a decent high school pretty close by, I had to attend Ridgemont High School because we lived on the other side of the train tracks, and they were the defining line. Literally, we lived on the wrong side of the tracks. It was kind of a drag, but now that I was in my last year of high school, it didn't bug me anymore.

Once I hit Bank Street, I made a left turn. My tunnel of trees was now gone, and I was on the section of Bank that had offices and businesses, like insurance companies and vacuum stores, nothing interesting. The sun was perched like a big, yellow ball in a cloudless sky, and it was shedding the perfect autumn heat that should have made me sing. But I felt only the weight of that big ball.

What am I going to do when I see Lacey? What can I say?

We told each other everything.

I shoved my hands in my pockets, lowered my head, and plodded forward, my feet feeling as if they had 20 pounds of mud caked on the bottom. I walked over the few dead leaves that had fallen, kicking them, and they crunched beneath my feet. Sometimes my visions were so confusing, and I had no idea what to do with them.

In the distance, I heard the bus barreling down the street, so I broke into a run, hitting the bus stop just in time. I trudged up the three steps, showed my pass, and made my way to the back. There were no seats, so I grabbed one of the handrails to keep my balance.

As the bus lumbered down Bank Street (it ran for miles and through tons of different neighborhoods and business sections, finally ending up in downtown Ottawa), my mind traveled as it always did when I was in motion. I thought about the stuff my mother had read to me over the years, in her valiant effort to figure out what was wrong with me. I could get past this thin veil of something that is supposed to lurk out there, and that was why I could actually see the dead—or ghosts, as most people call them—because I can move into the spirit world. I supposedly vibrated at a different frequency than most people. I quickly glanced at everyone on the bus. Why did I have to be different? Did anyone else on this bus have visions?

With my free hand, I gently touched the gold cross and chain that hung around my neck. My parents had given it to me when I was confirmed through the Anglican Church, and sometimes just the smoothness of the gold gave me comfort. I'm not sure I would say I was religious, but I did get some sort of weird protection from simple prayers and my cross necklace. I had been kicked out of Sunday school on a few occasions because of the things I'd said. One time, when the teacher said that after we passed away, we all went to heaven, I innocently said, "But my angels told me that some people stayed on earth, and that's why there are ghosts." Aggravated, the teacher sent me into the hall for a lecture. She said, "Indigo, angels do not visit little girls like you, they only visit the Men of God, because they are the messengers. Not little children, and especially not you. And there is no such thing as ghosts. You are scaring all the other children in class."

Yes, there are ghosts. I could see them, since they often appeared at the end of my bed.

So caressing my gold cross for support made no sense but then little in my life did.

My thoughts veered back to Lacey. A dull ache pounded my chest and kept pounding. It was as if her pain were a part of me, lodged deep in my muscles and bones.

When the bus lurched to a halt at my stop, I moved to the door along with all the other Ridgemont students, none of whom I knew, so I lowered my head and got off. Then I strolled slowly to the school's front entrance; Lacey's locker stood beside mine, and I had no desire to face her, since I now had such horrible news about Burke and Amber. If I took my time to get to school, the bell would ring. Lacey would go to class, and I could avoid her.

As I plodded along, I stared at the majestic maples and oaks, enthralled with how the leaves could turn from green to shades of red, orange and gold in just days. Fall was an amazing time of year in Ottawa, and it was a seasonal ritual to drive across the bridge to Gatineau in Quebec to see the colorful trees, because the valley view was absolutely stunning.

Lookout places situated along the winding road drew people from all over the world to visit and take photos of the mesh of colors that made one beautiful collage. I had only ever lived in Ottawa, the capital city of Canada. With all the federal money, litter was kept to a minimum, and Ottawa was labeled as the biggest white-collar city in Canada. Not that I cared about that, except it gave my dad a job downtown, where he worked with our National Defense as a mediator between the government and his union. He went to work in a suit every day, which he liked.

To me, Ottawa was home and a great city because all the heritage buildings and history gave it character. Since it was so old, many homes and businesses were made of stone and brick. Plus, there were the magnificent Parliament buildings downtown, near the Ottawa River and the Rideau Canal. But I only liked them for their stone walls and steeples and the Peace Tower Carillon, with its many bells that rang out the time. In other words, all the outside stuff, because inside they were haunted. And I mean really haunted. Every time I went close to them, I just couldn't go inside, even though they drew tons of international visitors. I had gone in only once and never made it past the front entrance.

Almost at my school, I saw the cops milling around the front entrance, leashes in hands, holding the drug-sniffing dogs that were about to walk the halls. Graffiti decorated the brick walls. I sighed. So much for enjoying the beautiful fall day. Back to reality.

High school had been a disappointment for me—not a place I enjoyed. If only I could go to the land of the Jim Henson's *Labyrinth* and be a warrior. *Labyrinth* was my favorite movie, and I loved how the heroine in the movie fought her way through the labyrinth to save her baby brother. There were days when I wished I could do something heroic, like use my sword to fight through all the knights at the Parliament buildings and rescue the poor people who were chained in cages and tormented by ghosts. I knew all too well what it was like to be tormented by ghosts.

I jumped when I heard a harsh voice behind me. "Indigo Russell, stop daydreaming. You'll be late for class, just like your brother."

I turned to see the vice principal of the school. Under my breath, I cursed Brian. Why did I have to be labeled because of him? His reputation had followed me for my full high school experience. I moved quickly into the school.

"Hey, Indie," said Lacey, when I approached my locker. She had her locker open and was looking in her little mirror, putting on lipstick, unaware that she too was late for class. "Did you get your math homework done?"

"Yeah." I nodded but didn't make eye contact. "But you know I'm not great at math." I unlocked my locker and opened the door. At times like this, I wished I had a mirror in my locker, too, but I didn't, so I pretended to pull out books.

She smacked her lips together, then looked at me, and I had to glance at her and smile at least a little. As usual, her dark, brown eyes danced and glimmered. She was happy to be here. When you were popular, high school was fun.

She had thick, curly, shiny, chocolate-colored hair and almond-shaped brown eyes. I had iron-straight, white-blonde hair and blue eyes. Plus, she was tall and willowy, and I had inherited my dad's short legs. She was a school athlete, and I was just a wannabe rocker who was in a band but had allowed it to die off just because.

"I don't care. Can I copy? Please. I just need to show I did it." She moaned. "I had volleyball practice last night, then . . ." She raised her perfectly shaped eyebrows up and down. "I went out with Burke." She leaned toward me and whispered, "We almost had sex. I swear it will be next time."

Breathe, Indie, breathe. Sex with Burke would have been wrong for Lacey, especially if he was cheating with Amber.

"Sure," I replied. "To the homework, that is."

"You are the best friend ever." She paused to flick her hair that moved like undulating waves around her shoulders.

"Yeah, right," I said.

She looked at me and laughed. "What's up with you?" She played with the best friend silver necklace I had given her for her birthday last year. Then her eyes widened, and she said, "Hey, there's a big party happening this Friday. You should go. I can't 'cause I have a tournament, but you should go for sure." She leaned toward me and whispered, "I heard John might be there."

And just like that, my throat closed up, making it hard for me to breathe. Sweat dripped on my neck and chest and pooled under my arms, and my cheeks scorched with heat.

I chortled loudly, probably too loudly, to mask my awkwardness. "Yeah, okay," I said. "And what do I do, just show up by myself?"

"You could go with Burke. Just for your entrance. Then you can, uh, y'know, put the moves on John." Lacey did a little shake with her shoulders.

"I don't have any moves," I mumbled.

"Don't look now, but here he comes," she whispered.

My face flushed, and my nerve endings fizzed.

"Hey, John," said Lacey.

"Hey," he replied, his voice thick, smooth, like maple syrup. Then he slowly added, "Hi, Indie."

I glanced at him through lowered eyelids and tried to smile. "Hi."

He gazed at me, longer than he did at Lacey, and his look penetrated my skin right to my bones. I couldn't avert my gaze and instead was mesmerized by his hazel eyes. There was this denseness to his pupils that I couldn't see through. I liked that feeling of not knowing. It made me feel normal.

But then, just like a light being switched off, he walked away, leaving me standing in the hallway like an idiot.

A big wad of something slid from my stomach to my throat, and I had to cough to catch my breath. My heart ticked, and I could feel it beating through my chest. My body trembled as I watched him walk down the hall, captivated by the sound of his crazy flip-flops smacking the floor, of his too-long jeans sweeping the dirty gray tiles, making swishing sounds. He didn't strut like Burke, but he had a distinct movement, like a James Dean lope, his long legs striding forward, his arms hanging loose by his sides, his sharp shoulders squared and uniform. And he wore those crazy flip-flops almost all year long. Who did that? John. John did that. He did everything that was different, and that was why I was breathing as if I'd just run a cross-country race. He pulled a book from the pouch of his sweatshirt and started to read as he walked. I wondered what he was reading.

Poetry?

Something philosophical?

Something profound and riveting?

"Did you *see* him look at you?" Lacey whispered. "You have got to go to that party, Indie."

I stood stock-still for a brief moment, unable to speak. I had to let my heart rate lower before I even attempted any words. No one wore plain sweatshirts with no logos to school but John. Logos were status. He didn't care about status. He had the confidence to be himself. He kept his head bowed as he read but didn't bump into a single person.

I turned and faced Lacey. "You're right," I said. "I *have* to go. Will Burke want to go with me, though?" Enough was enough; I had to make my move. If I didn't, high school would be over and . . . I shook my head. I couldn't think like that.

Then a thought hit me. Perhaps if I went with Burke, I could also stop him from cheating on Lacey. I would have another reason to be at the party, instead of just to see John.

I needed purpose to give me courage.

"Why not? He likes you. Thinks you're funny," said Lacey.

I laughed to appear normal. "You're kidding, right? I'm never funny."

Lacey laughed. "Yeah, you are. You're funny because you think you're not. Who else can lip-synch and play air guitar like you?" She held out her hand. "You let me copy, and I'll get Burke to take you to the party."

Chapter Three

As Lacey had promised, Burke picked me up on Saturday night. Normally, this is something that I would have tried to avoid, but since I didn't know where the party was, and Lacey had already set it up, I had no choice. I would suck it up and try to make conversation with Burke.

He knocked on the door, and I stepped outside and shivered. In the summer, the heat of the day carried into the night, but not in the fall. In the day, it could be beautiful and hot, T-shirt weather, but at night, a jacket was necessary. I did up the snaps on my jean jacket. Burke, of course, wore his Ottawa 67's logoed black hockey jacket, complete with name and position emblazoned on the sleeve, team logo on the front, and team name in letters on the back.

Once in the car, I did up my seat belt and asked, "How's your hockey team doing?" I knew enough about hockey to ask a few, hopefully correct, questions. To live in Ottawa and not be a fan of the Ottawa Senators NHL team was almost a crime, according to my dad and Brian and, well, the rest of the people in Ottawa. When Dad and Brian droned on about the

Senators, Mom and I would roll our eyes, smile, and start our own conversation.

"Great," replied Burke as he backed out of my driveway. "We're six and oh."

"Meaning?" Okay, so I didn't know that much.

Burke glanced at me out of the corner of his eye. "We've won six games and lost none."

I nodded. Why would he think I would know something like *that*?

We drove down my street and turned onto Bank. I glanced out the window, and we drove by a community arena, which resembled a big old barn. In our town, indoor hockey arenas sat on every corner, and once the temperature dipped below zero, the outdoor community hockey rinks were as common as the golden McDonald's arches. In the winter, kids played outside on frozen ice rinks until they couldn't feel their toes in their skates because it was such a *Canadian* thing to do. Believe me, I was never one of those kids. And the hockey player boys at school did nothing for me. Like Burke. Sure, I liked him and thought he was good-looking, but I preferred a guy who wore flip-flops instead of skates. A guy like John. He was puzzling and intelligent and always deep in thought and had long, thin legs instead of huge, muscular thighs like the hockey boys had. My body tingled, hoping he would be at the party. What would I say to him? Would he talk to me?

We were on our way to the Glebe, my favorite neighborhood in Ottawa because it was so funky. Both of us remained silent. Bank Street ran through some neighborhoods, then a business area, then more neighborhoods, right into downtown. The Glebe was one of the last neighborhoods before the downtown core.

"So," I said after we'd driven a little way, "what are your plans for next year?"

"It's my draft year," said Burke. "I'm hoping to go pretty high, then I can get to a rookie camp and hopefully a main NHL camp. I might have to play in the OHL again next year, but my big goal is to play NHL. So next year is hockey. What about you?"

I fiddled with the snaps on my jean jacket. *Good question, Burke,* I thought. I had no idea what my plans were. "Work for a year, maybe."

"You seriously have no idea *what* you want to do?"

I shrugged and slouched in my seat. "Maybe I'll travel. Who knows? I *definitely* don't want to go to school. Me and school don't mix."

I wished I could answer those questions. I turned my head and stared out the window again. Just because he knew exactly what he was going to do didn't mean that I did. A sudden flash of hot air surged through me, and I felt as if I were burning up. Thankfully, we were almost in the Glebe; I could get out of the car soon. I undid the top snap of my jean jacket and loosened my scarf as I continued to stare out the window, telling myself to breathe. I wanted to fan myself. What was I reacting to? His questions? My inability to answer anything about my future? Or his assuredness?

"Who do you play next?" I had to keep talking so he didn't notice that something was wrong with me.

"The Kitchener Rangers."

Then he proceeded to tell me all their stats and that they were a good team, blah, blah, blah. In a way, I was thankful for his rambling because then I didn't have to talk. As Burke chatted on, we drove into the Glebe, and I kept staring out the window as we passed upscale shops, specialty shops, bohemian shops, cafés, and tons of great restaurants: Thai, Vietnamese, vegetarian, and even trendy burger joints. My temperature began to return to normal, and I relaxed a little bit. The Glebe was a mix of old and new. Yes, there were beautiful old heritage buildings made of the classic red brick, but there were also newer condo complexes with large windows and modern features.

One day I wanted to have my own apartment in the Glebe.

Could that happen next year? Was that what I was going to do? Get a job and live in the Glebe?

"Maybe I'll get an apartment in the Glebe," I said, my words coming out of nowhere.

I snuck a glance at Burke. And then it happened. My mind went blank. I gripped the door handle of the car. *No. Not now. Please.*

But it was over so fast I didn't have time to blink. I saw a black and gold hockey jersey—then it was gone. Sometimes I got snapshots, still images instead of scenes. I breathed, thankful for the quick picture but totally bugged that I would see a stupid hockey jersey, as if I didn't get enough hockey just living in Ottawa.

"The Glebe would be a cool place to live. Expensive though, eh?" he said.

"Yeah, that's for sure." I paused. I didn't want the conversation to veer to me; I hated talking about myself. Plus, I wanted to find out more about what I had just seen. "What team do you want to pick you?"

"What do you mean, pick me?"

"Whatever you said before. It's some big year for you."

"You mean draft me?"

"Yeah."

"Pittsburgh Penguins."

"What color are their uniforms?"

He laughed. "You mean jerseys?"

"Oh, right," I said. "Jerseys."

"Black and gold."

I knew that.

I glanced out the window again. Why did I always know everything about everyone else but nothing about myself? Was I going to live in the Glebe next year? Was that what I was feeling? Some days I had 20 visions, then other days, it seemed like hundreds of snapshots clicked through my brain, and then on my busy, distracted days, I had zero come to me. And none were about me! Sometimes they were powerful and gave me headaches, like the one about Burke and Amber, and other times I just heard words or saw a quick snapshot, like the jersey. It was all so confusing.

After a few seconds, I turned back to Burke and glanced at his profile. I wanted to tell him not to get involved with Amber; it would not be the right thing to do. And I also wanted to let him know he was going to get drafted by the Pittsburgh Penguins, that'd I'd seen the jersey. But a big glob of something got stuck in my throat, and I couldn't speak. And I felt funny. My body started to shake, my palms started to sweat, and my throat felt dry. I placed my hands on my lap, holding them tightly to stop the shaking, hoping Burke wouldn't notice my white knuckles. What the hell was wrong with me?

Why couldn't I talk?

Why couldn't I help my best friend by telling her boyfriend not to mess around? And I had just seen a black and gold jersey. Why couldn't I just tell him that the team he wanted was going to draft him?

Was I supposed to just butt out and not use these stupid visions? The jersey was good news. Wasn't it? Was I missing something?

He'll think you're crazy.

Of course, that was it. I had to keep my mouth shut. We turned onto a residential street with nice big trees, including oaks and willows. The houses in the Glebe were different than in my neighborhood because they were much older, and most were the classic style: tall two-story red-brick buildings. Some of the houses here might have even been built in the late 1800s and early 1900s. When Burke drove up to the curb in front of a stately brick house, I exhaled. Finally, I could get out of the car and get some air.

We walked toward the house. Burke lifted the latch on the black iron gate and, like a perfect gentleman, ushered me through first. I walked down the narrow concrete walkway and climbed the four steps to the old-fashioned front porch that wrapped around the house. Outdoor wicker furniture sat empty on the deck, although I did notice the overflowing ashtray on the small table between the two cushioned chairs. Someone had been sitting in them recently. The noise from the party was emanating from the two front windows. My body started to vibrate, and my head ached. My body didn't respond to parties like Lacey's did. When she heard the music and loud noise, she would smile and dance and talk with animated gestures. For me, the walls seemed to move in and out and warp, and the only way I could stand it was to find a corner of the room and stay there all night.

I lifted my hand to knock on the door, but Burke laughed and just pushed it open. "I don't think anyone will hear you knock," he said. "This is going to be shaker."

I swallowed, trying to wet my dry throat. It had taken me an hour to decide what to wear, and in the end, I had on nondescript jeans and a plain V-neck. I had added a silver necklace and hoop earrings for dramatic effect. And I had tried to curl my hair—unsuccessfully, I might add—and put on eye shadow (borrowed from Lacey), mascara, and some lip gloss.

We walked through the front door, and I immediately saw the carved newel post and wooden staircase leading to an upstairs. Kids were looming over the staircase, looking me up and down. Then I looked down the narrow hallway to the kitchen. The house was packed, bodies milling over every square inch. Burke pulled a bottle of something out of his shirt, ignoring me. The guy obviously didn't want to babysit his girlfriend's friend anymore. I mean, we were past the front door, right?

What was I going to do now? Who would I talk to?

Was John here?

I glanced at the crowd, but all the faces and bodies melted together, like a buzzing blur of bees. The drone became louder and louder, and I stood in the middle of the room, my feet feeling as if they were glued to the floor. Why had I come? What was I trying to prove? I wished I were home in my room watching television or reading or . . . I took a few deep breaths to slow down my racing insecurities. I closed my eyes to escape for just a minute. Crowds made me crazy. It was like my blood absorbed everything that everyone was feeling, so I could feel their joy or sorrow, and it washed over me, making me either super hyper or totally depressed.

After a few good phys-ed-worthy inhalations, I opened my eyes and willed my body to calm down. I came to help out my best friend.

And to see John.

I jostled my way through the crowd and headed to the kitchen. Burke was ahead of me, weaving his way down the narrow hallway toward the kitchen at the back of the house. I walked a few steps behind him, so he wouldn't know I was following. I glanced around as soon as I walked in the kitchen.

Then I saw him.

He was alone, leaning against the counter, holding a red cup. He looked so out of place, exactly how I felt. He wore his usual: jeans, flip-flops, and the same plain hooded sweatshirt, no logos. From the pouch of his sweatshirt, a tattered paperback peeked out. From where I stood I couldn't read the title. I stopped moving, lowered my head, and stared at my feet. Had he seen me looking at him?

Someone pushed by me, and I stumbled a bit, which made me have to lift my chin and face the party. Immediately, I saw him staring at me—his hazel eyes pierced me, seared my skin. I thought about what Lacey would do in this situation, so I smiled. He raised his hand and coolly gave me a finger salute. The small movement made his thick dark hair randomly shift and move across his forehead in one small sweep. As if on autopilot, my feet started moving forward, step by step, until I stood in front of him.

"Hey," he said almost lazily. Then he smirked. "I'm surprised to see you here."

I shrugged.

"You don't strike me as the partygoer type."

"I could say the same about you," I replied.

He nodded, once. Then he tilted his head and stared at me. I wanted to look away, but I couldn't.

Finally, to break his gaze and the sweltering heat that had invaded me, I pointed to the book snuggled in his sweatshirt. "What are you reading?"

He pulled the paperback from his pouch, and when I saw the cover, I sank my feet in the floorboards and let my arms dangle at my side to maintain a casual look. The blood surged so fast through my veins that I might as well have been on a river raft fighting rapids.

"*The Sleeping Prophet*," he said. "It's about a guy named Edgar Cayce. You ever heard of him?"

I had. Because of my visions, my mom had a million books on different psychics, and we had many books on Edgar Cayce, too many. I knew Cayce was a visionary from the late 1800s who had died sometime in the 1940s, but that's about all I knew, because I tried not to be interested. My mother liked to tell me that I had what he had, and if I would just accept, blah, blah, blah.

I shook my head. "Nope. Never heard of him."

"He's interesting. Fascinating, actually." He shoved the book in his back pocket. "You want to go outside? Get some air?"

"Sure," I replied.

I followed John through the maze of bodies, moving steadily behind him, dodging arms, legs, feet, shoulders. Within seconds, we were outside, standing on the back porch. Translucent, silvery-blue light from the full moon lit the porch, and stars winked like gems in a clear ebony sky. A sudden eerie feeling washed over me, almost as if a burglar had crept into my body and stolen my energy. Since I was little, the full moon had had some sort of power over me. It used to stare at me through my bedroom window, and I would hide under my covers to get away from it. I shivered.

"You cold?" John asked.

"Not really," I replied.

He pulled cigarettes out of his pocket and tapped the pack on the porch railing. Once he had one in his hand, he rolled it around for a few beats before he leaned forward and cupped his hands to the autumn wind that blew around us. The cigarette sparked, and I stared at the tiny red specks. John threw his head back and inhaled, then he blew out a rush of smoke and handed the cigarette to me. I immediately took it and inhaled deeply, my lips touching the exact spot where his had been, tasting his mouth, wondering if this could classify as our first kiss. I let the smoke fill my lungs before I exhaled. When I handed the cigarette back to John, he had his head tilted to the side, and he wore a little smirk on his face, as if he were assessing me somehow, mocking me.

"What?" I asked.

"I didn't know you smoked."

I shoved my hands in my back pockets and shifted my stance so my hip jutted out. I didn't want to tell him I smoked to be part of something, a group perhaps. That as an outsider I needed to belong somewhere. That I practiced in front of a mirror so I could join the smoking crowd outside, and that I used it as a social tool to help my awkwardness.

John put his finger under my chin, forcing me to look him in the eyes, his touch sending quivers through my body. Butterflies invaded my throat, flying around as if they wanted to escape but couldn't.

He touched my hair, running his fingers down its length. When he got to the end of the strand, he rubbed it gently. Then he smiled. Immediately, I stopped shivering, and a rush of warm air spread through my limbs.

"Your eyes are the color of your name."

I tilted my head so I could feel his hand touch my cheek, unable to speak as he continued to stroke my hair. I couldn't believe he was touching me. I couldn't believe he remembered my name.

"Smoking won't take away your innocence," he murmured.

The back door flew open, and the moment evaporated. Sarah Sebert stumbled onto the porch. "Indie, I didn't know you were here," she slurred.

I stepped back. The cold resurfaced. I crossed my arms over my chest.

"I came with Burke."

Without saying a word to Sarah, John went inside, the back door thudding when it closed. I wanted to follow him, but Sarah grabbed my shoulder. "Is he not the coolest guy you've ever seen?" Her wild red hair and freckles glowed in the moonlight.

I didn't answer.

Then she whispered in my ear. "Come on, let's go back inside. I'll get you a drink," she said. "My big sis got it for me." Sarah was known as fun with a capital *F*. She always had booze, and she loved to laugh and dance, and she was nice to everyone. I'd never met anyone who liked to laugh as much as Sarah.

I allowed Sarah to lead me to the far corner of the room, where she picked up a stashed backpack. As I waited for her to retrieve her goods, I scanned the kitchen for John.

"Get a cup," she whispered.

Pretending to find a cup, any cup, I searched every room for him. But he was nowhere. Had he left? Had I said something to drive him away?

Finally, I headed back to Sarah, my hands shaking. Had I done something to make him leave without saying good-bye? With her back turned to the crowd, Sarah discreetly poured something into the red cup. I listened to the *glub, glub, glub.*

She handed me the cup, then quickly returned everything to her backpack. She stood and held up her cup. "To the funniest person I know."

"I'm not funny," I said.

"Oh my god. Yes, you are. When you slid into class yesterday, singing that Beatles song, I thought I would pee my pants."

"It wasn't that funny. And I honestly thought the room was empty. I would have never done it otherwise. I thought only Lacey was in the room." I kind of liked that Sarah thought I was funny; it made me feel good. Did John think I was funny, too? Probably not. Maybe he didn't like funny girls. Maybe I wasn't serious enough for him. Maybe he went for the bad-girl type.

Sarah interrupted my thoughts about John and, slurring her words, said, "We need to get our band going again, if nothing else but for fun. Remember how awesome we were last year?"

I laughed. Our all-girl band had been a blast, and rehearsals were something I'd really looked forward to, even if we weren't great. "We managed to get one song sounding decent," I said.

She held up her fist, and I fisted her back. "Let's do it," she said. "Let's play some rock and roll."

"Yeah, let's," I said with true enthusiasm. "What have we got to lose? It was fun."

I toasted her cup and tried to sound perky when I said, "Cheers."

"Indie, you're so great." She smiled a drunken smile. "And you're so pretty."

Sarah suddenly shifted her gaze from me to across the room. "Hey, there's Burke. I have to talk to him." As she moved to go around me, she slopped her drink all over my arm.

"Darn," she said. "Only one way to solve spillage problems." She lifted her glass and downed her entire drink. After grimacing and shaking her head, she slurred, "Come on, Indie. You do the same."

"I can't chug this. It's full," I said.

Suddenly I remembered my mission. I was at this party to keep Amber and Burke apart. My heart sank. What kind of friend was I?

Burke was standing extremely close to Amber—too close. I eyed them and immediately noticed her hand discreetly placed behind his back, her fingers hooking his belt like talons holding prey. She wore the same short skirt and T-shirt I'd seen in my vision. Hoop earrings much bigger than mine and high strappy heels finished the outfit. The middle of my forehead started to pulse, making me clammy and hot.

"Indie! Indie!" Sarah started to chant my name.

Within seconds, everyone in the kitchen was chanting, too. The voices saying my name reverberated through my head like bouncing balls. I felt dizzy, sick, as if the room were spinning around me. I didn't want to do this.

Would the booze lighten my heart?

Had John left because he thought I was too innocent?

I put the cup to my lips and tipped my head back. The liquid burned, my eyes watered, my stomach convulsed, but I drank every drop. Sarah pulled my arm and dragged me to the living room, where the music blared through the walls and ceiling, and the pounding bass pulsed into my feet from the floorboards.

After one song, I said, "I need water." What I needed was to find Burke and Amber. To make sure they weren't together.

I weaved my way to the kitchen, bouncing off a few walls on the way. I had never been drunk before, ever. My body just felt so strange and unearthly, like I was cruising on air. Once I was in the kitchen, I didn't see Burke or Amber.

"Have you seen Burke?" I asked a guy I barely knew. I had trouble forming the words.

"Whoa, girl, you're hammered."

I shook my head. The back and forth movement suddenly made my sensitive stomach convulse. Then I did the ultimate. I threw up.

The room started to spin. I grabbed my stomach and threw up again.

"Gross!" I didn't recognize the voice.

"I'll take her outside," said Sarah.

Sarah put her hand on my elbow and guided me through the kitchen, and once again I was on the back porch, only this time without John. She sat me down, and I put my head between my legs to stop the spinning.

"I have to go home," I mumbled.

"Who'd you come with?"

"Burke."

"Oh, that's right. You told me that already."

"Yeah, Lacey made him pick me up."

"Okay, I'll get him." Sarah left me on the porch by myself, and I lay down on my back and stared up at the sky and the stars and the big full moon. Like always, it just stared back at me as if it were alive or something. So freaky. Minutes clicked by. My stomach didn't settle and the spinning didn't stop and the full moon wouldn't stop laughing at me and nothing about this was funny. I had thrown up on someone. How embarrassing. I wondered who had to clean it up.

Why did John leave? Doesn't he like me? I wanted to cry.

Where was Sarah? I had to get home. Then Sarah flung open the door and, laughing, stumbled out on the porch.

"I found Burke. He was with Amber. They were up in one of the bedrooms."

I put my hands to my ears. "Lalala."

"Stop that," said Sarah, laughing. She sat down beside me and helped me sit up. I kept my hands over my ears. Just then, the door swung open again, and when I saw the familiar face, I dropped my hands.

"Hey, Indie, you okay?" Burke asked, sounding genuinely concerned.

I tried to stand up and almost fell, but he jumped forward and grabbed me.

"I'm so sorry." I could hardly talk.

"Hey, no worries. I'll take you home. I was leaving soon anyway."

"Business finished," chortled Sarah. She slapped Burke on the back.

"Can you drive?" I slurred.

"Yeah. I'm okay."

Burke guided me through the bodies at the party and helped me into his car, giving me a bag just in case I threw up on the way home. I rested my head against the headrest, and my world began spinning again, as if I were caught in one of those revolving doors at a big department store. I wanted this all to go away; I didn't want to be drunk anymore.

Why did John leave?

We didn't talk for the entire drive, mostly because I was too nauseous and my tongue wouldn't work. I had my head tilted back and my eyes closed as I tried to keep from barfing all over the dash of his car.

Why did he go without saying good-bye? Tears loomed under my eyelids.

When Burke pulled into my driveway, I tried to open the car door, but finding the handle became an issue. But Burke hustled around to the passenger-side door. When he opened it for me, he said, "What Sarah said isn't true."

I maneuvered my body so I could put my feet on the ground. I couldn't talk about this now. Burke held my forearm and helped me stand. Then he walked me to the front door, found my key in my purse, and opened the door for me. As I stumbled into the hallway, Brian walked out of the kitchen.

"Whoa," he said.

"Hi, Bri," I slurred. Then I crashed into the wall.

He immediately grabbed my arm to keep me upright. "Shh," he whispered. "Don't let Mom catch you like this. Keep quiet, and I'll walk you down the hall."

"I'm so sorry," I mumbled.

"Shh."

"But I really am sorry. John left without saying good-bye to me. Why did he do that?"

"Forget about the guy. Don't talk, okay? You'll wake Mom."

But I kept mumbling about John. We were halfway down the hall when Mom came out of her room in her pajamas.

"Indie," she said, "what's wrong?"

"What?" I put my hand on the wall. "Nothing's wrong."

"Are you drunk?"

"Nope."

"She's okay," said Brian.

"How many drinks did you have?"

"Onnnne." I held my pointer finger up in front of my nose, and it instantly turned into two fingers.

"Did you take her to a party?" Mom accused Brian.

"She only had one drink, Mom. She's a lightweight. What can I say?"

As I crashed toward the wall, Mom grabbed me by the back of my shirt. "I'll take over from here," she said as she guided me toward my bedroom. "We will talk about this in the morning."

"I'm not a kid anymore," I replied.

We entered my room, and I saw two Jim Morrisons on my wall. I stumbled and grabbed hold of my mom. Then I saw two black cats sitting on my bed and started to laugh. "Hey, Cedar has a twin." Cedar meowed at me like I was from another planet.

"Let's get you undressed," said Mom.

I allowed her to help me, but when I was down to my bra, I started laughing and whipped it off, hitting her in the face. Then I giggled as she put me in my pajamas.

"Indie, this isn't funny."

"I think it is. Do you know that kids at school think I'm funny? Me. Indie Russell. Funny." Then I started singing my dad's favorite Beach Boys song with my own lyrics. *"I wish we all could be Ottawa girls."*

I stopped singing. "Do you think Dad can hear me? He likes the Beach Boys. Not me. They're old farts."

"Let's hope he can't hear you." My mom's voice was stern. "He would not be happy about this. Now, get into bed."

Once I was in bed and under the covers, my laughter was taken over by bed spins and an incredible heaviness. As if Cedar understood, she curled into the crook of my legs. I mumbled to my mom, "I want John to like me. But I'm so weird."

"You're not weird," she answered.

"But I see things. It's dumb."

"That's just who you are."

"It soooo sucks."

"Shh. Indie, go to sleep." Mom spoke firmly. "We'll talk in the morning."

"Sometimes I wish I were a kid again." I hiccupped. "When I didn't know something was wrong with me." I sat up and almost fell off my bed. "Remember when Papa died? Remember how I saw him?"

"Indie. Enough."

"I was only seven."

Shaking her head, Mom left the room.

"I still see things!" I yelled after her. Then I flopped back on my bed, and the bed spins started again.

⸻

Chapter Four

I woke up to my phone painfully shrilling. It kept ringing and ringing—the two distinct rings that meant it was for
me. I yanked my covers off my head and glanced at the clock.
Then I groaned. It was only 10:30. The sun streamed through
my curtains, dappling my floor. My head throbbed and my
stomach . . . ohhh . . . it didn't feel so good. I knocked over a
framed photo of me with Sheena, Sasha, and Cedar as I picked
up the phone.

"Hello." The word scratched my throat.

"I heard you had quite the night last night," Lacey said,
laughing.

"Not funny."

"Burke said you got totally wasted."

I groaned, thinking of the high school rumor mill. Thankfully, today was Sunday, and by tomorrow, my sorry story
might be forgotten.

"At least you didn't puke in his car. He said it was funny,
since you're so straightlaced."

"Did you talk to anyone else?" I asked. Sometimes high
school reputations were ruined by just one party.

There was silence on the phone for a few seconds, and I wondered if I had done something really stupid, but I more or less remembered the entire night and most certainly hadn't blacked out. I waited for an answer, holding my breath.

Finally, Lacey spoke, and her voice was quieter, much more subdued. "I've got something serious to ask you."

"Sure." I needed water, a huge glass of ice-cold water.

"Did you see Burke and Amber together at the party?"

The question felt like a hard punch in the gut. I had been thinking only of my hangover and my own reputation, not of Lacey and Burke. Some friend I was.

Before I could answer, Lacey continued, "That bitch Adriana phoned me this morning and said she walked into a bedroom and they were making out. Burke called last night and this morning and told me how much he misses and loves me. He didn't sound as if anything unusual had happened. He just sounded like Burke. I mean, what guy would make that kind of call if he was just with someone else?" She paused. "Indie, did you see anything?"

"No," I replied. It wasn't really a lie. I had seen them together at the party, but they weren't making out.

Lacey sighed in relief. "Thanks. You're a doll."

"I was kind of drunk."

"Yeah, but you probably still would have heard something or seen something. I mean you do have that freaky ability to sense things. Anyway, I'm sure Adriana is lying. She's just trying to get to Burke because she wants him for herself. And anyway, there is no way he would hook up with Amber. She's not his type."

I thought of Amber's fingers secured into Burke's belt loops. I vaguely remember Sarah saying something, too.

And then, of course, *there were my visions,* as Lacey had just pointed out. But she wouldn't want to know about the one I had about Burke and Amber, that was for sure.

"I know Burke would never cheat on me," said Lacey. "We're incredibly close. Maybe I should just do it with him, because when you love someone, it is a beautiful expression." Her last line was said more to herself than to me.

"Don't just do it to do it," I replied.

"I won't."

"Do it when it feels right."

Lacey snorted. "Are you giving me advice on guys?"

"Hardly."

"I trust Burke, and no one is going to make me doubt him. I want him to be my first."

How to reply? I guessed I could own up to my vision. But she probably wouldn't have believed me anyway. Maybe Burke wouldn't do it again. Maybe it was a one-time thing that Lacey didn't need to know about. The guy had given me a ride home, and he had been so nice. Deep down, Lacey had to know something was wrong between her and Burke. Didn't she? Was it my place to tell her?

When I hung up the phone, I pressed my head back on my pillow and stared at the ceiling. This was when my visions really confused me. I wasn't sure what I was supposed to do with them.

Tell me what to do. Please.

I didn't want to be a bad friend. If it were true about Burke, she didn't deserve to have a boyfriend who cheated on her. But then I also didn't want to tell her something that wasn't true. Cold swirled around me as if a sudden flash of winter wind had arrived in my room unannounced. I shivered uncontrollably, goose bumps sprouting all over my body. I slid under my covers, wrapping my arms around my body. Even with my blankets pulled up under my chin, I couldn't get warm.

Why do I have to be cursed?

I closed my eyes, hoping that I could go back to sleep. But the sun shone so brightly that I could see it and feel it even with my eyes closed. With a huge moan, I got out of bed to pull my curtains shut. Our in-ground pool still had water in it, and the sun bounced along the surface, creating sparkles that momentarily blinded me and made my head throb. I shielded my eyes.

Indie, no one can figure out anything about you.

My stomach heaved. I closed my curtains and crawled back into bed. My head was buried under my covers, and I was almost asleep when the door banged open.

"Okay, miss. That was your one get-out-of-jail-free card. You're lucky your father isn't home. You know how he feels about drinking underage. I don't want to ever see you like that again." My mother stalked into my room and flung open the curtains I had just shut.

"Don't open the curtains." I rolled over to face the wall, the covers still over my head.

"I need you to help clean the pool."

"Now?"

"Not this exact minute but soon."

"Can't Brian do it?"

"You are both working today."

My mom sat down on the end of my bed. She was quiet for a moment. Then, in one gentle swoop, she drew the bedcovers off my head. She placed her warm palm on my cheek and asked, "Do you want to talk about anything?" Her voice had lost its edge.

"No."

"Are you sure?"

"Mom, I'm fine." I rolled away from her and closed my eyes.

"You mentioned a boy last night. Were you drinking with him?"

"No!"

She stood up and walked toward the door. "Well, if you're fine, then I definitely want you to help with the pool."

The door slammed, and I groaned. *Fine.* What a word. Was I fine? Hardly. I was hungover, I'd seen an unpleasant vision that would hurt my best friend, the guy I liked had left the party without saying good-bye, and I'd gotten so drunk I'd puked and made a fool of myself.

Let's face it, Indie, you've never been fine.

My mother probably thought my getting drunk was some sort of escape from my problems. I groaned again. If she made a doctor's appointment for me because of this, I would honestly freak out on her.

❖ ❖ ❖

At age seven, when I'd blurted out that I'd talked to my papa, my horrified parents had become "concerned." Before Papa's death, I had figured that everyone saw wavering bright colored lights above heads and had translucent people visit their rooms after dark. If I'd known then what I know now, I would never have admitted a damn thing to my parents. When their "concern" started, so did a bunch of my physical symptoms.

I pressed my hand to my stomach. When I started having stomach pains, at the age of ten, my mom carted me to our family doctor. "There's nothing wrong with her," the doctor said every time I went in. I swear he used to look at me cross-eyed, like I was one big hypochondriac.

That made Mom change doctors. The woman I saw next asked me questions that had nothing to do with anything physical. She asked about my boyfriends and my friends. I liked Dr. Z. That's what I called her. Then one day when I was in her office, I picked up a photo of her with her son, and I randomly said, "He's cute. He likes to draw." Dr. Z looked around her office, and there were none of his drawings anywhere. She gave me a funny look.

"Yes, he does," she said slowly.

Without thinking, I continued, "He has a hard time socializing."

This time she narrowed her eyes. "Yes, that is true," she'd replied.

Another day, we were sitting in her office, just the two of us, and she looked at me and said, "You are different. I think you have something like ESP."

I was different. That was my diagnoses? What the hell was ESP?

And it wasn't going away like the chicken pox did. I had told my mom about ESP the night after Dr. Z mentioned it to me, and she dismissed it—said I was "sensitive." Although I knew she did research behind my back.

This sensitivity I was supposed to have made my parents check out a psychologist for me on Dr. Z's referral. I'd been to my first therapy session in my early teens, and that guy had diagnosed me with ADHD.

❖ ❖ ❖

Another stomach cramp made me curl into a tight ball. From going to all the doctors and psychologists, I had developed ulcers. I rubbed my stomach, hoping that the lining wasn't inflamed again. My ulcers couldn't return. And if they did, I would hide the pain and blood so my parents wouldn't become "concerned" again. Pink Pepto-Bismol did wonders and was cheap. I could still hear my father's voice when my mom and I had come home from the doctor's. "What little kid gets ulcers?" he asked. "She should be playing with her dolls, riding her bike, coloring pictures with other little girls her age."

"She is a little girl who internalizes everything," my mother had replied.

I pulled my blanket over my head again. Fine, yeah, right. I was a walking freak. What guy would want to have anything to do with me? Especially a guy as smart as John. But I wanted him.

I would have to outsmart him and keep my secrets to myself.

Cozily snuggled underneath the blanket, curled in a small ball, I heard Mom's loud voice: "Indie, get up! Time to clean the pool."

❖ ❖ ❖

"You missed a spot," said Brian, pointing to a bug floating on top of the water. He was leaning back in a plastic pool chair, with his hands clasped comfortably behind his head.

"You're supposed to be helping," I retorted. "I wish Mom and Dad would just close the pool. It's fall, and no one swims anymore."

"I do," said Brian. "It's heated, you know." He paused. "Oh, right. You don't know, because you're scared of the monsters in the deep end."

"Shut up." I skimmed the pool strainer across the water, picking up the dead bug.

"Little sister, you owe me one. I saved your butt last night, 'cause there was no way you had just one drink. By the way, who's *John*? Should I beat him up for ditching you last night?"

"No! Stop talking and help me."

"Not a chance."

"You're not being nice."

"What can I say? I'm not a good Christian."

"What does being a good Christian have to do with help-ing me clean the pool?" I stomped to the other side of the pool and picked up the pool vacuum.

"Did I ever tell you I believe in the chaos theory? That every movement in the world creates change, and nothing is predictable. It's all very mathematical and not airy-fairy at all."

I glared at him. I knew he was taking a direct jab at my ability to see visions. He'd never believed me and thought I made everything up just to get Mom and Dad's attention. Feel-ing as crappy as I did, I had no desire to argue with him. I picked up the skimmer and tossed it at him.

"Okay, let's try your chaos theory or whatever it's called. Maybe your movement can change how this pool looks."

✢ ✢ ✢

Monday arrived more quickly than I wanted it to, and I swear I still had a hangover when I walked to the bus stop. The alcohol was slow to move out of my system. My bowels had acted up all day Sunday and were still messed up.

The nice autumn weather had changed, and now dark rain clouds hovered in the sky, but they suited my mood. I did up the snaps on my jean jacket and lowered my head to the brisk wind, knowing that soon I would have to pull out my winter coat. For today, the bright Indian summer had been replaced with dreary fall, and the warm winds had become a biting cold blast.

I arrived at school early, and the halls were empty. I didn't stop at my locker but went directly to the library, as I had something to look up for an English project I was working on for first period.

No one was in the library. I went immediately to the literature section and pulled out a book on the feminist movement. I had to do a comparison study for the novel we were reading in class, *The Handmaid's Tale,* by Margaret Atwood. It was a dystopian novel about the oppression of women and almost a warning to women about being complacent. It was also about indifference. Or at least that was my take on it.

I took the book back to a table and sat down to copy out a few notes for my essay on women being oppressed. My pen scratching on the paper was the only noise in the library until I heard footsteps.

Without looking up, I kept scrawling.

"Indigo." The familiar buttery voice made me jump.

"So I see you've scooped the book I wanted." John seemed to glide into the chair that was across from me, stretching out his long legs like life was just one easy movement. I glanced at him, allowing my hair to fall in front of my face. Even in the morning he looked hot, with his thick hair falling across his forehead and his hazel eyes appearing deep and brooding. I detected the familiar musky smell of man's soap and cigarettes.

"I'm almost done with it," I managed to stammer as I continued writing.

He pulled out a book from his backpack. "I'll wait."

I snuck a glance to see it was. I shuddered when I saw it was that *Sleeping Prophet* book again. But looking at it also made me remember the party and how we had stood on the back deck, under the full moon, and shared a cigarette.

"Are you reading that for some class?" I tried to ask nonchalantly as I kept my pen moving. I hoped he couldn't hear my voice tremble.

"Started off reading it for psychology, but now I'm reading it strictly for pleasure," he replied.

"Did you enjoy *The Handmaid's Tale?*"

"Yeah. I like Atwood. She's deep, and her work can be discussed on a lot of levels. I liked how she made me think about complacency and how if you just trust that everything will always be the same, you risk losing everything. There are so many complacent people in our society, and to me complacency breeds mediocrity. Do you want to just be mediocre? Or do you want to do something with your life that will help the world?"

I wasn't sure what I wanted to do with my life. Was I just going to be someone who did nothing, who as John said, was "mediocre"? Just recently a teacher had told me that I would never amount to anything.

"I liked her message about oppression," I said. "I'm looking at the feminist movement and how it has helped many women, but there are still countries today where women are oppressed." I finished writing and passed him the book, surprised that I had actually shared my thoughts with him.

"It's all yours," I said.

He pulled the book across the table toward his open binder. "I like your topic," he said. "Hey, do you take pysch?"

I shook my head. "Nope." There was no way I'd take psychology, even though my mom thought I should because it could have boosted my GPA. I probably knew more than the teacher from all my visits to doctors.

"It's a cool subject. And easy. Good GPA booster."

"So I've heard."

"Too bad you don't take it. I need some help."

I eyed him, checking to see if he was mocking me, like he did on Saturday night after I had taken a drag of his cigarette, but I detected none of that. Was he actually asking *me* for help? "Sorry," I replied.

He tapped his pen on the table. "It's a full-year course, and there are two midterms, two exams, and a huge paper due sometime in January. I want to do it on Edgar Cayce and how he had visions that came true. I want to compare him to Sigmund Freud. But it's a stretch, and maybe there isn't a basis for the comparison. Maybe I should just write on Cayce."

I shut my book. "January is forever away."

He grinned. "Yeah, I'll probably read the books I *like* for months, then write the paper the night before."

"I don't think I can help. I haven't heard of him."

"Freud?"

"Of course I've heard of Freud. I'm talking about Cayce."

This time he smirked instead of grinning. "You already told me you didn't know him on Saturday night. At the party. Remember? Or has the entire night escaped your memory?"

Had he heard about me getting drunk? Perhaps he had been at the party all night. Up in a bedroom somewhere. "Of course I remember," I replied. To change the subject, I started putting my books in my backpack.

"If you want to know more about him, I can lend you my book."

"That's okay," I replied. "You need to finish it first."

Why was he talking to me about this? Did he know something about me?

He leaned back in his chair, rocking it so he was balancing on the rear legs. "It's kind of unbelievable how he did it."

"Did what?"

He snapped the chair forward. Then he leaned toward me, his dark hair flipping across his forehead, his warm breath swirling in front of me. All I wanted to do was reach across the table and touch him. Feel his hair. Run my fingers through it. Touch his skin. Feel the stubble on his chin. Have it caress my fingertips. I wanted to be back on the porch with him when he stroked my hair, only this time, I wanted him to pull me close to his body. Or . . . I wanted him to lean across the table and kiss me. Right here in the library.

But he continued talking. "Had visions that came true. He was able to heal people of illnesses by seeing what was wrong when he was miles away from them. All he needed was a name. Do you know how utterly amazing and unbelievable that is?"

The heat in the room had risen to well over a hundred degrees, I was sure. I felt like I was sitting outside on a humid summer day. Sweat dripped under my shirt, and I could feel it running down my body. Was my face as red as it felt?

I wished he would stop talking about this stuff. And just focus on me. Look me in the eyes, and put his finger on my cheek and keep it there.

What he was talking about was too close to home. I felt like I should leave, get out of the library. But I couldn't move. It was as if he'd sucked me into a circle of energy that surrounded him. I wanted him to forget about schoolwork and ask me if I would share his cigarette.

"I would stick to doing your paper on Freud," I muttered. "That Cayce guy is probably not legit." I stammered when I talked.

"How do you know?" He stared at me, his eyes locking on mine. Stared. Without blinking. Just staring. His pupils were like deep, inky pools. I stared back, unable to look away from the wells of darkness.

Then he whispered, his voice husky and low, "You just said you don't know who he is." His words came out slowly, direct and almost critical.

I had to do something. Move. Shift. Anything. He was making me uncomfortable, but he had this hold on me. Then without thinking, without analyzing my words, I blurted out, "Well, he sounds like a flake." Then I pushed my chair away from the table.

And John moved his chair, too. Space hung between us. I'd ruined the moment.

With extreme coolness, he leaned back again, crossed his arms, tilted his head, and said, "You're judging the guy before you know anything about him? That's a bit presumptuous, Indigo Russell."

The tone of his voice confused me. Was he simply teasing me or deriding me? I was reminded of his comment about me being innocent. Was that how he viewed me? I didn't want him to think of me like that; I wanted to be his equal. Not a handmaid.

"I'm not judging," I said softly.

"Then what are you doing?"

I twirled my pen. "Expressing my opinion."

He nodded, slowly. Then one corner of his mouth lifted. "I like that."

Silence passed between us, the air still but the electricity hovering like a circling helicopter looking for something in the deep, dark woods. He broke the hush by tapping his pen on the table again.

"Cayce is an interesting study," he said. I wasn't sure if he was talking to me or to himself.

But then he looked at me, and I figured I was in the conversation. "I mean, you must think about these things," he continued. "Right?"

I shrugged.

He continued, "Is there a world outside of us that we can't see but people like Cayce can? He went into trances, you know."

I lowered my head, just slightly, and tucked my hair behind my ear. Again, I had this strong impulse to move, get away from this conversation, so I slipped my jean jacket on, and picked up my backpack and placed it on my lap. John was so absorbed in his thoughts that he didn't even notice I was getting ready to bolt.

He continued talking as if I weren't even there. "It's surreal."

I stood. "I gotta go. I can't be late again. See you in class."

With my backpack flapping against my legs, I left the library as quickly as I could.

⹔ ⹔ ⹔

The morning dragged. I couldn't stop thinking about John and his obsession with Edgar Cayce. We had books on him at home, but I had never read them; they were collecting dust in our den, a room I barely entered. I think Dr. Z had given my mom one. I had never read it because I just wasn't interested.

What would John say if he knew I had visions?

He mustn't find out.

He thinks Cayce is so fascinating but if he met the man in real life, he'd probably think he was freaky.

I caught up with Lacey just before lunch.

"You buying today?" she asked.

"Yeah. You?" I shut my locker door.

"Nah." She shook her head and looked like she was going to cry.

"Hey," I said softly. "What's wrong?"

"It's just this whole Burke thing." Lacey's voice trembled. "It's like everyone in school is talking about it."

When she looked at me, my heart ached, my arms and legs felt heavy, and my temples throbbed. I was feeling her pain. Her usually shining eyes were dull, and her radiant smile was gone.

"I need to tell you something," I said quietly.

As I opened my mouth to speak, I saw Burke strutting down the hallway toward us. He grinned at me and put his finger to his lips to shush me. He tiptoed up behind Lacey, put his hands over her eyes, and whispered in her ear, "Guess who?"

She turned and looked up at him, her eyes greeting his with adoration. Burke touched Lacey's face so tenderly I had to glance down.

"I'll catch you later," I muttered.

I turned my back on the lovebirds and walked away.

Chapter Five

The bell rang to end school. I don't remember walking to my locker, because my mind was so caught up in figuring out how to tell Lacey about my vision. I thought maybe I should read some of Morrison's poetry for help; perhaps he had written something that could make her understand the pain. He wrote a lot about pain. He also wrote about freedom. I liked his "The Opening of the Trunk" poem. It talked about inner freedom and opening the mind so the soul could wander. Maybe Lacey just needed to open up, and maybe her soul would realize that Burke was not good for her. If I did tell her, I had to be sensitive but honest, and then I wondered why I was thinking about telling her after they had looked so happy at lunch.

Because you're not normal, that's why.

What if she did have sex with him and found out afterward that he had been cheating on her? That would crush her completely. I had to tell her before they went all the way. I inhaled a huge breath of stale school air. I realized there was no way to make this go over well, but I had to do it anyway.

So, lost in thought, I was brought back to reality when I felt the bump.

"Hey, Indie." John was standing beside me. "You walk fast."

His shoulder rubbed against mine, the stimulating touch was enough to slow my steps. He fell into step beside me. "I'm finished with this Cayce book. I thought you might want to read it."

I glanced at him out of the corner of my eye and saw he was serious. Had I expressed some interest in this? I thought I had been clear that none of this stuff was on my radar. Nor did I want it to be. All I said in return was, "Oh."

He pulled the book out of the back pocket of his jeans, and when he passed it to me, our hands touched. There was that feeling again, the one that ran through my entire body like a jolt from an electrical storm. I loved the electrical storms that sometimes happened in Ottawa and the blinding rain that followed. I loved rain. Loved standing outside with my coat off, having the droplets run down my face.

"Don't worry about dog-earing any interesting pages," he said. "I got it at a used book sale."

"Sure," I said. Then I smiled at him. "If I get a seat, maybe I can read it on the bus."

"Yeah, let me know what you . . ." He let the end of his sentence trail off, raked his hand through his thick locks of hair, and exhaled, creating an odd noise I'd never heard come from him before.

Something about his raspy breathing and the sudden slouch of his usually straight shoulders made my body take on extra weight, like a barbell had been placed on my shoulders. His calm and cool demeanor receded, revealing a vulnerability that I'd never seen in him before. In that moment, I ached along with him, but for what—I had no idea. At a time like this, I wanted to see something, a snapshot to tell me what was bothering him. But all I could hear was him breathing and the end-of-school-day hallway noise. It all sounded so loud. And the pain I was feeling for him was so real, so intense. Why couldn't I focus? It was almost as if my pain for him overshadowed my ability to see what was wrong. But something troubled him. I knew that much.

He looked down at the floor and kicked a piece of mud before he said, "I gotta go. Enjoy the book."

Then he turned and left.

I watched him walk away, his steps heavy, his confident stride replaced with trudging tracks. I wanted to run after him, try to make him feel better.

But I didn't.

I knew he wouldn't let me in. Not yet, anyway.

I gathered my books and headed outside to my bus stop. It was a very gloomy day; clouds stalked the sky, and the sun didn't have a hope. It was that typical fall day that made you feel that winter was just around the corner. I did manage to get a window seat on the bus, but I didn't pull out the Cayce book. Instead I stared out the window at the drab gray clouds that hung low in the sky. Sometimes by Halloween there was snow. The darkness of the sky sheathed me in a damp cold. I sat alone with an empty seat beside me. In my mind, I replayed John's hushed voice and how it seemed to crack, his slouched shoulders and loud sighs.

The bus lurched to a stop, and the doors opened, letting in a gust of cold air. I hunkered in my seat and once again stared out the window. Three stops before mine, I saw the man enter, talking animatedly to himself. *He* would sit beside me. They always did—the ones with mental issues. A part of me wanted to get up, but I couldn't do that to the guy. I didn't want to hurt his feelings. Sure enough, he sat beside me and continued to babble. I didn't respond to him, but I also didn't try to shut him out.

When I got off the bus, I walked home with my head down. My legs were so heavy; they made my feet hard to lift. I was exhausted. I was always so tired after I sat beside someone like that guy—it was as if he sapped all my energy in just one bus ride. I knew if I were to lie down on my bed, I would fall asleep for hours. Sometimes, when I felt like this, I could sleep for 17 hours straight. To ease my tiredness, I shifted my focus to John. Everything about his body language had said he was headed someplace he didn't want to go.

But where?

My feelings for him were growing, and the mystery darkening him increased my obsession. I wanted to know everything about him. We were close to forging something, but not close enough. I wanted him to touch my hair again, and I wanted him to kiss me. How was I going to let him know that I liked him? Perhaps I could take the easy way out. Get Lacey to give him a note for me. What did I have to lose?

The wind whipped my hair around my face. I was in my last year of high school. Who cared about my reputation? I pulled a strand of hair out of my mouth, wondering about Burke's question about the future. What *was* I going to do next year? Some of my friends were planning on traveling, some were going to get jobs and work full-time so they could move out on their own, and a few others were planning to go on to college and university. But I had no plans, no idea what should come next. My grades weren't great, and I had no real skills.

Was I indifferent? Like the theme in *The Handmaid's Tale*? The math and science teachers often said I was indifferent to my education. I think I might have been labeled indifferent since I'd started school. How sad was that?

School wasn't my thing. That I knew. I'd almost failed grade four. What normal kid does that? Because I didn't speak, they thought I was a slow learner. I sat in the middle of the third row, daydreaming about living in some faraway fantasy land that wasn't earth.

"Indigo, you need to do your work." The teacher would come down the aisle and stop right in front of my desk. "You haven't even started. When were you going to get busy on this?"

I didn't answer. I looked down at the paper and all the numbers. What if I answered and somehow the kids found out I was different and that I saw dead people in my room, saw things before they even happened? They would laugh at me. Or run away from me. Look what had happened with my hamster, Teresa. Anna was traumatized, and she never came over again. Halfway through grade four, my parents were called in to see the teacher. Later that night, I heard them talking in the kitchen: the teacher wanted to fail me because I didn't talk.

Back then Lacey was the only constant in my life. She knew about my visions and stuck with me.

My steps slowed. Lacey. Lacey.

I'm so sorry, Lacey.

Snapshots of Lacey and me riding bikes, braiding our hair, and playing outside until the streetlights came on flashed through my head until I rounded the corner to my house. I knew we were drifting apart and had different interests, but we'd always been friends. I trusted her, and she trusted me to tell the truth.

Once I was home, I headed straight to my room and closed the door. Without taking off my jean jacket, I lay down on my bed. My room had always given me some sort of peace. Even when I was little, it was as if my bed had been my protector, a safe place to go to escape the craziness of my world. Of course, this was all so ironic. I hated feeling caged, yet I liked my room, which was a box with walls. Go figure.

You're so weird, Indie.

For a while, I lay quiet on my bed, thinking about way too many things.

What was I going to say to Lacey?

What was on John's mind when he left like that? Should I write him a note?

What was I going to say to Lacey?

Why was I crazy?

What was I going to say to Lacey?

I slowly sat up. Maybe playing the guitar would help. I pulled it out from under my bed and started to strum and sing random words that I tried to piece together to make a song that we could use with our band. It would be fun to get that going again. I strummed and sang:

Problem after problem,
Hurt after tears.
It's never going to go away,
That's what I fear.

I stopped singing. Today my words made no sense, and I didn't want to think about fear. I put the guitar away. I wasn't good anyway. And I was dog tired.

I stayed in my room, under my covers, until my mom called me for dinner. At the dinner table, I picked at my meat and pushed my potatoes around. She gave me a concerned look from across the table, so I sat up and shoveled some corn into my mouth. I did not want her coming to my room tonight asking questions, and she had that look that said she might. I refused to make further eye contact. When dinner ended, I helped with the dishes, all the while making small talk so she wouldn't pick up on my mood. When we were done, I begged off from any more conversation and headed down the hall to my room. Once in, I shut the door. Tightly.

I put on music and tried to listen to the lyrics for inspiration. Nothing helped take away the chill that I was now feeling. I wore two shirts, a sweater, socks, and sweatpants. My stomach ached, my head throbbed, and I kept glancing at the clock. I had to wait until nine to call Lacey. I knew she was out with Burke.

At least five times, I flopped down on my bed because I couldn't concentrate on anything but what I would say to Lacey. When I heard the beep on my clock radio, telling me it was nine, I sighed. I ran through my lines one more time before I punched in her number. She sounded breathless when she answered.

"Did you just get home?" I asked.

"Yeah. Literally like a minute ago," she puffed.

"Can you talk?"

"Give me a sec."

From the crashing sound, I guessed she had thrown her pink phone on her night table. The seconds ticked by, and they matched my beating heart. A delay was not what I needed or wanted. I heard a few more indistinct sounds, then finally her voice again. "Okay," she said. "I'm good." Although I couldn't see her, I knew Lacey had plopped onto her bed and was lying back on the pile of cushions and pillows that adorned it.

"I have something to tell you," I said. No sense stalling. I'd stalled long enough.

"Are you seriously going after John?"

"Maybe," I said.

"I saw you talking to him in the hallway today," she continued. "Indie, I swear he likes you. I'm not his biggest fan, but hey, you like him, and that's all that maters. I want to see you happy, girlfriend."

"I don't know about that, but I want to tell him I like him."

"Then tell him."

"I was thinking of passing him a note."

"A note? Like we used to do in grade seven?"

"Okay, so dumb idea."

"Not at all. At least he'd know. I'll do it for you."

"Yeah, at least he'd know," I said slowly. "And then I'd find out if he likes me back." I paused. Life was about truth. Lacey deserved the truth. "I have something to tell you," I said.

"'Kay." She paused. "Tell me what you have to tell me, then I have something super important to tell you." She giggled. "But you go first."

I breathed, swallowed, exhaled, then sucked in another big breath.

"Hurry up!" Lacey sounded so upbeat, but also really impatient. "What I have to tell you is so—just so amazing."

"I had a vision," I blurted out.

"Oh! Cool. Am I marrying Burke?"

"Not exactly."

"Okay. We got engaged, and he gave me a big diamond?"

Why was she talking like this? "You're only in high school. Do you really want to get married?"

"Burke and I are thinking of applying to the same university. We could live together. Lots of couples do that."

"But you're only seventeen." Sometimes Lacey exasperated me. She was not a person to think anything through, unlike me. I thought everything through to the last minute detail and then did nothing about it.

"We will be eighteen by then. Anyway, love isn't about age."

I tried to absorb her words—well, one word, really, the word *love*, which caused me to pause for a moment. She was madly in love with a guy who cheated on her. I decided to go for it so I spit out, "Listen . . . I'm so sorry, Lacey, but I saw him with Amber McKinnon before it happened."

The phone went silent, although I could still hear her breathing. Then, very slowly, she said, "Before it happened?"

"Yes."

"You mean you saw it in one of your visions?"

"Yes."

"When did you have this *vision*?"

"A few days before the party."

"So why are you just telling me about it now?"

"I don't know." I stumbled over my words. "I didn't want to hurt you—"

"Hurt me? And what you're doing now isn't hurting me? Do you have proof? Besides your *vision*?" Again she said the word like it was poisonous.

"Not really. But at the party they were standing together, and Amber had her fingers in his belt loop."

"For gawd's sake, Indie! That is not making out. Burke and Amber went to the same elementary school. They've known each other for years, and they're friends."

"She looked like she wanted to be more than friends," I said, not knowing what else to say. I'd really blown this.

"That's Amber. She's like that with every guy."

"I know. That's my point."

"Did you see them together in *real life*?" Her words were pointed and very sarcastic.

"Not completely. But she was leaning on him, if you know what I mean."

"Burke would never, ever sleep with her, no matter how hard she tried to get him into bed."

"What if they just made out a bit?"

She sucked in a sharp breath before she quickly said, "Made out a bit? Indie, making out is not standing beside each other. Well, maybe it is in your books, because you know nothing about guys. You've never even had a boyfriend."

Her words stung, but I was not going to react to the comment. "My vision was very real," I mumbled.

"Real? Are you freaking kidding me? You've lost your mind. Listen to me. Nothing—and I mean *nothing*—happened." Her voice came out like static, clipped and purposeful.

"I think something did happen," I whispered.

"You think! What do you mean you think? You either know, or you don't. And if you only *think*, then you don't know."

"Okay," I said. Confrontation was my worst enemy. I had told her, and now it was time to back off. Self-doubt crept into my mind. Maybe my vision was whacked. Maybe I was just a lunatic, like that Cayce guy. Did everything he saw come true?

"You know, Indie, I've always been your friend and never cared that you were different."

My stomach churned, and my hands started to shake. I had ruined the one true friendship I had. And for what? A stupid vision that may or may not be true.

"What? Did you have so much fun at the party that now you want in and to hell with me? Is that it?" She threw her words at me. "Or do you want Burke now because he was nice enough to drive you home?"

"No!"

"Are you sure?"

"I don't want Burke. He's your boyfriend. Why would I want him?"

"That's true, Indie. He is my boyfriend."

"He's going to hurt you."

She fell silent. It felt like an eternity.

"I'm so sorry." I could feel my throat closing in, making it hard to breathe. "Maybe my vision was wrong."

"It *was* wrong. Totally wrong. You know, I had something really important to tell you tonight, and you're the first person I wanted to tell, and now you've gone and wrecked my moment."

"You can still tell me," I said quietly.

"I don't want to, because you won't be happy for me. Well, maybe I will anyway, just to prove how wrong you really are.

For your info, Burke and I had sex tonight. It wasn't just a hookup, Indie; we made love. There's a difference."

Before I could reply, the line went dead.

I clutched the phone in my hand for a few minutes before I put it back in its cradle.

I wanted to scream; instead I did nothing but stare at the wall. Finally, I moaned and rolled over, and that's when I saw the book John had loaned me sticking out of my backpack. I got up and pulled it out. Slowly, I cracked it open and started to read. Cayce went into trances or some sort of sleep state to see his visions. I flipped the page, not wanting to read line by line. He was an average guy with a wife and kids, and he taught Sunday school. Yeah, right. What church would allow a guy who had visions to teach little kids? Give me a break. The church hated this kind of stuff. Another page. He hated taking money for what he did, and there were some who tried to extort him, make him into a sideshow, so he decided to help only those who were sick. Okay, that I could understand. Well, sort of.

I turned another page. He often didn't remember his readings because, he claimed, the unconscious mind had some sort of access to the information that the conscious mind didn't.

What!? That was so not true. I remembered things.

My blood gushed through me at the audacity of such a statement. Angrily, I threw the book against the wall and watched a couple of the pages fall from the spine. Obviously, it was a piece of crap.

Why couldn't I just forget, too?

My life would be far better. Lacey would still be my friend.

Chapter Six

I woke up in the morning feeling like crap. I hadn't slept all night because of what had happened with Lacey. In fact, I'd cried myself to sleep. I didn't want to go through my last year of high school without her. We had everything planned out for grad formal: limos, dresses, corsages, dates. I was supposed to go with John, and she was supposed to go with Burke. I would wear a short dress that was simple and sleek, but with cool accessories, like a feather boa. Lacey always wanted to wear a long dress, something frilly or lacy, like a debutante ball gown or like the dresses actors wore to the Oscars. Although we had different tastes in the dress department, we had both decided that we would go to the hairdresser and get updos.

Now I had wrecked everything. What was wrong with me?

Your stupid visions, that's what.

"Leave me alone," I said out loud. "Stop telling me what I did wrong and just tell me how to fix this."

Not a chance. Fix this yourself.

How was I going to face Lacey today? Especially when her locker was beside mine.

63

For the second day in a row, I got to school early. Only this time, I didn't go straight to the library—I went to my locker. I had to get my books before Lacey showed up.

My locker door was still open when I heard the familiar smacking of flip-flops on the tiled floor. My heart quickened. My pulse raced.

I looked up. "John," I said.

Casually, he leaned against the locker beside mine and gave me a lopsided smile. But through his smile, I saw something else. Red rimmed his eyes, like he hadn't slept all night. Was he stoned?

I inhaled. I didn't smell anything except fresh soap and cigarettes.

No, he was just exhausted. But I sensed sadness, too. It seemed to seep from the little red lines in his eyes.

"You didn't wear a hockey jersey," he said.

"Is it jersey day again?" I had totally forgotten. Hockey nets would be set up outside at lunch, and guys and some girls, the athletic ones like Lacey, would go out and play ball hockey with the teachers and students. The hockey boys like Burke would be treated like gods.

"Lame, eh?"

"So lame," I replied. "I hate all those dumb 'rah, rah, school spirit' days."

"Totally."

"Hey, did you read the book I gave you yesterday?" he asked.

"Just a little," I confessed.

My face flushed as I remembered throwing the book against the wall. I had to buy him a new one. I turned toward my locker, both to hide my red face and to get my books out so I would be gone before Lacey came.

"So?" he asked.

"So?" I replied.

"The book?"

"Right." I tried to act normal, searching for the stuff I need-ed for first period. "I didn't have time to read much, but . . . it just doesn't seem realistic." I hurriedly pulled out a book and, in the process, sent the entire top shelf of my locker toppling to the floor.

John bent over to retrieve everything that had spilled out. He handed me some books. "I betcha he really could see dead people."

My spine stiffened, and without looking him in the eye, I took the books and stacked them in my locker. Did John know something about me?

"No one can see dead people." I tried to laugh. "They're all just quacks. When people are dead, they are dead." I finally turned toward him, and although I wanted to flash a flippant smile, I didn't. The look on his face was so serious.

"I have to believe that there are people who can talk to the dead," he said quietly, shaking his head.

Why did he have to talk about this stuff? Most guys his age had zero interest in this stuff. Had he recently lost someone important to him? Shivers ran the length of my legs, up into my back, and all the way to my head, where I suddenly saw . . . nothing.

Blank.

Nothing but white.

No! I cannot, will not, have a vision in the school hallway. I clenched my fists and tensed every muscle in my body.

Stay in the present. Stay in the present. My mind chattered.

Then I caught a whiff of some sort of weird smoke. Was someone smoking in the school hallway? Had John just lit up a cigarette? The aroma was sweet, tantalizing. No, it wasn't cigarette smoke.

It was more like one of those cigarillos.

I glanced at John's hands but saw nothing. Next, I frantically scanned the hall.

It was then that I saw the white outline of a man standing behind John. I wanted to yell, tell him to leave me alone. Tell him to go back to where he came from.

But no words came out of my mouth.

Although his outline was fuzzy, I could see that the man was tall and extremely muscular. When spirits showed themselves to me, they were neither solid nor liquid. They always freaked me out because they were almost like Jell-O. A big fat cigar dangled from his mouth. The eyes were always unclear, so I couldn't see what color they were. When he reached up to take his cigar out of his mouth, he smiled at me. And it wasn't a nice smile. It was a leer. But he didn't speak, which was weird. Usually they talked. I gasped, dropping my books again on the floor, the thud echoing off the concrete walls.

"What's the matter?" John craned his neck to look behind him.

I bent down to pick up my books.

Keep cool. Keep cool. Just pretend that nothing happened.

John squatted to help me. Again. I was such a loser.

"Are you okay?" he asked. He was so close that I could feel his hot breath on my face. For some reason, it comforted me. My heart rate dropped, and my shaking started to subside. The smell of cigar smoke dissipated, and I breathed in and out, trying to bring everything back to normal. The man was gone.

"I'm fine," I replied.

John put his hand on my elbow and helped me stand. Then when he handed me my books, our hands touched, and this time, when the shivers coursed through my body, they were electric, full of surreal zapping energy. "Thanks," I said.

"You look as if you just saw a ghost." He smiled at me.

I held my breath. Did he know? I tried to smile back. And, really, his words had been said without any implication that he had figured out what had happened.

"Nah," I replied, trying to sound nonchalant. "I'm just a real klutz sometimes. Hey, is the cafeteria open this early?" I asked. "I'm not usually here until a minute before the bell goes. I need some coffee."

"Coffee," said John. "My breakfast staple. I'll buy you a cup."

I slammed my locker shut with my foot and snuck a glance down the hall. No man. Just an empty hallway. Maybe I could get through the day.

We didn't talk much as we walked down the hall, and that was a good thing because my mind was racing, thoughts pinging back and forth. Why had that guy just shown up? Who was he? My body felt drained. I was sure if I went home, I would sleep for hours. The secrets piling up inside of me were taking their toll.

And I had to keep them buried deep, deep, deep down.

I had to put them in the ground and shovel dirt over them to keep them silent. I decided the next time I had a vision, I would will it away, or if a dead person showed up in front of me, I would get rid of them with my mind. I could not let any of this destroy my life.

I glanced at John. His hair seemed to sway when he walked, almost as if he moved in slow motion. And I loved his profile—long masculine nose, full lips, and square jaw. His chin looked smooth today. He had shaved this morning. If I touched it, would it feel smooth?

Then just like that, my happy thoughts about John were crowded out by thoughts about the man in the hall. He hadn't looked like a particularly nice guy. Was he an old janitor? An ex-teacher who had done something wrong? Maybe he had sold drugs or molested students. If I dug in old school records, I bet I could find out. Wait! I needed to keep him buried. No digging. Whoever he was, I didn't like him and wanted nothing to do with him.

We entered the cafeteria, and John got me a coffee from the vending machine. It tasted terrible, but I couldn't help drinking it and smiling. The cafeteria was still quiet, and we sat next to each other on one of the tables. I struggled to keep the conversation light.

"So, what's your favorite band?" I asked, swinging my legs back and forth.

He tilted his head and squinted, thinking. "I like lots of music. Maybe Pearl Jam is my favorite band. Or Eric Clapton. The Kinks." He grinned. "I like songs with lyrics. How about you?" John asked.

I played with my paper coffee cup. The few sips I'd taken were scraping the sides of my intestines. "I love the Kinks. I'm totally into '60s rock 'n' roll. The Beatles. The Doors . . . and more modern stuff, too. I like the Police, too, and Pearl Jam. 'Just Breathe' is a great song."

"It's about death. Going to the other side."

Silence.

John leaned into me with his shoulder, and I didn't move away. I let our bodies connect. At first the tingles ran down my one arm, the one he was touching, but then they coursed into my stomach and through all the rest of my limbs. Then the tingles turned to a throbbing sensation that I felt all over my body. I could have sworn I was feeling my blood pulsating, through my skin and my clothes. My heart raced, ticking wildly. My face flushed. I realized that I had absolutely no control over my reactions.

I tried to catch my breath.

And I wondered if he was feeling the same thing I was.

"I like the Grateful Dead. Such a great name for a band." He paused, then looked my way. "You really don't believe in what we were talking about earlier? About people being able to talk to the dead?"

"No," I said. The heat in my body subsided a little, enough for me to answer his question. "I think it's all a bunch of hocus-pocus." I mimed the words *hocus-pocus* as if I were a Halloween witch, just to do something with my hands. "I think everyone dies, and that's it."

"But where do we go? Does anyone come back in spirit form?"

I swallowed. Papa had come to me when he died, and he still showed up now and again. He had told me that all the spirits who came to me were people who had died. People who couldn't for some reason leave the earth or, like Papa, just wanted to visit to tell me things. I kept swinging my legs. Back and forth. Back and forth. Who was the guy in the hall? Why had he come to me?

Because you're weird, thats why.

I didn't answer John, and silence hung around us like an uninvited guest.

John spoke first. "Well, I guess everyone is entitled to their own opinion." He shrugged, turned away, and stared at the drab beige cafeteria wall, deep in thought. I kept silent and continued swinging my legs. Then the bell rang.

"Time for class." I slid off the table. "Hey, you want to meet for lunch?" I blurted out.

"I can't," he mumbled, quickly looking away. "I've got something I have to do."

"Okay," I replied, trying to sound cool. "No big deal."

Crushed, I didn't go to my first class and instead went outside for a smoke. A brisk wind smacked me in the face, until I rounded the corner that led to the little concrete area beside the school that was designated as the smoking pad. It was sheltered from the wind. Kids milled about, red sparks sizzling like strobe lights. As soon as I entered, I saw Sarah, Zoe, and Carly, so I made my way over to them. I had started hanging out with Sarah shortly after grade ten, when Lacey made varsity volleyball. Through Sarah I had met Zoe and Carly. Lacey and I were clearly on different paths. Lacey had never smoked a cigarette in her life.

Lacey. I'm so sorry.

You did the right thing, Indie. The soft, kind man's voice poked through my thoughts.

"Hey, Indie." Sarah waved her hand in front my eyes, snapping her fingers to get my attention.

"Hey." I pulled out my cigarettes, thankful for the distraction. Smoking gave me something to do with my hands, took me outside of my head and away from the voices. I sparked my cigarette on Sarah's and inhaled. When I exhaled, I let the smoke out in one slow, steady stream. Mindless. Numbing. I listened to everyone talk about school, teachers, good bands, bad bands, new songs, old songs, while my mind chattered about other things.

Lacey hated me; John had rejected me.

I had seen a ghost at school.

I wanted to go home.

And do what? Lie on my bed? Listen to music? And think about how I was totally messing things up on a daily basis? I couldn't stop thinking about John. His saying no to meeting for lunch had really hurt. But maybe he really did have something to do.

Or maybe he just doesn't like you.

"Indie, we seriously should get our band going again," said Sarah, using her hands to talk. "Remember, we talked about it the other night at the party?"

"Ha ha," I said. "I wasn't sure if you'd remember."

"I wasn't that drunk. Not like someone else I know." Sarah hip-checked me.

I laughed. "I'm in," I said. Unexpected excitement spread through my body. To be back playing music in our band would be awesome. I had loved hashing over what songs we would do, then searching for the music, listening to it, memorizing the lyrics, and rehearsing. This was exactly what I needed. It would take my mind off John. I stubbed out my cigarette.

"Me too," said Carly. She too had excitement in her voice. "I just got a new keyboard."

"Count me in, too," exclaimed Zoe.

"Why don't we meet at Denny's after school today—the one in South Keys?" Sarah asked. "We can talk about songs and stuff like that. Get organized. I got a new drum set for my b-day last year. You're still playing your guitar, eh, Indie?"

"Oh, yeah."

"You still writing poetry, too? Maybe we could try some original songs."

"I guess we could try," I said, flattered that they thought I could write a song. "That would be pretty cool to create our own song! We could jam to figure out the tune."

Sarah, Zoe, and Carly all put up their hands for high fives. Then Sarah said, "Denny's it is for a meeting of the minds."

I high-fived everyone back. I was planning on heading to a bookstore anyway to try to buy a new book for John, seeing as I'd destroyed the one he'd lent me, and there was a bookstore close to Denny's, so this was perfect.

"I'm going early 'cause I don't have last block," said Sarah.

"I'd skip, but I got a test."

"Just meet us in there. In the smoking section."

I nodded. Then the bell rang. I walked back into school just as the halls started to fill with students. My fingers were frozen, so I shoved them in the pockets of my jacket. At least I had something to do after school and with my time.

As I walked to my class, I passed Lacey, and when I saw the hollowness circling her eyes, a pain flamed in my chest. My lungs burned so badly that I had to stop walking to lean against the wall. Hurt seeped through my skin to my bones, and my chest felt as if a rubber band were tightening around it. Lacey had this way of walking tall with her chin up and shoulders square, but I could see through that. Her heart was broken.

I had just gotten back into step to get to class when I saw Burke approaching from the other side of the hall. Was he going to blast me? Embarrass me in front of everyone? Had Lacey told him? He passed, smiled, said hi, and kept moving.

Thank you, Lacey.

All day I kept looking up and down the halls in search of John, but when school ended, I hadn't seen him again. Had he skipped? My heart burned in pain, and something crazy invaded my limbs: numbness, heaviness, sadness. Why did I get these overwhelming feelings of sadness all the time?

I headed to the bus stop to go to the mall. As soon as I got there, I saw Nathan Carroll huddled off to the side, standing alone as usual. He was teased mercilessly for being small and nerdy and having pimples and braces. I always felt for him. He didn't deserve to be the butt of everyone's jokes; it wasn't fair. I walked up to him.

"Hi, Nathan," I said.

"Hi, Indie." He glanced at me, then quickly looked away again.

"Do you usually take this bus?" I asked, wanting to make conversation.

He hunched his shoulders. "Yeah. I live close to the mall."

I nodded. The bus approached, and we both moved to board. Then out of nowhere, a big brute of a guy pushed by Nathan, making him stumble. I grabbed his arm to help him keep his balance. "Come on," I whispered. "Let's sit together."

Once we were seated, he looked out the window, then turned to me and said, "I hate this weather. It's so gloomy." He turtled his head into the collar of his jacket.

I laughed to make him feel more at ease. "I like the gray and the dark," I said.

"You do?" He frowned.

"Yeah, I do."

He shoved his hands into his pockets. "That's kind of funny, because to me you are like a butterfly, light and free to fly in the summer sun from bush to bush. I'd think you would like the sun."

I laughed at his comment. "Me? A butterfly? You're funny, Nathan."

He laughed along with me, the metal in his teeth gleaming, and I could see a spark of happiness in his eyes, which made me feel lighter as well.

"I like the gray, because sun all the time is kind of boring," I said. "Don't ya think? I bet even butterflies like the gray. It's like life. Some days are light, and some days are really dark."

Nathan stopped smiling and lowered his head. "I have dark days all the time, so I guess that's why I like the sun so much. Just makes me feel a little better."

"Life can't be that bad," I said.

He glanced at me. "It's not that good." Then he brightened a bit. "Well, not at school anyway. But it's better when I'm sitting with you on the bus!"

I nudged him with my shoulder. "I read the weather forecast, and tomorrow is supposed to be sunny."

He grinned. "Good."

As we chatted for a few more minutes, I felt lighter and freer because Nathan was happy. It was funny how my moods were so dependent on others.

Nathan's stop was two before the mall.

"Thanks, Indie," he said as he stood to get off.

When he looked at me, I thought he might cry—and not tears of sorrow, but more of happiness, because someone had been nice to him. I didn't understand why people thought it was fun to hurt others. It made no sense.

Had I hurt Lacey? That is the last thing I want to do.

I lifted my hand and gave a little wave. Within seconds, he was out the bus door. I slid down in my seat, thinking about

Lacey. Then my thoughts veered like a car making a sharp turn, and I thought about John and the man in the hallway. I tapped my fingers on my thigh, over and over, waiting for my stop, my thoughts streaming through my mind.

Who *was* he?

Finally, the bus stopped, and I stood to get off. My legs were heavy, and I felt like I'd walked uphill for an hour. Over the years, I'd been tested for mono at least five times, but the results were always negative. I was tired for no reason. My energy was so crazy. One minute I felt great and light, and the next I felt as if I weighed a million pounds.

As I walked to Denny's, something nagged at me, made me feel uneasy, so I hurried. I turned to look behind me. No one was following. What was wrong now? It was broad daylight, and not a single person was walking behind me.

When I was close to the door, a sudden throb hit my forehead, nearly making me gasp for air. I looked behind me again and still saw nothing. There was no one nearby.

Relax, Indie. Breathe.

I rushed so I could get to the table, meet my friends, have a cigarette, and stop this insanity. Sometimes with people around me, I could push all this internal stuff aside.

Suddenly, I started thinking about a flight home from California, a year ago, when out of the blue, I had heard my cousin's name. I remembered how I had felt on that day—I was feeling the same way now.

✧ ✧ ✧

I had been on an airplane, staring out the little window at the clouds floating like gauzy mist. Brian wasn't with us, because he had to work. As I watched the clouds, my mind went blank, white. Then, I had heard the word *Curtis* loud and clear. I sat forward and blinked. I had a cousin named Curtis. For the past five years, he'd had so many drug problems, and everyone in the family worried about him.

Once we landed, we got our bags and then picked up our car. I sat in the backseat feeling uneasy. Something wasn't right.

In the backseat of the car, I had swung my legs back and forth as I stared out the window, until my mother yelled at me from the front, telling me to stop kicking her seat. When we arrived home, my head pounded. Brian met us at the front door, his face red and blotchy from tears. He *never* cried.

"Curtis is dead," he sobbed. "Overdosed."

✧ ✧ ✧

What was wrong with me? I had to stop thinking about all of this. I was going to meet my friends. I started running.

This isn't close to the same, Indie. You are imagining everything.

But it is, Indie, it is. Remember the feelings. That's your job.

By the time I saw Sarah waving at me from a table way in the back, my breathing was coming out in pants, like I'd just finished phys-ed class and the run test. Ignoring the hostess who usually seated people, I hurried down the aisle to get to the booth where Sarah, Carly, and Zoe sat.

Sarah laughed when she saw me. "Did you run here?"

"Nah, I just walk fast." I sat down beside her and tossed my backpack on the floor. Then I immediately took out my cigarettes.

I lit up, inhaling deeply. *Relax. Relax.* The smoke somehow stopped my thoughts from getting out of control and numbed my body so panic couldn't set in.

"So, we've been talking about our band," said Sarah. "We should have a rehearsal soon. And then once we get good enough, we could find somewhere to play."

"Like a real concert?" I asked. "We need a lot of practice before we play in front of people. But, wow, that would be so cool."

"We could do some type of fund-raiser." Carly tapped her fingers on the table.

My mind went blank, then I saw a dog, and he had the saddest eyes. The vision disappeared like a puff of cigarette smoke. "Animal shelter," I said. "We could do something for stray dogs and cats. They often have events, and maybe we could play at one of them and help them raise money!"

Sarah held up her hand. "You rock, girl. That's a great idea."

"I'll phone them," said Carly. "My friend works there, and I know they have one event in the fall, which we have probably already missed, one at Christmas, and one in the spring."

Sarah pursed her lips before she said, "I dunno. Christmas doesn't give us much time. Last time we rehearsed a million times before we perfected one song. If we are going to do this, we have to do it right."

The smell of lilacs hit me. "I think spring would be great," I said. "And I agree that we need the time. What songs are we thinking of?" I took out a pen and paper from my backpack to write everything down.

The conversation around the table escalated and became animated as we continued with our plans. Time ticked by. We would go to the animal shelter and offer our services, see if we could do something in, like, six months, which would give us time to put together a set. Five songs would probably be enough.

While I was excited to talk about the band and totally got into it, my head continued to throb, and my stomach ached. I smoked and listened, talked and laughed, but on the inside, I had a rolling uneasiness that just kept rising and falling, over and over again. After our band conversation was over, we started to do our usual talk about parties and crap.

"Hey," said Carly, leaning forward and directing her words at me, "I heard Burke was necking with Amber at that party on the weekend. Does Lacey know?"

I gave a noncommittal shrug.

Sarah laughed and jostled me with her shoulder. "Indie was so drunk, I doubt she remembers anything."

"You were the one who gave me the drink." I laughed. "Like, four drinks in one."

"You were so funny. I laughed so hard when you threw up on that guy's shoes."

"Which guy?" Carly asked.

"That preppy kid with the starched pants."

Zoe burst out laughing. "I must have missed that."

"Indie was on the porch with John." Sarah almost sang her words. "He is so hot. And I think he likes you, Indie."

Just the mention of his name made my heart race. "I don't know about that," I replied, trying to look cool.

"We got to get him to ask you out," said Sarah. "You guys are perfect for each other."

Without thinking of any consequences, I yanked a notebook out of my backpack and ripped out a piece of paper. Then I wrote: *I like you. Do you like me?*

I folded it in half and gave it to Sarah. "Give this to him for me."

"Are you kidding me?" Sarah's eyes were wide with shock. "You got balls."

"What the heck?" I said. "Might as well find out before I waste any more time."

Sarah took the note and carefully put it in a little zippered section on the front of her backpack. Then she motioned for me to scoot out. I stood, and she also slipped out of the booth, swinging her backpack over her shoulder. "Tomorrow morning, first thing," she said. "Now I gotta go, or my mom will kill me."

"Me too." I picked up my backpack as well. "I have to go to the bookstore first and pick something up."

Once we were all outside, I went one way, and Sarah, Zoe, and Carly went the other. Alone, walking over to the bookstore, which was in the same little outdoor strip mall, I wondered how John was going to react to the note. I was deep in thought about this when something crashed through me, like I had been tossed into a huge snowbank while snowboarding and I was trying to get to the top for air. I stopped walking and clutched my chest again. What was wrong with me now? This was the second time today. First when I passed Lacey, and now this. Cold eddied around me. I felt as if I were suffocating.

Blank.

No. This can't be happening.

I quickly staggered to a seat on a bench outside. My vision narrowed until I had only a hole to look through, a long tunnel. Then everything went blurry. Maybe it wouldn't come on.

My head pounded. I squeezed my eyes shut, then remembered how that hadn't helped last time, so I opened them wide. At this point, I needed to try anything to get these visions to go away.

I focused on a spot on the ground, and just when I thought it was over, that I had managed to squelch it, outsmart it, the throbbing began again. My sight grew longer and thinner, the fishbowl getting closer and closer. I shifted my gaze upward, looking for another spot to stare at. My gaze landed on a parking sign. No! That wasn't going to work. I needed to look down again. The square concrete tiles on the sidewalk started to twist, and the picture started to form. It was blurry at first, then suddenly it was crystal clear. I saw a big red heart pulsing, in and out. Almost like a cartoon depiction. Pains pushed through my chest, and I could hear the heart beating, a loud sound like on a heart monitor.

Thump. Thump. Thump.

The thumping got faster and faster.

Thump, thump, thump, thump, thump.

Faster, faster, until I could hardly breathe. It wasn't normal. The heart was beating too quickly. It had to slow down.

Thump thump thump thump thump thump thump.

Then it stopped. Just like that. My mind cleared, the noise abated, and as quickly as the vision had arrived, it left. My headache suddenly dissipated, until all I felt was a dull ache through my entire body.

Shifting back to reality, I looked around the small strip mall. Nothing. What was wrong with me? How many times a day did I have to ask myself that question?

First there was the uneasiness when I walked into Denny's and now this. I thought about Edgar Cayce. He purposely went into trances. I wondered if next time I could purposely *not* go into a trance. I had no desire to see anything in the future, nor did I want to tap into the spiritual dimension.

Look what happened when I did. I lost my best friend.

Suddenly, I realized I was shaking so hard my teeth were chattering, and it wasn't even that cold out yet. I had to go home to the comfort of my bedroom. Finally, after my heart rate had returned to normal, I slung my backpack over my shoulder. To heck with the bookstore. I would buy the book tomorrow.

I had just gotten up when I noticed a woman walking into the bookstore I had planned to go to. I couldn't move. I stared at her. I didn't know her, but I couldn't take my eyes off her. The thumping of the heart suddenly sounded in my head again. The sound got louder and louder, until I was sure my head would burst.

The heart.

Her heart.

No! She's going to have a heart attack!

Instead of moving, I stood in one spot. I didn't know what to do. The woman, dressed in a red trench coat, had grasped the door handle and started to pull on it when she stopped in mid-yank and put her hand to her forehead, wiping her brow.

Go to her, Indie. Help her.

You idiot, you saw her red coat that's all. That's what the heart was.

I shook my head. *Had* I just seen a red heart because of the red coat she was wearing? She wasn't touching her heart; she was pressing her hand on her forehead like she had a headache. If I wasn't crazy before, I was now.

I took one step to walk away, but suddenly the woman grabbed her chest. Even from where I was standing, probably 30 feet away, I could hear her struggling to breathe.

Then she collapsed, her body thudding as it hit the ground.

I sprinted to her, screaming, "Call an ambulance. This woman just had a heart attack."

The flurry of activity started as a man who had been heading in our direction yelled that he would make the call. After that, everyone who passed by or was coming out of a store got involved, even if it was just to watch. A crowd gathered around us. I got down on my knees and held the woman's hand. She was short of breath, so I knew she couldn't talk to me, and her face had turned a horrible gray color.

"Don't talk, okay?" I said softly. "Help is on the way."

She wheezed, and I wondered if air was even getting to her lungs. Her eyes remained wide open, and I could read the panic in them. I absorbed her fear through her fingers, and an electrical current ran through my blood, giving me the adrenaline to stay with her. It was fight or flight, and I had to fight for her.

"The ambulance is coming," I whispered. I squeezed her hand. "Hang in there."

I didn't leave her side. Murmurs filled the air: buzzing, talking, asking questions.

Come on, air—get to her lungs.

Relief washed through me when I heard a siren wailing. I kept holding her hand, talking to her softly.

Then the paramedics rushed onto the scene, pushing through the crowd with their stretcher, yelling at everyone to move aside. They looked down at me.

"She had a heart attack," I said.

The paramedic knelt beside me and quickly assessed her. Then he put an oxygen mask over her mouth.

"She's had a heart attack," I repeated.

"We won't know anything until they run tests at the hospital," he replied as he worked, strapping the woman on a stretcher.

I squeezed her hand one last time before I let it go. Then I said, "You're going to be okay."

As the paramedics walked away carrying the stretcher, their strides long and purposeful, I watched, not moving. Everything was fine now. The woman would be okay. Someone came up to me and said, "What happened?"

"Heart attack."

"How do *you* know?" asked another voice in the distance.

The ambulance door slammed, and I watched it speed away, red and blue lights flashing, siren shrieking.

"I just do," I replied. Then I walked away.

Chapter Seven

The first thing I did the next morning was telephone the hospital. The receptionist on the cardiac unit said the woman was going to be fine. Then she asked if I was the girl who had helped her, and I stuttered and answered no, it had been my friend. The woman went on to tell me that the family had been wondering who the girl was because the woman had talked about her all night, and they wanted to thank her.

I had hoped she wouldn't remember me.

That morning it took me longer than usual to put together an outfit. In the bathroom, I put on more makeup than I normally wore for no other reason than to waste time. What would John think when he got the note from Sarah? I swept blush over my cheeks like Lacey had taught me, then applied lip gloss, smacking my lips like Lacey did. When I finished, I stepped back from the mirror to evaluate myself and realized I looked like a clown. What was I thinking?

As I was scrubbing my cheeks, Brian knocked on the bathroom door. "Move it, Indie," he said. "I'm gonna pee in the hallway if you don't hurry."

I opened the door and stormed out.

"Who are *you* trying to impress?" He was wearing only his boxers, and when I passed him, he raised his eyebrows. Laughing, he shut the bathroom door in my face before I could smack him.

✤ ✤ ✤

At school I walked to my locker with my head lowered, counting the tiles on the floor, my gaze darting around to make sure I wouldn't bump into anyone. I also looked and listened for flip-flops.

Then I heard Lacey's voice calling my name. My body tensed. Could we possibly forge some new ground, make our friendship work again? I lifted my head. She held out her hand and said, "I forgot to give this to you."

The silver best friend necklace was dangling from her index finger. I took it.

"I don't wear it anymore," she stated. "For reasons both you and I know." Although I could clearly see that she was still angry with me, I also detected something else. Suddenly, I heard the man's gentle voice in my head.

She needs you.

Before I could say anything, Lacey turned and walked away.

I watched her leave, knowing if I chased after her, she would cause a scene. The necklace burned my skin. I hoped she might look back at me so I could tell her I was sorry, tell her I missed her. But she didn't. When she was out of sight, I carefully tucked the necklace in a safe spot in my locker. One day I would give it back, and when that day came, I didn't want it to be tangled. I took out my books, slammed my locker shut, and leaned my shoulder against it. For a moment, I had thought we would be friends again.

Tears sat behind my eyelids. I missed her, missed the one person I could trust.

What did the voice mean by telling me she needed me? I needed her just as much.

Warm air misted my neck.

"I like you, too," John whispered through my hair.

My body calmed, my tears dissolved, and I pivoted slowly to see John staring down at me. He winked but didn't touch me. And I really wanted him to. Our eyes connected, like, really connected, and it was the first time I'd noticed how his hazel irises were flecked with tiny dots of gray. Behind his eyes lurked deep mysterious emotions, and I liked that about him. I swear, if the bell hadn't rung, I would have kissed him in the hallway.

At lunch I looked for John but couldn't find him, so I met up with Sarah and Zoe in the smoking area.

"Hey, did you hear some woman had a heart attack last night by the bookstore near Denny's?" said Zoe, blowing out one of her famous smoke rings. "The ambulance flew by us. Rumor was she just collapsed."

I nodded as I blew out smoke, tilting my chin up to look cool. "I saw her," I said.

"What happened?" Sarah asked.

"She just grabbed her chest and went down." I flicked the ashes off my cigarette.

"Were you, like, close to her?" Zoe's eyes widened.

"No," I said quickly. "But there was a crowd."

"I heard some girl saved her. The family was on the radio this morning. The woman who had the attack wants to find her to say thanks. Said she was like this angel sent from heaven or some crap like that. Angels are so in right now. Who believes that shit anyway?"

"Not me." I tried to laugh, hoping I sounded convincing. "I sure didn't see any angel swoop down." I used my hands to mock the word *swoop*. The gesture must have worked, because Sarah and Zoe laughed.

"Yeah, like, who really wants to be classified as an angel, anyway?" said Zoe. "It's more fun being baaaad girls. Hey, that's what we should call our band! Bad Girls."

"I'm with ya, sister," I said, bumping her with my hip.

✢ ✢ ✢

Nothing physical happened between me and John all week long, and I found that both confusing and annoying. I kept waiting for something, anything—a touch on the arm, a hug—and I couldn't help thinking he didn't like me, despite what he'd said.

Finally, Friday rolled around, and I wondered what his plans were for the weekend. He'd told me he liked me, so why was he being so evasive? I had no idea if I should ask him about his plans or just leave it and go about my own business.

At lunch, when I was heading out to the smoking area, I saw him sitting under a tree engrossed in a book. The weather had changed again, and the autumn sun had returned, heating the ground, drying up the moisture. The colored leaves were now in full regalia, shining against a cerulean sky. John looked romantic, sitting there reading. I sauntered up to him, trying to be cool. "Hi, John," I said.

He shut his book so I couldn't see the cover. Suddenly all my romantic feelings were gone, because I got the distinct feeling that he didn't want me to know what he was reading. What was he hiding?

"Sit down," he said, patting the grass like I was a child.

I sat beside him.

We didn't talk for a few moments. He picked at the grass and threw some into the air.

"You going to Zoe's party tonight?" I finally asked.

He shrugged. "Not sure." He paused for a few seconds before he asked, "Are you?"

"Maybe. I'm supposed to sleep over so we can rehearse tomorrow."

"Rehearse?"

"Yeah, we kind of have a band."

He gave me a funny little smirk. "Like a lame chick band? Please don't tell me you're the drummer."

"No. Sarah is."

"What do you play? Tambourine? Or the"—he clapped his fingers together—"castanets? Or maybe you're the triangle girl."

I laughed, even though it was a little insulting. "No," I said. "Guitar."

"Hey, I'm going to the junior hockey game tonight," he said, totally changing the subject.

Surprised that John would like hockey or any sports for that matter and a little ticked he had been so sarcastic about our band, I replied with one word: "Oh."

"I know a couple of guys on the team, and they gave me some free tickets. I might go to Zoe's after." He looked at me. "You want to come to the game with me?"

Was this going to be our first date? "Sure."

"Great," he replied.

Silence hung between us for a few seconds, and then I asked, "What were you reading?"

He playfully pinched my cheek, the touch of his fingers almost sending my body into spasms. "Philosophical stuff. Nothing you'd be interested in."

John brushed off his pants and stood. Then he held out his hand to help me up. Just the feel of his skin sent shivers cascading through the length of my body, and I physically craved him in some surreal way.

We started to walk back to the school, and we were partway there when I smelled . . . the cigar smoke. My skin got clammy, and my heart raced like a speeding car. *No. Not now. Please.*

This was the second time I'd sensed this guy when I was with John. Why? And where was he? Not in my field of vision yet. There was only the smell of smoke. Determined not to let him in my view, I stared straight ahead. I didn't want to see him sitting under a tree or lurking by the back door. With my eyes lowered to the ground, I tried to appear normal, letting John carry the conversation. Thankfully, he was on a roll about the value of a socialist government and how we should treat homeless people with more respect.

Keep walking, keep walking. Ignore the smell. Hang on. You can do this.

But then there he was, standing by the door we were about to enter. Sweat trickled down my face. My throat tightened so I could hardly breathe. I braced myself to walk by him. I had to do this, get through this without John suspecting anything. As I passed through the doorway, I tried to maintain my composure, and I didn't make eye contact with him. Oddly enough, like before, he didn't try to talk to me, not one word.

And then, although I tried to avoid him, he stepped into my path. He put his hand to his throat. I just lowered my head and kept walking.

"I won't see you after school," said John once we were inside. "I have to leave early." He looked away. I sensed he didn't want to go wherever he had to go.

"Okay," I answered, not wanting to say more, in case he detected nervousness in my voice.

"How about I call you?" He turned back to me.

The cigar smell still lingered, but it was faint. Had the spirit followed me into the school? "Great," I managed to spit out.

"I need your number," John reminded me, smirking.

I took a pen from my pocket, then took out a matchbook. My hands shook as I tried to rip the cardboard back off the matchbook cover.

John eyed me, his eyebrows slightly furrowed. "Your face is white. And you're shaking. Do you feel okay?" He took the matchbook from me and tore the cover off. Then he handed it back.

"Yeah, I'm fine." I wrote down my number, willing my hand to stop shaking. "It's the sun," I said as I wrote. "I'm fair, and it doesn't always agree with me."

"Okay." He didn't sound convinced. "You were out in it for all of a second."

After he took my number, we parted, and as soon as I hit the main hall, the cigar smell faded completely and my heart rate returned to normal. I hurriedly headed in the direction of the library, praying that I could get on a computer. Forget biology—I had some school history to look up.

I tried every search engine possible but couldn't find anything about a middle-aged guy who had been arrested for harming any students or staff. I learned all about the history of the school, when it had been built, who was the first principal, blah, blah, blah. For an hour, I read about my school in minute detail and didn't uncover one single lead about the man with the cigar. But I did find out about Brian and the food fight riot he had led in grade nine. Although his name wasn't mentioned, I knew the article was all about him. I tried to contain my laughter in the hushed silence of the library.

Disappointed and discouraged, I logged off the computer when it was time for me to head to my last class of the day.

If there was nothing on the Internet, how was I ever going to find out who this guy was?

✣ ✣ ✣

That afternoon, with the sun streaming through my window, I crawled into bed thinking my life was like a yo-yo, constantly going up and down. Last night I'd helped save a woman who was having a heart attack, then today I had seen the creepy ghost again, and for no good reason. One good thing, one bad thing. Why couldn't my life just be normal, or at least make sense? As I lay in bed counting the dots on the ceiling, a funny but very familiar smell wafted through my room.

Wool and Old Spice cologne.

"Because you're you."

At the sound of the hoarse, gravelly voice, I sat up in my bed. "Papa!"

There he was, in his dress slacks and shirt and black felt fedora, sitting on the edge of my bed, just like when I was seven years old. I smiled and felt my body instantly relax. When I was little, I'd loved crawling up onto his lap to absorb the smell of his Old Spice and his wool jacket. I wanted to be seven again, when I didn't know that I was different, when I thought everyone was like me.

"You haven't visited me in so long," I said.

"You didn't want me to, my little sweetie pie."

I hugged my pillow to my body. He always called me his little sweetie pie. "I'm sorry."

"Don't apologize, child."

"Did you come because you have something important to tell me?" I wondered if he was going to tell me who the man was so I could stop obsessing about it.

"Your mother is worried about you."

I sighed. Not exactly what I wanted to hear. "She's always worried about me. I'm weird."

"Tell her a smile can brighten up a dull day. And tell your dad that Curtis says hello. And me too, of course."

"I'll tell my mom about the smile," I said. "But Dad won't believe me. You know what he's like."

"I'm working on him," he replied. "Through his dreams."

I laughed. "You're funny, Papa."

"So are you, my dear. Keep making your dad laugh for me. He likes your singing."

"Tell me something, Papa. Who is the man at the school?"

Papa wagged his finger at me, then said, "You always have to negotiate." He disappeared in a split second, leaving me sitting in an empty bedroom, hugging my pillow like I was a child. Only I wasn't a child anymore. I was a teenager in my last year of high school.

And I had been a teenager when Curtis had died. After Curtis had passed away and the funeral was over, Papa had come to me, just like he did today. "Curt is okay," he had said. "He is with me now. Tell Aunt Cathy and your mom and dad that we're fishing all the time."

A few days later, when Aunt Cathy came over for dinner, I approached my parents and her in the kitchen. "Oh, by the way, Papa told me to tell you that Curt is with him. And that they're fishing together."

Silence encased the room. Then Aunt Cathy's eyes welled up with tears, as did my dad's. My dad went over to his sister and hugged her hard.

"I didn't know they fished together." My dad tenderly patted his sister's back.

"He had some happy times fishing with Dad."

Aunt Cathy wiped the tears from her cheeks, disengaged herself from my dad, and stepped toward me. My father remained where he was with his arms crossed.

She grabbed my hands in hers. "Thank you, Indie," she said, squeezing my fingers. "Thank you."

Aunt Cathy had believed me, but my dad hadn't.

I continued to hang on to my pillow for a few minutes. Why wouldn't Papa answer my question? Was I not supposed to know? Was I being tested? Was I supposed to figure it out on my own? Sometimes I wished my brain had an off button, or at least one for pause, so I could silence the thoughts for a while.

The minutes ticked by as I lay staring at the clock, waiting for John to call. Finally, at 5:30, just an hour and a half before the game was supposed to start, the phone rang and it was my two rings. I immediately picked it up, holding my breath. It had to be him.

The sound of his smooth, sleek voice made me sink into my mattress. For so long I had dreamed of getting my first phone call from John, and now here I was talking to him, arranging our night. I pulled my legs up and sat cross-legged on my bed, pressing the phone against my ear. I loved how his voice sounded so deep and sexy on the other end. We didn't talk long, and the conversation ended with John saying he would pick me up. I had never had a guy pick me up at my house for a date before. After I hung up, I hopped off my bed.

Then I started to jump up and down. I stuck on my Police CD and found the fastest song. I danced around my room, singing into my pretend microphone.

Halfway through the song, I stopped. "What am I going to wear?" I rushed to my closet.

"What about this pink top?" I took it off its hanger and threw it on the bed. "No. It's too . . . blasé." Then I pulled out a blue pullover-type top. "The arena might be cold. This one could work."

I kept pulling and tossing clothes on my bed. I must have tried on clothes for 20 minutes. In between outfits, I danced and sang, dressed in just my underwear. Finally, I decided on the pink top, the first one I had picked. It wasn't blasé; it just needed some accessories. Lacey would have accessories.

I grabbed for my phone without thinking. Then as quickly as I picked it up, I put it back in its cradle.

"Not tonight. You will not think of her tonight."

Don't worry. Things with Lacey will work out when they are supposed to. It was the man's voice again, so soft and kind.

"Who are you?"

When you're ready, you will find out.

⁓⁓⁓⁓⁓

Chapter Eight

When I was finally dressed to go to the game, I took one last glance in the mirror. I looked okay. My new purple eye shadow seemed to highlight the blue in my eyes. And for once, my straight hair had curled the way I wanted it to. Now, to get to the kitchen before John rang the doorbell. I did *not* want my parents opening the door. I was almost to the kitchen when I saw them in the dining room, peeking out the window. No way! They *were* waiting for the doorbell. At least Dad had changed out of his work suit and was wearing jeans and some type of shirt, and Mom wasn't wearing her nurse scrubs.

I tiptoed up behind them and screamed, "Boo!"

My mother immediately put her hand to her chest, and my dad jumped practically a foot into the air.

I laughed. "Scared ya."

"Indie!" screeched my mother. "You could have given us both a heart attack."

Just then the doorbell rang, and I ran to the front door. When I opened the door, John looked as cool as he did at school, only he had made a wardrobe adjustment. He had ditched his flip-flops in favor of a pair of cheap-looking, generic high-top runners. I bit my lip, trying to contain my laughter.

Then my parents walked out of the kitchen together, looking a bit stiff and predictable. John stuck out his hand to my mom first. "Pleased to meet you." His line sounded extremely rehearsed. Then he did the same with my dad, only their handshake lasted longer. My dad looked like he had a viselike grip on John's hand.

"So do you think the Sixty-Seven's will win tonight?" My dad sounded so corny.

"It will be a good game," replied John. "Two top teams."

"We should get going," I said.

My dad ignored me. "Are you a Senators fan as well?"

"Dad," I said, slightly exasperated, "what is this, like, twenty questions or something?"

John turned to me and gave me a funny little lopsided but sad smile. "It's okay, Indie. I don't mind."

Just then to make things worse Brian burst through the front door with energy to burn.

"Hey," he said when he saw our group huddled in the hallway. "What gives?"

"John," I said, "this is my brother, Brian. Brian, this is my friend John.

Where my dad's handshake was firm but stable, Brian's looked like he was some real-estate agent desperate to close a deal but making all the wrong moves. Brian pumped John's hand so hard, I thought John's arm might fly out of its socket. "So, *John,* is that your wreck outside?" Brian winked at me.

"We better head out," I said, lowering my head. This was *so* embarrassing.

John took my cue. "Well, it was nice to meet you."

"You from Newfoundland?" my dad asked. "You have a bit of an accent."

"Um, yeah, sort of. I spent my first few years there."

"Come on," I said, tugging on his arm.

Outside, I could hardly look at John—that is, until we were in his "wreck" of a car and he lifted one side of his mouth in a funny little smirk.

"What?" I asked.

"You have that perfect Hallmark family."

"Shut up." I playfully punched his arm, and he grabbed my hand. The tips of his fingers ignited my skin, zapped me into feeling alive. The feeling seemed to spread quickly through my entire body. If he only knew who I really was, he wouldn't think we were so perfect.

"You're lucky to have such a great family." He squeezed my fingers before he started the car engine and drove away from my house, his car rattling and clanging.

The Civic Arena was located on Bank Street but miles away from downtown and close to my house, so it hardly took any time to get there. John parked on the street, and we walked to the arena. He didn't take my hand, and it was so baffling. As we entered the arena, the energy from the crowd milling around the concourse hit me square in the face, giving me a giddy, bubbly feeling.

We found our seats and sat down, and immediately our thighs touched; every nerve in my body prickled and twitched. Neither one of us did anything to break the connection.

While I was immersed in how I felt about our legs touching and how he made my body react, John looked at the ice and didn't speak to me. My mind raced with lustful thoughts of us standing alone in the middle of some snow-covered field and of him kissing me. We were the only ones in the field, and the only light was from the sliver of the new moon.

Suddenly, I sensed someone staring at me. I scanned the crowd and spotted Lacey, sitting with some of the other hockey players' girlfriends. I lifted my hand to wave, but she just swiveled her head and looked away. Who cared about her tonight, anyway, when I was at the game with John? My heart tightened.

Who was I kidding?

Then I felt John move, and our shoulders touched. I needed to forget about Lacey for tonight. Energy buzzed around us from the fans chatting, eating popcorn and hot dogs, drinking beer. I absorbed the energy and jiggled my leg. The lights dimmed when the referees, in their black and white zebra shirts, made their entrance, and the crowd booed. I joined in. After three laps, the low voice of the announcer belted out from the speakers, announcing the teams.

One by one, hockey players soared onto the ice, flying with grace and speed. They announced the first line, and when Burke's name came over the speakers, I searched for Lacey again. Facing forward, staring at Burke, she obviously wasn't going to acknowledge me.

Then a 12-year-old girl, a budding star with a phenomenal voice, sang "O Canada!" I almost cried. I hid my face from John, so he couldn't see the tears threatening to spill. What was wrong with me? One minute I was giddy, and the next I was ready to cry. Crowds made me lose all sense of my emotions, and I could go from high to low in a matter of minutes. I absorbed everyone's energy, just like I did at parties.

The puck dropped. I watched the players rush up and down the ice, chasing the small black round thing, crashing bodies against the boards. Then suddenly big purple lights flashed in front of my eyes, and I saw the numbers 4 and 1 loud and clear.

I blurted out, "We're going to win four to one."

John took his eyes off the game for a second and gave me a funny look. "You're predicting?"

Caught in the moment, I replied, "Yup!"

"Nah," he replied back. "It'll be two to one. The other team is good, too, first in the league, and we have yet to beat them. But I have faith that tonight we will win by one goal."

I stuck out my hand. "Bet ya ten bucks: four to one." I knew I was being a total brat, but I was having fun.

Then the crowd started to cheer, and we both jumped to our feet to get in on the action. The crowd and the energy electrified me, almost made me feel as if I were high. I was absorbing everything, from the fluorescent lights to the loud cheers to the bursting crowd, and the energy from everyone and everything soaked my skin and made every nerve in my body spark.

At the end of the first period, the score was 2 to 1.

John and I left our seats to grab some snacks. Usually my visions were a pain and I hated them, but tonight I was having some fun with it all.

"One more goal, and *you lose the bet,*" I sang my words as we hiked up the stairs.

Once on the concourse, we jostled the crowd, and I followed John's lead—that is, until we came into the opening and I saw Lacey standing by herself, drinking a soda pop.

She threw her cup in the trash just as we walked by.

"Hey, John," I said, "I'm going to say hi to Lacey. I'll be out in a sec."

He nodded, and I headed over to Lacey. "Hi, Lacey," I said. "Burke's playing well, eh?"

She nodded—kind of curtly, though—and said, "Yeah. Not that you would care." She paused for a second. Then she said, "It sure didn't take you long to replace me."

I frowned. "I didn't replace you."

"And after all I did for you."

"What do you mean?"

"Oh, come on, Indie. I got you to all the cool parties. You would never have been invited if it wasn't for me persuading everyone. Some gratitude."

"I've always thanked you for everything."

"Whatever." She put up her perfectly manicured hand, palm facing me, to tell me the conversation was over. Then she turned and walked away.

As I stepped outside, pulling out my cigarettes, I couldn't help wonder what *that* conversation had really been about. Had I not shown enough gratitude when we were friends? Had I been a bad friend? Did she honestly think I was hanging out with John to make her mad?

For the rest of the game, I tried not to let my conversation with Lacey ruin my night. And for the most part, I was successful, but that was because John was beside me. His intense interest in the sport made me realize that there was a lot about him I still didn't know. He was starting to appear a lot more complex than I'd first imagined. I mean, who would have thought such a loner, who liked to spout off about social responsibilities and read crazy spiritual books, would also like a wildly popular team sport that was sometimes a little rough? There was definitely more to him.

In the third period, the score was 3 to 1. Suddenly Burke got a breakaway. The crowd went nuts. Everyone stood and screamed and cheered. He skillfully stickhandled down the ice and, when he was close to the goalie, rifled off a shot that sailed into the top corner of the net. The crowd exploded. I looked at the score clock: 4 to 1.

"I bet Amber liked that," said John.

"Amber? You mean Lacey."

John shrugged. "He's got them both hooked."

I squinted as I looked at him. "And you think that's okay?" I asked.

"I didn't say that."

I couldn't help but glance at Lacey. She was on her feet, cheering for Burke and high-fiving the other hockey girl-friends. Among them, she ranked highest; she was the girl-friend of the star who would get drafted and perhaps one day play in the NHL. But at what expense?

The buzzer sounded, ending the game. I stuck out my hand and grinned. "You owe me ten bucks." Then I did a little dance.

He gave me a slow, quirky smile.

I held up my hands. "My stars aligned. What can I say?"

"I thought you didn't believe in that stuff."

I looked at my watch. "It's only nine thirty. Let's go to Zoe's."

Once in the car, John suddenly said he had to go home and take care of something. I was so full of energy that I really wanted to go to the party. If I went home, I would just pace in my room or bounce up and down on my bed.

But no go. I couldn't convince John to go to the party, and I didn't want to ask him to drop me off. I just didn't feel as if I should ditch him after we'd been on a date. Zoe would under-stand. He took me straight home.

Parked in front of my house, he tapped his fingers on the steering wheel, the noise bouncing off the car's tin roof. I had no idea what he was thinking.

"I wonder if Cayce could have done that," he finally said.

My body tensed, froze almost. Light from the streetlights shone like flashlight beams into the car, and I could see from the look on his face that he was deep in his thoughts, and they weren't going away. It made me really nervous.

"Done what?" The conversation made my head spin. I didn't want to talk about this again. I wanted to go to Zoe's and have fun. I tapped my fingers on my thigh.

"Make predictions on lottery tickets. Think about it. I know there were no lottery tickets in those days, but if there had been, he could have made millions."

"No one can do that." I really wanted him to shut up and kiss me.

"It's such a mystery," John said as if he were talking to himself. "It's like I'm being drawn toward finding out more about it. It's something that I can't explain."

I wanted to say, "That's because there is no explanation," but I kept my mouth shut. I put my hand on the car door handle. "I better get going."

He turned to look at me, and when our eyes connected, my skin flushed and my body ached for some contact with him. Why wouldn't he stop talking about this stuff—actually, just stop talking, period—and kiss me?

At last he put his hand on my forearm. He traced his finger up and down it, pushing my jacket up so he was touching my bare flesh. My skin tingled, sending unearthly shivers through my body as I enjoyed every little movement.

"Tonight was fun," he said.

"Yeah," I replied, slightly dazed.

"I'll call you tomorrow."

"Sure."

Then he took his hand off my arm.

I got out of the car and walked slowly up my driveway, thinking about how badly I wanted him to kiss me. I also thought about how I continually lied to him to hide who I was.

"Why am I lying?" I whispered.

He won't like who you are.

Chapter Nine

"Where you off to?" My dad was sitting at the kitchen table, drinking coffee and reading *The Globe and Mail*.

"Sarah's," I said. "We're reviving our band." I slung my guitar case over my neck.

"You need a ride?"

"Sure," I said.

I put my guitar in the backseat and got in the front. For the first few minutes on the drive, Dad and I talked about the weather and how it was going to be a long winter because they were predicting early snow. Then out of the blue, he said, "John seems like a nice guy. Seems to know a little about hockey."

"Yeah, he does." I picked at some lint on my jacket.

"Did he ever play when he was young?"

I shrugged. "I'm not sure."

"Does he play any sports?"

Again I shrugged. "Not that I know of."

"Not that it matters," said Dad. He took his eyes off the road to glance quickly at me. "What matters is that he treats you right."

"He does," I said.

My dad turned his gaze back to the road ahead of us. "Does he golf?"

This time I laughed. "Enough with the questions." My dad was an avid golfer. It was like an obsession with him.

"I should be able to get a few more games in this fall," he said. "If this nice weather comes back. Maybe tomorrow the sun will shine."

I knew the conversation about John had ended, and for that I was glad.

✤ ✤ ✤

The Bad Girls' rehearsal went well, and it felt great to be doing something creative. I loved the energy and enthusiasm and passion we all shared for music.

We didn't complete any songs, because Sarah was getting used to her new drumsticks, and Zoe couldn't get her bass guitar tuned properly, and I ended up phoning home three times to see if John had called. It didn't matter, though, because Carly had called the animal shelter, and they said they were definitely interested but were booked solid until March. So we fooled around a lot at our first rehearsal, knowing there was tons of time.

I arrived home at around 4:00 P.M. and, after finding out no one had called me, went right to my room and started pacing like a caged animal. Back and forth. Back and forth. And I talked to myself, trying to think of song lyrics. "I'm always said to be wrong and doing strange things. But it's not me. It's someone else I'm being."

I pulled out a pen and paper and wrote down my words. Then I looked at them. I didn't want to use those words for a song. They were about me and the fact that I had visions. I got up and started to pace and talk to myself again.

"He's all I think about. All that I love. My heart bleeds year after year. Being left alone again is what I fear."

I flopped down on my bed. "He's not going to call."

Suddenly, my phone rang, the noise startling me. I grabbed it at the first ring. But it was Sarah, wanting to talk about Zoe and how she wasn't pulling her weight in the band. I didn't want to talk to Sarah, not if John was going to call. Finally, she had to go, so I hung the phone up and pulled out my guitar.

I had strummed a few chords and sung a few of my lyrics when my phone rang again. Two rings. I snapped it up again, fumbling as I said hello.

As soon as I heard his voice, my shoulders loosened. I lay my guitar on the floor and fell onto my bed, my body feeling as if it were liquefying into a pool of calm.

Yes, I wanted to go out again.

What time?

Where?

Just us.

Sure.

A few hours later, I was in the passenger seat of John's car as he drove through downtown toward the Rideau Canal, a waterway that feeds from the Ottawa River and starts at the Parliament buildings. He parked his car on a side street, and we both got out.

"Let's walk around the Parliament buildings," he said.

"Sure."

A cool fall evening breeze brushed my face as we walked into the huge grounds. There were only a handful of people walking, and I liked that—made it kind of quiet and solemn. We headed to the Centennial Flame, directly out front of the Parliament buildings, and John dug his hand in his jeans pocket, pulling out two loonies. "Here," he said. "Let's make a wish."

The eternal flame burned in the middle of a fountain that was surrounded by shields of all the provinces and territories in Canada. People loved to throw money in the fountain and make wishes, and all the money collected was used by an organization that helps support Canadians with disabilities. I clutched my loonie in my hand. I knew exactly what I wanted to wish for.

"On the count of three," said John.

I squeezed my eyes shut and said, "One, two, three." Then I threw the gold coin in the water. *I wish for John to kiss me tonight.*

"What did you wish for?" I asked John.

He laughed and took my hand. "Not a chance," he replied. "What did you wish for?"

"No way I'm telling you!" I laughed along with him.

Hand in hand, we walked toward the majestic Parliament buildings, then we veered right and followed the path along the stone wall at the back of the buildings, which gave us a view of the Ottawa River and Hull, Quebec. The red, orange, and yellow of the maple trees provided an absolutely breathtaking backdrop for the fast-flowing river.

"The trees are so beautiful," I said in almost a whisper. "It looks like a postcard."

"Yeah. It's something to see." Then he turned, leaned against the stone wall and looked upward. "I love these buildings," he said. "Every year I take the tour and think about what it would be like to have lived back then."

I didn't want John to know that I had never been inside because the buildings were haunted and that so many of the people from back then were stuck on earth. "I love the stonework," I said. "The etchings and the spirals." Then I grinned. "And I love the guards out front in the summer. You know, the ones in the red coats and big furry hats? Lacey and I jump around like monkeys in front of them, trying to make them laugh, and they never crack a smile."

John shook his head at me and laughed. "You would do something like that?"

"Lacey says I do the best monkey impression."

"Show me," he said.

"No way."

"Come on," he teased.

He stepped toward me and wrapped his arms around me, tenderly maneuvering me so that he was once again leaning against the rock wall, but now I was in nestled in his arms with my back pressed to his chest. His breath warmed the nape of my neck, and I let my body lean and relax into his, knowing his strength would hold me.

We stayed like that for a few minutes, just looking up at the buildings, wrapped in our own world. Then we pulled apart and he said, "You want to get a BeaverTail, then walk the canal?"

"You bet," I replied.

We walked to ByWard Market and went right to a little BeaverTails hut, which had these amazing pastries shaped like beaver's tails that came with all kinds of different toppings: cinnamon, sugar, lemon, chocolate, bananas, and so on. I ordered my favorite, the original cinnamon and sugar, but John opted for a lemon-sugared one, although he spent a couple of minutes waffling between strawberry and lemon.

As we ate, we walked out of the Market and toward the canal. The Rideau Canal is a major tourist attraction in Ottawa, and in the summer tons of boats cruise up and down it. Some are pleasure crafts and others are tourist boats giving people a view of the city. In late September it's always quieter, and there are fewer boats. We walked five minutes before a boat floated past, playing loud music. I wiped the sugar off my mouth with my napkin before I said, "Someone's trying to get in the last good days before winter."

"Yeah. Soon the canal will be frozen," replied John. "Hey, maybe we can skate the canal this winter."

My heart skipped. Was he thinking ahead . . . about us being together in winter?

"Sure," I said.

Finished with his BeaverTail, John threw his napkin in a metal trash can. Then he raised his eyebrows. "Can you skate?"

I playfully slapped him on the arm. "Of course I can skate." Then I threw the remainder of my pastry in the trash. In the winter months, the canal froze, and it became known as the world's longest skating rink. Huts dotted the sides, serving BeaverTails, as well as hot chocolate and hot dogs. Bonfires burned to warm cold hands, parents rented red sleds for children, and lovers skated hand in hand.

I stared out at the sunset. An orange hue was swirled with a cobalt blue and pink-lavender and a hint of gray that reminded me of smooth stones. The combination of colors was spectacular. I liked being by the canal at this time of year. We'd only seen the one boat. When a jogger passed, I moved over and let my shoulder connect to John's. The atmosphere was serene, and we didn't talk.

He took my hand in his. At school he barely touched me. He was a hard guy to figure out, but I guessed that was what I liked about him. I liked not knowing, his unpredictability.

We meandered quietly for a few minutes before I said, playfully, "I didn't know you were from Newfoundland. You don't really have a Newfie accent."

He swung my hand a bit and avoided looking at me. "I wasn't there long."

"Did you move directly to Ontario?"

"Yeah, pretty much."

"How old were you when you left?"

He shrugged. "I dunno. Around four, I guess."

"Do you have any brothers or sisters?"

He shook his head. "No, it's just my mom and me."

"Do you . . . have a dad?" I asked quietly.

He dropped my hand. The sound of the wind rustling through the trees, shaking the leaves, took over the silence that had followed my question. I was just about to change the subject, figuring I wasn't going to get an answer, when John said, "He's never really been in the picture."

"Oh," I said. I shoved my hands in my pockets. "I'm sorry to hear that."

"He left my mom when I was little. Just before we moved. From what she tells me, he just took off and she never heard from him again. She thinks he must have changed his name, because she could never find him. That's when we moved here. We lived in a car for the first few weeks. I do remember bits and pieces of sleeping in the backseat."

"That's so sad," I said.

"It's life. You make do with what you got."

"Would you like to see him one day?"

"Not really. He was such an asshole. I remember little things, like him screaming at my mother and pushing her into their bedroom. They fought a lot." He paused momentarily, long enough for a bird to fly overhead and land on a branch.

Then he continued, "But sometimes I think of finding him and telling him what a lousy dad and husband he was. He really hurt my mom. Killed her spirit." He looked up and stared at the bird on the branch. "It angers me to think of him being abusive to her."

Oh yes, he hit her. His voice sounded in my head and before I could shake my head and get rid of it I heard more. *He was physically and sexually abusive to her.*

I wrapped my arms around my body. I didn't want to hear any more. "She must be strong to raise you on her own," I said.

"He drank a lot, I guess. That's when he was mean." He stopped talking for a second before he said, "I don't know how my mom will survive without me next year. She's had it rough. Sometimes she doesn't cope real well. But . . . I want to go. I want to get away from here. I want to go to London, England."

"You have to live your own life," I said. A vision of me living with John in some bohemian apartment in London skirted through my mind. I gave my head a little shake. What was wrong with me? I hardly knew the guy. Just days ago, I had chastised Lacey for thinking about being with Burke next year, and here I was doing the same thing.

Falling.

Was I falling into a big hole with no way out?

The scary truth was . . . I wanted to fall.

"Sometimes I think of trying to find someone, like Cayce," said John, "who can see things so I can just ask the person if they can see my dad and where he is now."

I lowered my head and stared at the ground as I walked.

John continued. "Maybe if I found out he was not such a bastard and had turned his life around, I'd try to find him. And maybe the person could look ahead and see my mom next year and tell me she was going to be okay if I went away somewhere."

I knew he wanted answers but why did he think he needed to get them this way? Surely, there was a relative he could talk to, someone in his father's family. I inhaled, and when I exhaled, I said, "I read once where some of those people who do that kind of stuff are called charlatans."

"Fakes?"

I shrugged. "My aunt went once and said it was expensive and not worth it."

John stopped walking and turned to look at me, his s knitted together. "You know something about this?"

"Not really." I stumbled over my words. "My aunt just talked about it briefly. Said she wasted her money."

My answer must have placated him because he nodded. "Maybe I just have to find the right person."

Cold air swept through my hair and circled my body. It was getting dark, and that meant the warmth of the autumn sun would be gone for the night. Thoughts filled my brain. His mom had huge stuff to deal with. What, I wasn't sure. But I was feeling something cold and damp.

John sighed and ran his hands through his hair. A pain hit me hard in my chest, making me realize that the darkness I saw behind his eyes was a massive burden he carried regarding his mother.

"I'd like to meet her one day," I said.

"Who?"

"Your mom."

He scratched the back of his neck before he uttered, "Maybe." He paused for a moment, then stood a little straighter and turned to look at me. "Enough of me," he said, trying to sound cheerful. "Let's talk about your normal family."

Normal? Yeah, right. Little does he know. At least he didn't seem to suspect anything about me.

After we both had sparked our cigarettes, we started to move again. By now the sun had fallen below the horizon and the colors had all but disappeared, leaving a prewinter sky that was turning blacker by the minute. The new moon in the sky looked as if at any moment it could plummet to the earth because it wasn't strung up properly.

The moon reminded me of my relationship with John; it hung by a thread. I gave my head a tiny shake.

Do not think like that, Indie.

Even fewer people were out now, and the joggers seemed to have called it a night. We walked aimlessly with no real destination in mind. A lady with a golden retriever passed us, and we stopped to pet the dog, but that was it. I liked the tranquility, the lack of people, and with John beside me, I liked the darkness. Once our cigarettes were out, John took my hand again as night descended upon us.

"You ever think about nature versus nurture?" he asked solemnly. "We're talking about it in psychology. It's an interesting topic. Are we destined to be who we are the product of? Or are we the product of how we are brought up, of our environment?"

I hesitated before speaking, trying to think of the right answer. "I don't know what I believe," I replied. I thought of my own life. I wasn't like my parents. But I had been told by my mother that my great-grandmother, my mother's grandmother, used to see things, too. Had I inherited a genetic trait the way Sarah had inherited her mother's flaming red hair? "I think there are arguments for both," I said, "but I would argue for nature. We're born the way we are."

"I don't want to be the product of either," said John. "The product of my old man or how my mom raised me."

Again, the cold enveloped me, and I knew that something about his mom was off—like, really off. "If you're neither, then what do you want to be?"

He kicked a stone with his foot. "Independent. My own person. Just me."

We walked for a few more minutes, silence trailing our footsteps. Then he glanced at me out of the corner of his eyes. "You wear that cross all the time. Do you believe in God?"

I reached up to touch my gold cross. Was there a God?

I shrugged.

"I believe religion is manmade," said John. "You must believe in God to wear a cross all the time."

Say something, Indie, say something.

"I guess it's for luck," I said.

"That's an odd reason to wear a cross. Are you Catholic?"

"I was confirmed Anglican, but I don't go to church."

"Me either. My mother's parents are Catholic. Most people in Newfoundland are. They disowned her when she married my dad. He wouldn't convert. Now only her brother talks to her."

"Every religion has its place," I said, spewing words like I knew what I was talking about. "At least that's what I think." Did I really think that?

The conversation was getting me down, and I didn't want to talk about heavy stuff anymore, so I let go of his hand. "Race you to that post."

I took off running, and within two strides, John was ahead of me. Then he spun around to run backward in front of me.

"No fair," I laughed, huffing. "You got way longer legs than me."

John stopped, and I ran right into his arms. By now there was a chill in the night air, and the sky was raven black.

His lips grazed my ear, and he whispered, "You're so different than the other girls."

If only he knew how different.

I didn't answer; his warm breath seemed to cover my mouth. I didn't want to tell him anything that he didn't need to know. I just wanted him to hold me and touch me.

He lifted my chin with his finger and then he lowered his lips to meet mine. At first I gasped at the heat that flowed through my body. I wanted this, and nothing was going to stop me from having it. I relaxed to enjoy every single feeling that coursed through my body, and for once, I allowed myself to be malleable and soft. I wanted to feel his hard muscles, his smooth skin. We separated for a moment but then he pulled me back into him even tighter. The small crescent moon drifted above us, and I couldn't help thinking about how the wish I'd made earlier in the evening had just come true. I wanted him even closer, so I pressed my body into his, and he responded by stroking my hair and resting his cheek on the top of my head.

I loved the feel of his arms around me, how he smelled like fresh soap, and how our bodies fit together so perfectly, like the colors of the sunset.

Part Two

Chapter Ten

October 1997

My shirt was almost off when I heard the front door slam. I pulled it down and jumped off the bed to look at myself in the mirror. My hair was a tangled mess, my face had a reddened, scratched look, and my lips were puffy and swollen. "My mom's home," I said. "I'll be right back."

John had also gotten up and was hurriedly tucking his shirt into his pants.

"Indie," yelled my mother from the kitchen

"Yup. Just doing some homework," I yelled back.

"Go and make nice," I whispered to John, finishing the buttons on my shirt.

He tried to kiss me again, but I pushed him away. "Stop. My mother is going to know."

As John went down the hall, I raced to the bathroom. I splashed water on my face, then put on some face cream and a little shiny face powder, which seemed to take away the redness. Next, I ran a brush through my hair, hoping these small measures would hide the evidence that John and I had not, in fact, been doing homework.

When I was satisfied that I looked okay, I made my way to the kitchen.

"John's been telling me about a project he's working on for his psychology class." Mom stirred a big pot of sauce that was on the stove.

"Oh, yeah?" I said as nonchalantly as I could. "What's for dinner?"

"Spaghetti, salad, and garlic bread." My mother looked at John over the rim of her reading glasses. Why she needed her glasses to stir spaghetti was beyond me. "You're staying for dinner, John?"

John shrugged. "Sure. I'd better phone my mom first." John left the room to use the phone in the hallway, and I could hear him leaving a message on an answering machine.

"She's not there?" I asked when he came back.

"She's probably in the bathroom or something." He spoke without looking at me, and from the way he tapped his fingers on the kitchen counter, I picked up his nervousness. In the month we'd been going out, I had yet to meet his mother or even see where he lived. He always came to my house, and every time I asked to meet her, he clammed up and offered some lame excuse.

"John and I were talking about his project on Edgar Cayce," my mom piped in.

I was sipping a glass of water and nearly choked on it. Since we'd started dating, I'd always managed to steer the conversation away from Cayce. His paper on the guy wasn't due until well after Christmas.

I glanced at my mother.

Please don't blow it for me. Please don't tell John about my visions. He is my life right now. I need him. Want him. He is everything to me. And I mean everything.

"Do you believe in his work?" John asked my mom.

"Of course I do. I think he had special abilities and that he used them for the good of mankind."

"Mom, do you need help with the salad?" I butted in.

"No, I'm fine, honey. I made it earlier." She turned back to John, and I wanted to scream. "Some people just have that ability to tap into another dimension. They use their senses to do this."

John sat forward on his chair, like an eager scholar. I clicked my fingernails on the counter.

"The guy was a visionary," said John, "but I've also been reading about some other contemporary psychics who use smell, hearing, or even touch. Sylvia Browne and John Edward are two I've been trying to compare. At first I started the paper just looking at Cayce, but I've decided to put in some modern-day psychics just to show how things have changed and progressed."

I sank in my seat and stared into space. Why did my mother have to get involved in this? And why couldn't John just do his paper and be done with it? Or pick a topic that had something to do with psychology and not psychics.

"You should see the project we're doing for film class," I blurted out. "Sarah, Zoe, Carly, Monique, and I are going to perform a Spice Girls song, and Brent—you know, Brent from math class—he's going to film it. It's going to be hilarious."

I jumped up and starting singing the Spice Girls song "Wannabe," and I also did all the dance moves we had thought were so funny and so stupid when we practiced in class.

John gave me an incredulous look. "You hate the Spice Girls."

I kept singing and dancing. *"If you want to be my boyfriend, you gotta be nice to my mom."*

My mother turned and rolled her eyes. "I doubt those are the words," she said.

John laughed. "No, they're not the words. Not even close. Nor is that the tune. I hope you're not the singer in your band."

I ignored John's snide comment and kept singing and making up words. Then I started laughing so hard I couldn't continue singing. When I could catch my breath, I said, "You should see my costume. I picked some of it up at Value Village the other day. I'll go put it on." As I ran out of the room, I yelled over my shoulder, "And, yeah, I hate the Spice Girls."

I raced into my bedroom and put on the fake leopard print coat. Then I ran to Brian's bedroom, grabbed his Union Jack flag from the back of his chair, draped it around my neck, and ran into the kitchen. When I entered the kitchen, I knew Mom and John were talking again, so I slid on the floor and yelled, "Miss Geri Halliwell." Then I started singing again.

"I thought she was the redhead," said John over my singing. "Does your band sound like this? I sure hope not."

I continued dancing and quickly answered, "I'll wear a wig to be Geri, and no, our band does not sing these songs." I started singing again. Then I pretended to play air guitar. "We play rock 'n' roll!"

John started howling like a dog along with my singing. Sheena started whining, and Sasha wagged her tail. The cacophony of sounds made us burst out laughing.

Mom smiled and shook her head at us. "You kids are crazy." Then she pointed at me with the kitchen tongs. "Did you really get that jacket at Value Village?"

"Yup." I stuck my nose in the fake fur. "It smells like old people."

"Who smells like old people? Indie?" Brian strolled into the kitchen but stopped as soon as he saw me. "*What* are you doing with my flag?"

I twirled around. "I need it for a project."

"A *Spice Girls* project," John added.

"You're shittin' me."

John held up his hands.

Brian glared at me. "You've lost it, little sister. Don't wreck the flag."

"Dinner will be on the table in fifteen," said Mom. She pulled a pan out of the oven and placed it on a pot holder. Then she turned to John.

"We have lots of books in the den on that topic we were discussing. Get Indie to show you where they are while I'm finishing dinner. You're more than welcome to take any that you think might help with your paper."

How could she do that? How could she just switch topics? I thought I'd successfully moved them both along.

In all John's visits to our house, he had never once set foot in the den, because I had made sure that was one room we avoided. I always closed the door or just simply skirted around it, telling him it was my dad's study and he didn't like anyone in there. Now I had to take him in there myself. And all because of my mother.

"Indie," said my mom, pointing her finger, "the den. Dinner will be on the table in minutes."

"Do you really want to do homework now?" I said to John. "Let's talk music instead. I *promise*, no Spice Girls. Over at Zoe's the other day, we practiced this great Pearl Jam song, and it sounded pretty good."

He frowned at me. "For what it's worth, I think you should quit your band. And we can talk music later. I'll take any book I can get now. If it's one I don't have."

The den was near the back of our house, off a hallway near the laundry room. I trudged down the hall with John on my heels. Once we were out of sight of my mother, he said, "How come your mom knows so much about Cayce?"

"My mother has books that I know nothing about."

When we entered the den, John whistled. "Man, oh, man. Talk about books! This is amazing." John immediately went to the shelf while I stood at the doorway, my feet glued to the floor, unable to venture into the room. I hated this room. Reminders of my elementary school days flooded my mind and made me dizzy: doctors, diagnoses, ulcers that ripped my stomach apart and made me spit blood. Why was I being dragged through this again and again? Why did I have to fall for a guy who liked this stuff?

I watched as John went from book to book, totally absorbed. He'd open one and read a bit then open another and read, and within the span of minutes he had a stack beside him. From the doorway, I could feel his energy, his vibrations, and there was no doubt about it—he was buzzed.

And I was deflated.

Then he pulled out the exact book he had given me when we first met: *The Sleeping Prophet*. I didn't even know we owned a copy.

"That's your book," I said. I had never given one back to him because I didn't want him to know that I had never read it.

With a quizzical look on his face, he opened the cover. "No, it's not," he said. "Mine was from a secondhand store, and someone had written in it."

"You're taking all of those books?" I asked, trying desperately to change the subject.

He turned and stared at me, and I saw something in his eyes that made me want to sink through the floor and into the basement to hide. I shuffled my feet, trying to uproot them, and I crossed my arms, hoping to keep all his energy away from me.

"You really know nothing about these books?" he said accusingly.

"Nothing," I answered with conviction. Then I looked him in the eyes and said, "It's my mom's deal, not mine."

❖ ❖ ❖

"I want to meet *your* mom," I said to John after dinner when we were outside and he was about to drive home.

John opened his car door and jiggled his keys. "Okay," he finally said. "I'll talk to her. See if a night works this week."

I waited for him to kiss me good-bye, but he didn't. He waved, got in his car, and drove away, leaving me standing on the curb, watching the red of his taillights. I was quite sure he didn't look back at me either.

The next day at school, we set a date for Thursday night for me to come over to his house and meet his mother.

Thursday night arrived, and I dressed in jeans and a nice shirt. I couldn't help but wonder what Lacey would have thought of the purple shirt I had chosen. If only she could forgive and forget. It had been well over a month now since we'd talked. She was still with Burke. I was with John.

John picked me up and we drove out of South Keys and toward the Alta Vista neighborhood, a mix of suburban homes, high-rise apartments, and town houses. As we drove, we listened to music. My stomach flip-flopped. I was so nervous.

We only drove for 15 minutes, then John parallel parked his car on the street and in front of a small but nice-looking town house that had no garage. From the outside, it looked a bit worn but cute and comfortable. Mature maples and oaks, some with a few straggling leaves, lined the street. I sucked in a deep breath and undid my seat belt.

We walked up the small walkway, but he didn't hold my hand. He was too busy jingling his keys. Staring at him, I realized he was way more nervous than I was. He unlocked the front door, then walked inside ahead of me, almost pushing me behind him and scanning the hall as if he were casing his place to prevent me from seeing something I shouldn't. I couldn't help but glance around to see if anything was out of the ordinary, but there was nothing. Perhaps the cleaning standards weren't on par with my mother's, but then, whose were? She was obsessive. The furniture was simple, nothing elaborate, but it was livable.

"Mom," John said. Not loudly, like I would have done if I was searching for my mother and couldn't see her right away.

"I'm in the kitchen," said a voice.

Right away John's tense shoulders relaxed. He turned to me, took my hand, and smiled. "She's in the kitchen," he repeated. As if this was a really good thing, an unusual occurrence. My mom was always in the kitchen.

I smiled back at him and squeezed his hand. Then we walked down a small hall and into a tiny kitchen with big windows that overlooked a small backyard cluttered with stuff, including an old rusted tricycle. I was staring out the window so intently that I walked right into a counter just as I entered the kitchen. The pain shocked me, and I screeched. John's mother turned from the stove to look at me.

"Are you okay?" she asked.

I was such a klutz! "I'm fine," I replied. I rubbed my hip bone. What would his mother think of me now?

"Mom," he said, "this is Indie."

She wiped her hands on a dish towel. "It's nice to meet you, Indie."

I hadn't been able to get any picture in my mind of her at all before tonight. I had tried, but nothing came—my mind stayed blank. Dressed in jeans, a pink T-shirt, and casual moccasins, she was slim and attractive, with long, thick, brown hair. From the way John spoke about her, I was sort of expecting her to be downtrodden and a bit ragged. How could I have been so wrong?

"Sorry for the entrance," I said.

She smiled, and it was then I noticed her glassy blue eyes and how they appeared vacant, and dull, almost as if a layer of fog covered them. Bags hung underneath her eyes. Had she not slept in days or was she missing some sort of vitamin in her diet? She had high cheekbones, a cute nose, straight white teeth, and beautifully shaped eyes—it was the look behind them that threw me. Her raggedness was hidden inside her.

When she did smile, I noticed a little flicker in her eyes, but it faded as if the light had sputtered and died. Something wasn't right, something I couldn't pinpoint.

"I'm just glad you're okay, Indie," she said, sticking out her hand.

I shook her hand, and I could feel it trembling. Her fingers were tiny and frail, and although I wasn't big, I felt like a giant shaking her hand. Just the feel of her clammy skin made me start to sweat. My breathing grew shallow.

I inhaled, trying to get air into my lungs.

Act normal, Indie.

My throat kept closing.

"Hi. It's nice to meet you," I replied, as if on automatic pilot.

Do I sound okay? Do I sound too breathy?

Bring some air into your body, Indie.

A pulsing started in my forehead, and my eyes burned as I tried to keep them open and focus on John's mom. Oh, great, now I was having a vision. I was totally spazzing out.

Go away. Go away!

Stronger, stronger, the pulsing hammered my forehead. My vision grew narrower, and tunnel-like, the telescopic lens getting closer and closer to the fishbowl. I let my arms hang to my sides, hoping to stop what I knew was coming. This was not going to be just a snapshot—the pulsing was too intense. It was right in the middle of my forehead, in what some people called the third eye.

John went to the stove. "I'll flip these for you, Mom," he said.

"Can I get you something to drink, Indie?" Mrs. Smith asked.

"Water would be great," I managed to reply.

When I looked at her face, I tried to smile to appear normal, but all I could see was a garden shovel, one of the spade ones like my father used for digging dirt. Dirt covered the spade as if it had just been used.

This was crazy. A garden shovel?

As she turned to get me water, the shovel started to dig. And dig. And dig. Faster and faster. But I couldn't see anyone holding it. Just the shovel. Then I started to smell dirt. Dirt. Why dirt? It was as if I were on a farm somewhere. The scent wafted through my nostrils. Fresh dirt. The shovel was digging a hole and dirt flew, creating a big pile. The hole got bigger and bigger.

Why was I seeing a shovel?

Why was I smelling dirt?

Was I still smiling? *Say something, Indie. Speak.*

As suddenly as the shovel had appeared, it vanished, and I found myself standing in the middle of John's kitchen, shaking, my knees almost buckling under the weight of my body. Mrs. Smith still had her back to me. The tap ran, and water trickled into a glass. Good thing I was wearing jeans, because I was sure my knees were knocking together. And it was a darn good thing I had taken a wide stance, because I was so dizzy I could have lost my balance and ended up a big heap on the floor.

Inhaling and exhaling as quietly as I could, I tried to slow my breathing down and get my heart rate back to normal before she turned and gave me the water. I had no idea if my face was white or red or yellow, but I suspected it didn't look normal because it felt so clammy and hot. John still had his back to me and hadn't noticed a thing.

When I thought it was safe to move, I stuck my hands in my jeans pockets.

"Have you been gardening?" I asked.

Stupid question, Indie. Stupid. Stupid.

My throat was dry, and my tongue seemed to be stuck to the roof of my mouth.

"Gardening?" Mrs. Smith turned from the sink and, laughing, handed me a glass of water. "I'm not much of a gardener," she said.

With a plastic cooking flipper in his hand, John also turned to look at me. "Why would you ask that?" he asked. "Sometimes you say the craziest things."

What the heck was I supposed to say? I say crazy things because I *am* crazy?

"I thought . . . I smelled dirt." I tried to laugh, trying to at least sound semi-normal, if that can happen after asking such a weird question. What was with the shovel? And the dirt? Now my visions were bordering on ridiculous. Were there house plants around that I smelled?

"Dirt?" John raised his eyebrows, obviously thinking I was nervous, which, if I hadn't been so freaked with the vision, would have been kind of cute. But nothing about this moment was cute.

"I'm not a gardener or a cook," said Mrs. Smith. "I've made sandwiches for dinner." Then she laughed. "Grilled cheese."

"I love grilled cheese," I answered. And I did. It was my favorite sandwich.

I tried to scan the room for houseplants without them noticing. Perhaps there was a cactus or some creepy vine plant or even just a flowerpot.

Although my heart rate had slowed and the shovel and dirt smell had disappeared, I still felt off: dizzy, unbalanced, and nauseous. I tipped the glass of water to my mouth and managed a sip, allowing it to soothe my parched throat.

"Can I help?" I asked John.

"Indie, it's grilled cheese. I can make these blindfolded. I eat them, like, every other day."

"That makes me sound like a horrible mother," said Mrs. Smith.

John didn't reply and kept his back to his mother. An awkward silence filled the small kitchen.

Mrs. Smith wrung her hands before she turned to me. "Are sandwiches okay, Indie?" Concern laced her voice, as if she hadn't made the right food for my visit.

By now, I was starting to feel better, so I smiled and said for the second time, "Mrs. Smith, I love grilled cheese sandwiches. They're comfort food to me."

John finished frying the sandwiches, slid them onto plates, and dumped the pan in the sink. We sat down at the dining-room table with our sandwiches, the ketchup bottle, a jar of pickles, and a big veggie tray. John got the two of us a beer (which was totally weird for me but kind of cool, too) and gave his mother water, even after she told him that she wanted a beer. When he gave her the water, he avoided her gaze, and she didn't say anything to him about not getting her what she had asked for. I thought the role reversal was strange, so unlike my relationship with my parents.

Dinner went well, and we discussed trivial things, like the weather, a few television shows and movies that we had all seen, and our favorite and not-so-favorite actors. We even talked about a few of the new fashions coming out, which was kind of funny because his mom and I both agreed that we liked more of a casual style and that Winners was our favorite store. I liked his mother; she was shy, like me.

But . . . why the shovel? Why the dirt? I was baffled.

At the end of the meal, she said, "Indie, thank you for coming over. John doesn't bring many friends home."

"It was nice to finally meet you, too." I smiled at her. Under the table, I put my foot on top of John's. "Thank *you* for dinner."

When she looked at me, her eyes were misty. "It wasn't much. It was really more like lunch." She glanced John's way. "I'm very lucky to have a son like John."

John stood and started gathering the plates. "I'll do dishes."

"I'll help," I said, trying to lighten the mood that had suddenly settled over the table.

"John said you were different than most girls." She put her hand on my arm.

Something about her touch burned my skin, as if I had been seared by the frying pan. Although I was shocked, I didn't pull my hand away. Instead I let the pain flow through me, because I didn't know what else to do but let it all happen. After what was probably only seconds, but seemed like minutes, she removed her hand. Free to escape, I picked up my plate and walked into the kitchen.

John was huddled over the kitchen sink. I sidled up beside him. "Need help?"

"I'm good."

I nodded, even though he didn't look at me. I circled my arms around his body and hugged him, resting my cheek on the middle of his back.

He stopped rinsing the dishes and just stood at the sink with his back to me for a few seconds. Then he turned to face me, pulling me toward him to kiss the top of my head. "You made my mom happy," he whispered.

If I made her happy, why do I feel so drained?

I looked up at him, and our eyes immediately connected. I saw his pain. Then he lowered his head, and we kissed until we heard a couple of loud coughs at the door.

I only stayed about an hour longer, because it was a school night. We both had homework to do, and John still had to drive me home.

On our way out, Mrs. Smith said, "Please, come over again, Indie. I'd like to get to know you better." She smiled. "John tells me you're in a band. I think that sounds fun."

Again, my throat felt like it was a desert, and my heart started to pound. "Sure," I replied. "Next time I'll tell you all about the band."

Once in the car, my body relaxed. Exhausted, I leaned my head back on the headrest.

"My mom liked you," he said.

"I liked her, too," I replied. Cold air washed over me. My stomach churned. My head suddenly throbbed. *Know me better?*

Was that why I saw the shovel? Was my vision trying to tell me that she was going to dig up the dirt I had thrown over my past and who I really was? That would make sense.

Is she going to be the one to burst my bubble?

I got home, said hello to my mom, begged off answering her 101 questions about my visit, and told her I was going to my room to do my homework. Instead of opening my books, I flopped onto my bed and fell right to sleep.

When I woke up, groggy and disoriented, my room was dark, and the red lights on my alarm clock said it was 3:00 A.M. I was still in the clothes I had worn to John's. When I stood up to change into my pajamas and wash off my makeup, my legs felt as if I were wearing ankle weights.

What is going on? The shovel!

That was it. If Mrs. Smith managed to dig up that I saw crazy visions and dead people, she would tell John, and he would drop me ASAP. The thought of not having John in my life made me nauseous.

First Lacey. Then John. What would I do if I lost him?

I had never been in love before, but I knew this was it. I spent all my waking moments thinking about John, and when I was near him, all I wanted was his touch, his hands on my body and his lips on my skin. He had this crazy power over me.

I fell back into a fitful sleep and had horrible dreams about shovels and dirt and holes in the ground and Lacey's necklace. Everything intertwined and nothing made sense, and when I woke up for the second time, the sun was streaming through my window and my pajamas were drenched in sweat.

⟞⟡⟝

Chapter Eleven

My mother was sitting at the counter with her coffee, newspaper, and one piece of toast with peanut butter when I walked into the kitchen. She immediately glanced my way, looking at me over the rim of her reading glasses. "So, how was your dinner last night? You didn't say too much when you got home."

"I had homework." I poured cereal.

"Did it not go well?"

"Why do you always have to think the worst?"

She folded her newspaper and placed it on the counter. "I'm not thinking the worst. You just seemed like you didn't want to talk about something. I worry when you bottle things inside."

"His mom was nice. Everything went well."

She paused and folded her napkin, which I knew meant she was thinking about what she wanted to say next. I hated when she did that. Finally, she said, "You haven't told him yet, have you?"

I stood up and threw my cereal down the disposal. I had lost my appetite. Then I stared at her. "No, Mom, I haven't. And don't you tell him either."

"Indie, I think he would understand you."

"No, he wouldn't. He would be like everyone else and think I was a freak."

She held up her hands. "Okay. Let's drop the subject." She paused, but only for a second. "Oh, I forgot to tell you, I ran into Carol. She says she misses you and wonders if you and Lacey had a bit of a tiff."

To get out of this conversation, I slung my backpack over my shoulder. "I'm not thrilled with her boyfriend."

"Neither is Carol. She is worried about Lacey. She says Lacey doesn't hang out with her girlfriends anymore, and this boy has alienated her from everyone. She's even thinking of quitting the volleyball team. And she might have a scholarship. Maybe you should try to patch things up."

"I'll try, but I'm not promising anything. I have to get going."

Then for some reason, I thought about Papa's visit from a month ago. Perhaps it was the worry lines stretching across my mom's forehead that made me remember. As I walked out the kitchen and toward the front door, I said over my shoulder, "By the way, a smile can brighten a dull day."

My mom gasped, and I turned to look at her. By the expression on her face, I knew she had figured out that Papa had been to see me again. I laughed as I stepped outside and slammed the front door.

When I got on my bus, I was surprised to see Nathan. Of course, he had an empty seat beside him even though the bus was jammed.

I sat beside him. "I've never seen you on this bus," I said as I put my backpack on my lap.

Nathan pulled his finger out of his nose. Kids teased him constantly for that habit. Although he was just one grade younger than me, he acted like an eight-year-old. "My parents divorced, so I've moved," he said.

"That sucks," I replied. "At least you didn't have to switch schools."

"I wanted to," he whispered. "Ridgemont scares me. I wish I didn't have to go swimming today in phys ed. I hate phys ed."

Something in his hushed tone made me glance at him. The poor kid had fear stamped all over his face; he was a walking target for ridicule. To put on a bathing suit in a locker room full of macho guys must be so awkward for him.

"Just pretend you're sick," I said. "And sit and watch from the sidelines. I've done that before." I faked a cough, and Nathan laughed.

Suddenly, I felt a push on the middle of my back and I had to brace my hands on the seat in front to stop from flying forward. I turned around. The girl behind me was slouched in her seat with headphones shoved in her ears. Her feet were on the ground and not on the seat. Had she kicked my seat?

"What's the matter?" Nathan asked.

I faced front again. "Did you feel that girl kick the seat?"

He shook his head. "Sometimes they do that to me." Then he smiled broadly at me, showing a mouthful of metal. "But not when I'm with you. Thanks again for sitting with me *and* for giving me advice on my stupid swimming class."

He faked a cough, which made us both burst out laughing.

❖ ❖ ❖

John didn't meet me at my locker, and I had no idea why. Since we had started going out, he'd met me every morning. I stuck my pager in my pocket, just in case he called. My brother had just given me his old pager, and I had given John the number. When he called, I always pretended I needed to use the bathroom to step outside and get to a phone. In my hurry to get my books, I knocked a bunch of stuff out of my locker.

I bent over and randomly gathered everything, and that's when I saw Lacey's silver best friend necklace on the tiled floor. I threw all the rest of my crap on the shelf then bent back down to pick up the necklace.

It was tangled, with several small knots and one really big one.

I shoved it in my pocket, threw my books in my backpack, and slammed my locker door shut.

As I walked to class, my mind was a jumble of thoughts. I had felt a kick to my seat even if Nathan hadn't. What was with that? And I'd seen a shovel last night at John's? And I'd dreamed about everything, even Lacey's necklace. And now it was tangled in my pocket.

I hardly heard a word in math, and by the end of the class, I had a full page of doodles. Still immersed in my thoughts, I got up to leave and shouldered someone, causing me to lose my balance and sending my books tumbling to the floor.

"Watch where you're going," Lacey muttered.

"Sorry," I mumbled, bending over to pick up my books for the second time that day. Of the 30 people in class, I would have to pick Lacey to smack into. I thought about the necklace. Had that been a sign that I was going to run into her today? Was I supposed to pick up on these signs?

When I stood, I was so hoping she would have vacated the room, but she was still standing there. Now she was eyeing me instead of glaring.

"I wish you hadn't ruined our friendship," she said, holding her books in front of her.

"I was honest with you," I said.

"Honest?" She paused. "You lied to me."

"It wasn't like that."

"Yes, it was!"

"No, it wasn't. I was trying to warn you. Help you."

"Warn me about what? Burke? Just admit it, Indie, you were jealous of my relationship with him. That he took me away from you."

"Jealous? I was happy for you." I pulled my books around in front of my chest.

"He doesn't cheat on me, you know," she said. "He drove you home from that party, and you wanted him for yourself, so you said that to me."

"What?"

"That's it. Isn't it? You made up the vision. And took John as second best."

I couldn't believe what I was hearing. She had no right to bring John into this. I was about to scream at her, when I caught myself. I didn't want to hurt her any more than I already had. Plus, I remembered the man's voice coming to me, telling me we would one day be friends again. I lowered my voice and said, "I valued our friendship and was never ever jealous. I admired you. I still do. I only ever wanted what was best for you. I wanted to tell you the truth."

"Truth?" She laughed, mean undertones lacing the sound. "And, tell me, are you sharing the same truthful relationship you had with me with your new boyfriend? Does he know about you? Like, really know? Like *I* know?"

"John and I have nothing to do with you and me."

"Girls!" A loud voice boomed from the front of the room. Both Lacey and I turned at the same time. Mr. Leonard stood by his desk with his hands on his hips. "Take your catfight outside my classroom—preferably outside the school grounds and somewhere far away. Go to the mall."

Without looking at Lacey, I ran from the classroom, down the hall, and straight to the girls' bathroom, where I pushed by the makeup queens who felt it necessary to reapply blush and lipstick between classes. I locked myself in a stall, put the toilet seat down, and sat with my head in my hands. My body shook. My head throbbed. And sweat dripped from my pores. In all our years as friends, Lacey and I had never had a fight. I pulled out the necklace and tried to untangle it, but my hands were trembling so much that it was useless. Tears slid down my cheeks. This was all because of my stupid visions. Would my visions also ruin my relationship with John? I couldn't let that happen. I would kill myself if we broke up. Would I ever have anything normal in my life? I looked at the chain. It was really tangled.

I wanted to be normal.

Normal.

I shoved the necklace back into my pocket and hugged my knees. I didn't want to be me. I was stupid, crazy, a freak of nature. I sat on the toilet for a few more minutes, rocking back and forth, waiting for the queens to head off to their next class. When I was convinced that no one was in the washroom, I wiped my eyes with toilet paper and unlocked the stall door. At the sink, I ran the water and splashed it on my face, then I reached for a paper towel. As I dried my face, I glanced in the mirror.

It was then that I saw the words, written in lipstick in big red letters: INDIE IS A FREAK!

I gasped. Everything swirled around me. The sinks, mirrors, and brick walls went around and around me, and it was as if I stood alone in the center of a tornado. The red lipstick words flashed, like a blinding neon light. I closed my eyes to get away from it all, to make it stop. I pressed my feet into the floor to keep my balance. The room moved in slow motion, and the spinning got slower and slower with every second. It was as if it were running out of batteries. Within a few seconds, calmness surrounded me, cloaked me almost. Still shaking, I opened my eyes and again stared directly into the mirror, only this time, there were no words. They were gone. Just like that.

I grabbed the sides of the sink, bent my head over, and tried to breathe. This was so crazy.

Don't hate yourself for who you are.

The man's voice. Why didn't he leave me alone? "Don't talk to me now," I whispered softly. "Not at school. Please."

I heard the washroom door open and managed to stand upright. Whoever it was could not hear me talking to an imaginary voice. I played with my hair in front of the mirror.

Sarah ran in and headed straight to the stall. "I gotta pee so bad."

I faked a laugh and said, "And I gotta get to class."

Her stall door shut, and I hurried out, pushing the red words to the back of my mind. I had to. What else could I do? If I took them as a sign that something bad was going to happen to me, to John and me, then I was doomed. The hall was empty, and I walked in a daze toward my next class, thankful that today was Friday.

For the entire class, I checked my pager. John still hadn't called. What was wrong?

Secrets. They have a way of being dug up with spade shovels.

By lunch, I still hadn't heard from John, and I must have checked my pager 100 times. The bell rang, and I tossed my lunch in the garbage and headed out to the smoking area, scanning the school grounds to see if John was reading under a tree somewhere, even though it was freezing outside; winter was definitely on the way.

But he was nowhere. I breathed the cold air; the temperature had to be hovering around freezing, and there was a mist that clouded the air and made visibility difficult. Almost like my relationship with John; nothing was ever clear.

I shivered and wondered if it would snow before Halloween. I sure hoped not. Of course, Sarah, Zoe, Carly, and the rest of their friends were hanging out in the smoking area. I approached them, although I wasn't sure I really fit in. Sure, we had our band, but was I really one of them? Who did I fit in with?

John. I fit in with John. He made me feel normal. He made me feel alive and free. It was ironic in a way, because even though he was dark and brooding, he made me feel lighter. I loved the Police song "Every Breath You Take" because that was John and me. He was my every breath. I had to have him in my life.

Where was he today?

"Hi ya, Indie."

I waved and pulled out my cigarettes.

"We were thinking we should have another rehearsal," said Carly. "March will be here before we know it."

"It's not even Halloween yet." Zoe laughed at Carly. "But you're right, we need to think of some new songs," said Zoe.

I had a hard time focusing on the conversation, because I was so worried about John. He liked to skip, but usually he let me know. Empty, hollow, I missed him and needed him, especially now with all of this Lacey stuff.

"So what are you up to tonight?" Sarah asked, interrupting my thoughts. "You going out with John *again*? We really need to rehearse."

I shrugged. "I don't know."

"Do you not want to be in the band?" Carly asked.

"Yeah, of course I do," I replied.

"Well, come hang with us girls for one night," said Sarah. "My parents are gone. We can make as much noise as we want."

I pretended to laugh. "You saying we just make noise?"

Sarah bumped me with her shoulder. "Yeah, but if we're drunk enough, it will sound good. We can start with Baileys and coffee after school."

"Maybe," I said with reluctance.

"Come on, Indie. You always have an excuse. We need you in the band."

"Okay," I conceded. How would I tell John that I couldn't see him because I had a band practice? He hated the band.

Time crept by, and I doodled at least five pages in my afternoon classes. I must have scrawled John's name out 50 times. He didn't show up at school, nor did he page me. I tried to call him a few times, but there was no answer at his house.

So I went to Sarah's after going home to get my guitar.

True to her word, Sarah produced a big bottle of Baileys from her parents' liquor cabinet, and from the refrigerator, she pulled out a carton of chocolate milk. "We'll throw this in the bottle. It will go sour, and my mother will think the booze is bad and say she's going to take it back, but she never does. Then it will get tossed, and no one will know."

"You know all the tricks," said Zoe.

We drank the Baileys, then we went downstairs. I slung my guitar on my shoulder and tuned it while Sarah set up her drums, Zoe changed a string on her bass, and Carly played around on her keyboard.

"Okay," said Sarah. "Are we ready? Let's start with 'Superman's Dead.' One, two, three . . ."

I started to play and sing with Sarah, although I was a little unsure of the words because I had missed the last rehearsal because of John. Sarah was our lead singer, and I did backup. We made it through the entire song, which was a feat for us. Usually, we ended up stopping halfway through.

"Wow," said Carly when we hit the last chord. "That was *amazing.*"

"Yeah," said Sarah, holding up her drumsticks. "We rock!"

"We are going to have those animals at the shelter dancing!" Carly ran her fingers down her keyboard, ending with the lowest note and a snap of her fingers.

"That was so awesome!" I said. My body vibrated with energy. I could feel my heart beating, and in a good way. It was exhilarating.

"You need to stop missing rehearsal, girl," Sarah said to me.

Then she did a drumroll before she said, "All we need is five songs. Just a quick set. And playing at this fund-raiser will be way better than playing at the school talent show in May."

"I wouldn't play at the school if they paid us," I said.

"Why?" Zoe asked. "Would *John* not approve?"

"You've missed so many rehearsals because of him," uttered Carly.

Sarah glanced at me quickly, then said, "Well, Bad Girls, I think the success of that song deserves another drink."

I hadn't eaten all day, so after the next drink, which I chugged, I started to feel the effects of the alcohol. The girls just didn't understand what it was like to be involved, like I was, with John. But, they were right. I was missing practice because of him, and I really liked being in the band. When I went to the bathroom, I checked my pager again. No call. Was he avoiding me? We went downstairs, played a few more songs, and then attempted to do a new one. It bombed, and we laughed hysterically.

"I'm done," said Zoe, taking her guitar off her shoulder.

"Me too," said Sarah placing her drumsticks on her drum. "I'm starving. Are you staying, Indie?"

"I'm not sure," I said.

"Figures," said Carly. "Gotta go see the boyfriend."

I ignored her, put my guitar away, and went to the bathroom, where I sat on the toilet seat and checked my pager again. Why hadn't John answered any of my calls?

Upstairs, I quickly used the phone but got his voice mail. Sarah threw a frozen pizza in the oven. I decided to stay and drink, because I needed to forget about John.

After downing more than I needed, Zoe put on the Police, and we danced in her kitchen, laughing as we stumbled and fell. I liked the numbing feeling of the alcohol.

"Hey," I slurred, "play 'Every Breath You Take.' That's my favorite song of theirs."

When the song came on, I sang along with it, thinking about how I wanted John to belong to me and how my heart did ache with every step he took. I wanted to sing to him, tell him how I felt.

At the beginning of the song, the girls laughed, then about halfway through, they quieted down and just listened. When it was over, Sarah pumped her fist and said, "We have to do that song with our band! Indie, you can be lead."

"Sing it, girl," yelled Carly. She started the song all over again.

This time I didn't want to sing to John; I wanted to be funny. I used my fist to make a pretend microphone, then I slid across the kitchen floor as if I were a true rock star. This made the girls howl in laughter. On the outside I was funny, but on the inside I was hurting. I kept the show going for the entire song.

When the Baileys bottle emptied, Sarah pulled out a big bottle of vodka. Orange juice replaced chocolate milk. I got drunker and drunker, and my life got hazier and hazier.

Our conversation veered to Halloween and our costumes, and we planned the party that was going to be at Zoe's. Tonight the booze was fun and made me forget about John and . . . that I was a crazy freak of nature. Had he found out about me? Was that why he wasn't calling me?

When we were all really drunk, Sarah slung her arm around me and asked, "So, have you and John had sex yet?"

Everyone stopped dancing and started giggling. "Yeah, we're all dying to know if he's any good," slurred Zoe. "We think he'd be so amazing."

"Yeah." Carly almost fell into the counter, which made me giggle along with the girls. "Tell us, Indie," urged Carly.

I shook my head and put up my hands. "Noooo way." I pressed my hands to my heart. "What we have is sacred."

"Oh. My. Gawd," squealed Sarah. "You're so in loooove."

"I'd like to be in love," slurred Zoe. "No one likes me. What's it like to be in love?" Zoe tried to sit on a chair, but missed it by a foot and landed on the floor. "I want a boyfriend, too."

I raised my arms in the air and danced in circles. "It's the best feeling in the world. The best feeling in the world." I kept repeating myself. Then I pressed play on the CD player.

"Not again," said Carly. "We've listened to that song a gazillion times."

I held up my finger. "Just once more, 'kay?"

Again, I sang, pretending that John belonged to me. I kept singing until the spinning made me lose my balance. The girls helped me stand up then walked me to Sarah's bed, where I must have passed out.

❖ ❖ ❖

At noon the next day, I caught the bus home from Sarah's. The alcohol sloshed and swished in my stomach, and I just wanted to throw up. Because it was Saturday, only three other people were on the bus. I made my way to the back and sat down, sliding over on the vinyl seat to be close to the window and putting my guitar beside me. The window glass was cold; condensation bordered the bottom. The weather was hovering at the in-between stage, where it wasn't quite winter yet but the nice fall weather was over. I ran my finger through the water droplets, making swirling marks. Were John and I done, just like the warm autumn air? Were we a one-season couple?

Soon it would be nothing but cold outside, every day, every hour. Was my winter going to be cold without him? The cold would match my insides. Cold. Ice cold. Why hadn't John paged me? Had I done something wrong? Said something he didn't like?

Only my mother had paged me.

I tried to close off my mind, get a picture of John and where he was. But nothing happened, and I couldn't get my mind to still long enough to even see the white page. Too many questions ran through my brain. Why did I have such a hard time seeing anything for myself? I was so immersed in thought that I didn't hear anyone approaching me. Then I heard the small, squeaky voice. "Can I sit with you, Indie?"

When I looked up, Nathan stood by my seat, clutching a violin case. "Sure," I replied. I put my guitar case on the seat in front of me.

He sat down and carefully put his black violin case on the floor beside him.

"You play?" I asked. I wanted to make conversation so he wouldn't see how hungover I was.

He nodded. "Yeah."

"How long?"

"Since I was three."

"Wow, you must be good."

"I didn't know you played guitar," he said.

"If you can call it that," I replied. "We have an all-girl band. We might do a short set for the animal shelter at their fund-raiser."

"I'll come watch," he said. "When is it?"

"Probably not until March."

"I'll still come," he said. "I want to be a concert violinist." Then he sighed. "I just have to make it through high school."

"You have good grades," I said.

He shook his head. "Making it through high school has nothing to do with grades."

Suddenly, just like the last time I had sat with Nathan, I felt a shove on the back of my seat and flew forward, almost nose-diving into the metal bar in front of me.

The muscles in my arms tensed as I grabbed the bar. Then it happened. What I had been trying to make happen: my gaze clouded over, my mind went blank, the spinning started . . . and I saw a pool of water.

"What's wrong, Indie?" Nathan put his hand on my shoulder.

The touch made me return to the bus. I leaned back and exhaled, clutching my stomach. "Did you feel that?" I whispered.

"Indie," said Nathan, "no one is sitting behind us." Then he glanced at me, his eyes wide and innocent. "Are you high?" he whispered. I sensed a disappointment in his tone.

"No," I replied, trying to smile. "I think I have the flu."

"That's good," he said. "Well, not good that you have the flu, but good that you're not like the others. Are you still going out with John Smith? He's always nice to me, too."

I smiled at Nathan. "Yeah, he's still my boyfriend."

But is he? I had felt a kick and seen a pool of water. *Is that for John or Nathan? Is John kicking me away? Is our relationship drowning in a pool of water?* I was so confused.

✤ ✤ ✤

John didn't call that afternoon, nor did he call that night. I had no idea what to do with myself. I locked myself in my room to sleep and get rid of my hangover. But I couldn't sleep, and the four walls of my room throbbed in and out. Finally, darkness arrived, and I curled under my covers.

Dreams invaded my sleep.

John and I ran along a beach and then Lacey was running beside us. But she stopped and started choking because her necklace was too tight. She clutched her chest and fell. John started to do CPR on her. Then Lacey became Burke, and John still did CPR. I just stood there doing nothing. Nothing. Nothing.

I woke up in the middle of the night, shaking and breathing so hard I had to sit up. A glass of water sat on my nightstand, so I picked it up and took a sip.

Suddenly cigar smoke stung my nostrils.

I immediately looked in the direction of the smell. I put my hand over my mouth to stifle my screams. At the end of my bed was the man I had seen at school. The glass in my hand dropped, water soaking my covers. I didn't care. He just stood there, motionless, staring at me with a sneer on his face. I was so repulsed that I inched to the back of my bed. My teeth chattered, and I wanted to throw up, but most of all, I wanted to scream and scream loudly.

"Who are you?" I snapped.

No answer. He crossed his arms and let his cigar dangle from his mouth.

"Why are you here?

He took his cigar from his mouth and gave me an evil smile that hit my bones.

"Answer me!"

Still nothing.

"Why won't you talk to me? Say something, anything. You're supposed to talk to me. Every other dead person who has visited me has talked. Why won't you speak?"

He just stood there staring at me, my body.

I pulled my bedcover up to my chin. "Who are you?" I asked again. "Who are you? Tell me!" I flung my words out fast and furious.

His vindictive smile made me cringe.

Could ghosts rape? The thought crashed through my mind, because that is exactly what it looked like he wanted to do to me. Every part of my body shook.

I yanked the covers up to my nose and curled my legs to my body, trying to become as small as possible.

"Get out of my room!"

He reached up and made a slashing movement to his throat. Then, with a horrible glint in his eyes and a mocking look on his face, he started to undo his belt.

"No! Get out!"

I threw my pillow at him. It went right through his body and landed on the other side of the room. Then I threw my doll. She crashed against the wall and fell to the floor. I screamed and screamed. Then I threw the glass. It crashed against the wall and splintered into tiny shards. I would not let this happen to me. I couldn't.

The knock on my door rattled me back to reality. Suddenly, the man's face changed, and his evil sneer was gone. I saw some sort of remorse. Then he disappeared.

"Indie! Are you okay?"

The smell was gone. The man was gone. I had to get out of my room. I had to feel my mother's arms around me, and I couldn't wait for her to come into my room. I had to get to her now. I needed her. I tried to stand so I could walk to the door. My mother barged into my room.

"Indie, what's wrong?"

I saw her face as my legs gave way and I fell to the floor. Then the room went black.

When I awoke, the light was bright, and a cold, damp cloth was on my forehead. My mom was sitting on the edge of my bed, with my dad standing behind her.

When Mom noticed that I was awake, she readjusted the cold cloth.

"How do you feel?" she probed.

"Okay," I answered, my throat parched. "What happened?"

"You were screaming. Then you fainted. Do you remember anything?"

My dad moved to the end of my bed and began massaging my feet.

"I had a bad dream."

"Do you want to talk about it?"

"No."

"Indie, you fainted. This is not good."

"I have my period, and it makes me have nightmares. And my cramps make me weak." Why was I making up excuses? Why couldn't I just tell them that I had seen a horrible ghost? I glanced at my mom and saw her worry lines. That was why. She would worry about me and send me to the doctor.

"That would explain a bit," said my mother, obviously not convinced.

My dad stood. "I'll let you girls talk this one through. I'll go get you some water." The lines on his face softened, and he smiled like he had a little joke sitting on the end of his tongue. "How 'bout a popsicle?" He asked, raising his eyebrows.

I tried to smile back. "I'm not five, Dad. But sure."

Although my dad had broken the ice, my mother still eyed me. A tissue box sat on my desk, and she pulled out a few and started picking up the big pieces of glass.

"Don't worry, Mom," I said, trying to reassure her. "It was just a dream."

Mom put the tissue with the glass inside of it on my desk. Then she picked up my pillow and gave it to me when she sat down beside me again. "It must have been a bad one."

I hugged my pillow and closed my eyes. Who was that man? Why did he keep coming to me?

She stroked my hair. "Indie, you are who you are for a reason."

"I wish it would all go away." I stopped to catch my breath and hug my pillow closer to my body. "Mom, what if . . . what if John drops me because of the way I am?"

"I don't think he will, Indie. But if he does, he's not worthy of your love."

"I'm just so afraid of what will happen if I lose him."

Chapter Twelve

At 2:00 on Sunday afternoon, I still had not heard from John. I couldn't stand not knowing what was wrong. Stashed in my purse was a bus map. Within seconds, I had figured out what buses I needed to take to get to his house. With my pager in my purse, I grabbed my jean jacket and told my mom I was heading out.

The weather had taken a drastic turn. The sky was ash gray, the clouds were definitely snow clouds. Little particles of ice hovered in the air. Yuck. I hated the cold. I lowered my head and did up my jacket, wishing I had worn a scarf or even a turtleneck.

Two buses later, I was in John's neighborhood. Ten minutes after that, I arrived at his town house, my hands and toes frozen. I should have worn gloves and thicker socks. I lifted my hands to my face and blew on them, trying to warm them up. The curtains were drawn, and the place looked dark. But there did seem to be a light on around the side of the house, which, I was sure, was John's bedroom. This time there was no jingling of keys as I walked up the front walkway.

I rubbed my hands together before I knocked on the door. Once. I waited, and when no one answered, I knocked again. Footsteps sounded from inside the house. The door cracked open slightly, and John's eye peered out. When he saw it was me, he opened the door a little wider, but not much. In one small movement, he stepped outside, quietly closing the door behind him. I was so cold I wanted to go inside to get warm. Wearing only a T-shirt and jeans, he crossed his arms to the chill of the day. "What are you doing here?"

His tone shocked me. Was he not happy to see me?

"I haven't heard from you all weekend," I stuttered. He didn't want me here. I shoved my hands in my pockets. "I wondered if you're okay."

"I'm fine. I have a ton of homework."

"Why didn't you answer my calls?"

"I was going to call tonight." He shivered. "You should probably go."

Go.

Go?! Suddenly the word hit me. Was he serious? I had come here on the bus, in this crappy cold weather, to see him, and he wanted me to go. Tears threatened to spill down my face. I couldn't let him see me cry. I straightened my shoulders and nodded. "Do you think I could use your bathroom first?"

He didn't answer me. Did he have someone in the house with him? Another girl? I had to find out.

"Please," I said. "I really have to go. I won't stay. Plus I'm freezing."

He sighed, ran his hand through his hair, then said, "Okay. But my mom's sleeping."

I stepped inside his house and immediately noticed the gloomy darkness. I wondered if anyone *was* in his room with him. Had he brought another girl home? I slipped out of my shoes and tiptoed to the bathroom. As soon as I closed the bathroom door, my blood rushed to my head. And I couldn't breathe. I clutched my throat. What the hell? Afraid to even look in the mirror, I sat on the toilet. I trembled and shook and placed my head in my hands. But I did pee. Finished, I knew

I had to stand, so I braced myself by placing one hand on the side of the sink.

"Okay, Indie." I decided to talk myself through whatever it was that was going on. "It's just that the room is small. You're just feeling claustrophobic. Wash your hands and get out of here."

I managed to get my pants done up, then I turned to the sink to wash, refusing to look in the mirror, afraid of what my face would look like. I kept my gaze on the little ledge above the sink.

"Focus, Indie. Focus. And you will be okay."

I turned the water on hot and stuck my hands underneath the tap. It felt so good to warm up my hands. If only my heart could warm up this quickly. It still felt cold as ice from John's rejection.

Something in front of me glistened and glimmered.

Shone like a bright halogen light.

The light pierced my vision, and I kept rubbing my hands under the water, washing them clean. Was it the tap that was shining? I couldn't figure it out.

I turned the tap off. Then I closed my eyes.

I held on to the sink. "Open your eyes, Indie. Open your eyes."

You're a crazy girl. Crazy in the head.

At the sound of the mean voice in my head, I opened my eyes. "No, I'm not," I said firmly. "I'm not crazy. I'm just tired. And this stuff with John is making me out of sorts."

Nice try.

Then I saw the locket sitting on the little ledge next to a bottle of pain relievers. It was gold, real gold from what I could see, with a long gold chain. The locket itself was oval in shape and had some etchings on it. Was that what had been shining so brightly? The locket?

Suddenly, I was blinded! I covered my eyes and drew in a deep breath to stop whatever else was coming my way. I kept gripping the side of the sink. But a feeling so powerful overcame me, and I desperately wanted to touch the locket, hold it, open it. Mom had always told me not to touch other people's things, that it was rude. But something about the locket drew me in. The magnetic appeal overpowered me and any common sense that had been given to me by my mother.

I just had to reach for it.

Touch it.

Hold it.

My fingers inched forward, slowly, and when the tips of my skin came in contact with the necklace, they burned, sending painful electrical currents through my body. Scorching pain. But even the pain didn't stop me from picking the locket up and opening it.

I gasped. And shut the locket until it clicked.

I had to be wrong. Had to be. This couldn't be right. I held the locket tightly in my hand, squeezing my fingers, pressing the chain into my skin. It burned my skin, but I kept digging it into my palm, hoping that next time I looked inside I would see a different photo. I had to believe that what I saw was wrong.

"Okay," I whispered. "I'm crazy. I admit it."

There was no answer from the voice in my head.

I have no idea how much time passed before I opened my hand again. Seconds, minutes. Was John going to knock on the door soon, wondering if I was okay? The necklace sat in the palm of my left hand. I stared at it. Just stared. Then I sucked in a deep breath. And with my right hand, I clicked the latch and opened the locket again.

I glanced down again at the small photo, praying, hoping, desperate to see something different.

No!

The same face stared back at me.

The locket fell from my fingers to the floor. The room swirled and twirled around me. Spinning, spinning, I moved around and around, my body feeling as if it were some kind of liquid. When I glanced in the mirror, I couldn't see my face. Everything was a blur, and all I could see was a blank wall behind me. "Get a grip," I whispered. "You have to get under control. John is going to wonder what is wrong with you."

But I couldn't stop the room from spinning like an out-of-control merry-go-round. *Stop. Stop. You have to stop.*

I sucked in air as fast as I could and tried to breathe it out just as quickly. In and out. In and out. *Keep breathing, Indie. Keep breathing.* In and out. In and out. I hung on to the sink for dear life.

Finally, the spinning slowed and stopped. And when it did, the vertigo started. I clutched my stomach and vomited in the toilet. I heaved and heaved until everything was out of me. Then I turned on the tap again and splashed cold water on my face. How long had I been in this powder room?

I dried my face and slowly lifted my head to look in the mirror. My skin had a horrible gray tone to it. I pinched my cheeks.

"Come on," I whispered. "Give me some color."

Within seconds, I looked a little better. As I went to unlock the door, I remembered the necklace, sitting on the floor, below the sink. I didn't want to pick it up, touch it again. But I couldn't leave it on the floor.

I snatched a toothbrush out of a plastic holder and used the end of the brush to lift the necklace off the floor. Once it was back on the ledge, I put the toothbrush away, smoothed my hair, and opened the bathroom door.

The waft of fresh air that hit me almost made me recoil. I had been stuck in that small room with evil, of that I was convinced.

Before I walked into the hallway to face John, I inhaled and exhaled three times. The magic number three worked. Then I tried to walk as if everything were okay.

Act normal. Say something intelligent. Don't say something stupid. Don't mumble. And for shit's sake, don't faint. Just get out.

I was almost to my shoes when I heard the voice. "John," his mother screamed, "I need another drink. Please! They're coming for me again. I can't stand it. The pain. Please!"

All the warmth I'd felt when I entered the house disappeared, and icy cold air circled me. I stumbled to my shoes.

"You have to go," whispered John. He grabbed me by the upper arm, digging his fingers into my skin as he almost pushed me through the front door.

Within seconds, I was running hard down the street, my purse flapping against my body, my lungs burning. A bus came, and without looking at where it was going, I jumped on.

I slid into the first seat and tried to catch my breath. Then I rubbed my arm where he had grabbed me. I wondered if it was going to be bruised.

Did I dream the photo? Was I delusional? I had looked at it twice. Twice. Maybe I should have looked three times.

And the pain in his mother's voice had been unbearable. Awful. Horrible. What had happened to her? I shouldn't have gone over, should have waited until Monday to see him. Now, I wondered if he would ever talk to me again. I couldn't tell him about what I had seen. I just couldn't. I had to keep this all to myself. My stomach ached. I closed my eyes. I didn't want my ulcers back.

It took me three buses to get home and more than two hours because I got so messed up I couldn't read the schedule right. As soon as I arrived home, I grabbed some dog treats from the kitchen cupboard and lured Sheena and Sasha into my room. Then I shut the door, locking them in.

"Protect me," I whispered. "You have to stay with me all night." I patted my bed, and Sheena jumped up. When I was changing into my pajamas, I noticed my upper arm; there were distinct finger marks from when John had grabbed me. I quickly put on a long-sleeved pajama top and got into bed. I curled up in the fetal position, and Sheena found her spot right behind my legs. Her body felt warm against mine.

I left my light on.

Scared of the night. Scared of the ghosts.

And scared of the man in the locket.

The same man who kept visiting me from the dead. The man with the cigar.

❖ ❖ ❖

I didn't go to school the next day. I couldn't get out of bed I was so exhausted and listless. It felt as though every ounce of energy had been siphoned out of my body. I told my mother I had the flu.

She carried a tray of food up to my room before she left for work: a bowl of chicken soup for comfort, saltine crackers to help digestion, and a big glass of ice water for rehydration. Once a nurse, always a nurse.

All day I watched mindless television. I couldn't concentrate on even the shallowest of shows, and my mind constantly wandered to the man in the locket. I wondered about John and his family. He'd never mentioned anyone other than his mother and her brother. John had said that he was the only relative who talked to his mom. But the brother was still alive, so it couldn't be him. Was that guy in the locket a relative? An old boyfriend who had died? An uncle? Perhaps he was John's grandfather?

Or . . . was I imagining everything? I should have looked a third time. But the repulsion had been too strong, its effects making me violently ill. I was still sick today.

I flicked through television stations. "Push it from your mind." I talked out loud. "Push it. Bury it. Forget about it."

Flick, flick, flick. There was nothing to watch.

Around midday, the phone rang. I thought it was my mom, so I picked it up. When I heard the low, velvety voice, I swear I thought I'd stopped breathing.

"John," I whispered.

"Sorry about yesterday," he said quietly.

"It's okay."

"Can I come over?"

"Sure."

By the time he arrived, I was sitting at the kitchen table, slicing an apple, dressed in sweats and a long-sleeved T-shirt to hide the bruises on my upper arm. I knew he hadn't meant to give them to me.

He pointed at the apple. "My mom does that."

"Cuts her fruit with a knife?"

"She often has the knife by her bedside."

Silence hung over us like a big puff of air that needed to be pricked.

Finally, John said, "My mom, she has some problems."

I put down the knife, and the clanging sound echoed through the kitchen. The pain in his eyes almost made me cry. I put my hand on his forearm. "It's okay, John."

He slowly shook his head. "She's struggled for years."

"She has a disease."

"I think she drinks to hide her loneliness."

"Does she have *anyone* besides you? You've only ever mentioned her one brother. Is there anyone besides him to help her through this?"

I searched his face to see if I had gone too far. All afternoon I had thought about the man in the locket, and about his mother, and who she was avoiding with alcohol.

John moved away from me and blew out a big breath of air. "My uncle might move here. That would be so good for my mom. I talked to him the other night. I wish my father hadn't just taken off like he did."

"Does she ever talk about your dad?"

He shook his head. "Never. If I bring him up, she shuts me down and says he's never coming back and that he probably has a new family somewhere."

"What about any relatives on your dad's side? Do they ever keep in touch with her?" I cut a piece of apple and pushed it over to John.

"She never stayed in touch with any of them." John spun the apple slice in circles.

"You might have an entire family out there. Are you curious to find out who they are?"

Again, silence. After a couple seconds he said, "I've looked for traces." He didn't look at me and instead just kept spinning the apple slice around and around. It started to turn brown.

"Find anything?" I asked softly.

He shook his head, still spinning the apple, almost as if he were hypnotized.

"Maybe I can help you." I put my hand on his to stop his repetitive movement. "We could search together."

"My mom hates it when I look for him. Sinks her down. Last time she got really mad and told me to stop and to never look again."

"Has your mom ever had any boyfriends?"

"Never," said John. "I wish she would find someone, though. It's as if she can't get close to anyone. I just feel so sorry for her. She's always alone. She only has her bottle. She's tried to stop, but when she's sober, she's almost lonelier. Alcoholism is horrible."

This time, I put my hand on his face, letting it rest on his cheek. He tilted his head and gazed at me. The sadness in his eyes sank to the core of my heart. I looked into his eyes, wanting him to know I was there for him.

Then he leaned forward, and our lips touched, ever so gently at first, but building, building, until we were locked together, intertwined, my hands wrapped around his body, his swathing mine. He lifted me and gently sat me on the kitchen counter, circling his arms around my lower back. I draped my arms around his neck, and our noses touched. Then we kissed again.

When we separated, he whispered, "I heard there's a Halloween party on the weekend." His warm breath lingered around my lips. "Let's have some fun. You want to go with me?"

I kissed his forehead. "I'd love to."

✤ ✤ ✤

I loved Halloween and all the fun of dressing up, but every year I got totally agitated the night before Halloween and couldn't settle down or concentrate on anything. Sarah wanted me to go over to her house on Halloween Eve, as she called it, and watch scary movies, but I made up an excuse. I just wanted to be in my room. All those horror movies were too real for me because spirits and ghosts existed for me and the scary movies were generally all about ghosts. Plus, I knew Sarah would scream and I wouldn't be able to because I would be shaking under a blanket. Then she would think I was a party pooper. I could hear her voice in my head. "Indie, what's wrong with you? Aren't you scared? You have to scream to make this any fun!"

So I had to hide. And my room was the best place for that. I didn't even want to be with John, in case he detected my strange mood. I had been successful in keeping my weirdness away from him, so there was no reason to show him anything on Halloween Eve. I wasn't totally sure what happened to me on that particular night, but it was as if all the pores in my body opened, allowing every type of energy to enter me and swish through my blood. I read once that the thin veil that I was supposedly able to get through got thinner on Halloween Eve, which allowed all kinds of spirits to visit me. It was just so weird. And scary. I hated it.

I sat on my bed staring at the walls.

"It's just one night. Just one night," I told myself. "I can do this. Tomorrow will be different, and I will have fun. I just need to get through tonight." I breathed in and out. "Let's do homework."

I opened my books, stared at the pages, and . . . nothing. I couldn't concentrate. I threw my pencil on my night table.

"Okay, let's read, then."

I picked up the easiest novel sitting on my table. And I must have read the same page ten times.

"I know. I'll play the guitar."

I pulled it out from under my bed, but it just sat on my lap. I tried strumming a few chords, but it sounded horrible. So I put the guitar away.

Then I saw my Halloween costume in my closet. I got off my bed and put on my costume, pretending to be a witch in front of the mirror. I tried cackling and shrieking, and for a while, I did amuse myself and forgot about my edginess.

As soon as I took the costume off, though, the fidgeting started again and my agitation returned. Maybe if I breathed. I sat cross-legged on my bed and tried to relax; tried to get air into my lungs, but it seemed to catch in my throat. Finally, I fell on my bed and did my usual staring at the ceiling, counting the stucco dots.

One, two, three, four . . . "Tomorrow will be better." I stared at my walls.

Five, six, seven, eight . . . I remembered when I was little, Mom always worried about me on this night, and she would sit with me in my room as I quivered and shook. Sometimes when she finally left me alone, shutting off my lights, thinking I was asleep, they would come. The translucent people I had called them. One time there were hundreds of them, walking in a straight line, heading for my bed like an army of ants, but at the foot of my bed, they split and just disappeared.

Would they come again tonight?

I would hide under my covers. Nine, ten, eleven, twelve . . . I breathed in again and out.

By morning I will be okay. By morning I will be okay. By morning I will be okay.

No. I couldn't just lie on my bed counting like I was in kindergarten. I got up and paced. As I wore down my carpet, I picked up the witch hat, running my fingers along the outside of the silk brim, then up the ridge and to the top of the point. Then back down again. Over and over.

"Stop pacing, Indie. Just stop already."

Finally, I forced my feet to halt, and once again, I stood in front of my full-length mirror. I put the hat back on my head and stared at myself. My contorted face softened as I wondered what John was going to wear as a costume.

Maybe if I just thought about John, I would be okay.

✢ ✢ ✢

When John picked me up on Friday night, I was much more relaxed, having made it through Halloween Eve.

I laughed when I opened the door. Typical John: his costume was a Zorro-type mask. John was John, and he always had to be different.

"Nice costume," I said. "I bet *that* didn't break your bank account." Then I cackled and swished my witch cape.

"I thought you'd be wearing your Spice Girls outfit." He pulled me into his arms and kissed me. After we separated he whispered, "I like you better as a witch. Makes you sexy."

By the time we got to the party at ten, it was in full swing. Loud noise blasted my ears, and I froze for a second as the visual overload started. The party was a mesh of colors from the many costumes: Superman, Batman, Catwoman, Sailor Moon, the Hunchback of Notre Dame, Pokémon, *X-Files* characters, and animals of all sorts, including a lot of sexy cats. Shades of blue, green, yellow, pink, purple, and tons of other colors became like one big kaleidoscope.

My head buzzed, my palms seeped sweat, and my stomach flip-flopped, but I was determined not to let the massive amount of energy bother me. I wanted to have a good time.

I'm having fun tonight.

John immediately swerved into the kitchen, leaving me trailing three bodies behind and smack in the middle of the crowd. Without him, I felt vulnerable and a bit dizzy from the bodies around me.

"Hey, Indie!" Sarah grabbed my arm. "You look amazing," she said.

I performed my best cackle, which made her laugh and made me relax. Dressed in a super-short red skirt, red fishnet stockings, and a red silky tank top, and sporting a long red tail and a red mask with pointed ears, Sarah looked like the prettiest devil I'd ever seen. Her red hair clashed with the bright color of her costume. "Love your costume!" I said.

"Oh. My. Gawd," whispered Sarah, touching my arm. "Look what Amber is wearing." Sarah put her hand to her mouth and laughed hysterically. "Unbelievable."

I turned, and when I saw Amber, I frowned. She wore a green garbage bag—and I don't think there was much underneath but a black bathing suit—and she had a hose wrapped around her body. "I don't get it," I said.

"She's a hosebag! You know, a slut."

"Why would she wear something like that?" I asked, shocked.

Laughing, Sarah shook her head. "Who knows? She's Amber."

Just then, John came out of the kitchen and went up to Amber and whispered something in her ear. I wondered what they were talking about. Amber put her hand on his arm. I eyed them until I remembered that Sarah was still talking to me.

"I wonder if she's still after Burke," I said.

Sarah shrugged. "Maybe. Maybe not. She moves on pretty quickly. Come on, let's get you a drink."

I watched Sarah weave over to a corner of the room, where she probably had her stash. As I was standing there by myself, I felt the bump from behind and then something trickled down my back.

I turned to see Burke, dressed in a Batman costume, holding up a bottle of beer. "Sorry, Indie."

"It's okay."

"How are you?"

"Great. Fun party."

"Yeah." He sipped his beer. Then he said, "For the record, I wish you and Lacey were still friends. She misses you. She mentioned how you guys always went out for Halloween together when you were kids."

"I miss her, too," I said. Then I reached out and touched his arm. "Tell her that for me, okay?" The simple touch made me think that perhaps Amber touching John was the same thing.

He genuinely smiled at me. "Yeah, I will."

Just then someone bashed him from behind and he fell forward, spilling the rest of his beer all over the front of my costume. My heart raced, and I felt a jab in the middle of my forehead. I sucked in a deep breath, and it went away. I relaxed my shoulders.

In typical hockey-boy style, Burke grabbed the guy who had pushed him and put him in a headlock. They tussled for a few seconds before I decided that I really needed to wipe the beer off my costume.

In the kitchen I found a roll of paper towels so I ripped off a few. As I tried to get rid of some of the beer, I scanned the kitchen for John, wondering where he was. When I spotted him, he was alone, leaning against the counter. His mask was stuffed in his pocket and he looked totally out of place.

Did he want me with him? Or did he want to be alone? He had ditched me as soon as we entered the party. At least he wasn't with Amber. If I joined him, would that make me a clingy girlfriend?

"Indie, you look like you could use a sip." Dressed as a pirate, complete with the black eye patch and red bandana, Randy, a good friend of mine from elementary school, was standing beside me. He had pulled out a flask of rum from the large leather belt he wore around his waist. Once he offered the flask, I felt obligated to have a sip.

"Thanks," I said.

Not one to stay in the same spot long, Randy left me to move on to someone else. Once again, I glanced over at John, and through the maze of people, I saw him scowling at me. What was wrong?

The party had doubled in size, so I had to dodge bodies on my way over to John. Halfway there, I heard Lacey's voice, sprinkled with laughter. I lowered my head and let my hair fall forward, then I looked to see where she was and who she was talking to.

Dressed as Catwoman in tight black leather shorts, black fishnet stockings, an amazing black fitted corset, and a gorgeous jeweled mask, she looked stunning. Suddenly, the room started to spin on me. The pulsing started in the middle of my forehead. And it was strong, like someone was pounding nails into that spot. My stomach somersaulted. My forehead started to sweat. And my throat felt as if it were closing.

I stood in the middle of a room with nothing to hold on to. Vomit surged inside me but couldn't get through my throat.

No, no, no. Don't do this to me.

I tried to move my feet, but I couldn't. I had to get to the washroom. Now.

Go, Indie. Go. Move. Walk. Run. John can't see you like this. No one can see you like this.

But I couldn't budge. My feet felt as if they were nailed to the floor. The pulsing bashed against my forehead. Instinctively, I knew, there was no stopping this one. Not this time. It was not a simple flash but a full-blown vision. My telescopic lens narrowed, and my body felt as if I were swooshing down a waterslide to the fishbowl. I was out of control and couldn't do anything about it.

Bodies hit me, and I just stood still.

I couldn't see John. I couldn't see anything but a bright light. It flashed in front of me. Then blank. I saw no one. Felt no one. Only saw the white.

Then the picture changed, and I was looking through my lens. I heard ice scraping, scratching. A crack. Slam. Cheering, and a hushed silence. Bright lights, stadium lights, and Burke in his hockey jersey. My stomach turned and flipped, and I crashed against something. It felt as if I had been hit with a huge cement block and I was being heaved into the air with no support. My head ached, and I wanted to throw up, especially because I could smell blood.

Then I felt myself careening, sliding, flying across something hard, and I tried to grab on to someone, but I fell face-first to the floor. The lightbulb zapped, my stomach heaved, and my world went black.

I heard voices.

"Gross," said someone.

"First puke of the night."

Laughter swirled around me. I felt arms under me, strong arms. My legs were weak, and my muscles didn't seem to work. John held me under my armpits and almost dragged me out of the house.

Snow fell from the sky, but not the nice, big, fluffy drops that were pretty and romantic. Instead it was hard, crystallized drops, because the temperature had dropped so quickly. They hit my skin like little knife jabs, and the cold jolted me. Shame seeped through every one of my pores. But then the shame dissolved to tears, flowing fast and furious down my face.

In silence we walked to the car, John holding on to me because the cement sidewalk was glazed with a sheath of ice: hard, treacherous ice. His hand gripped my shoulder hard, and I tried not to wince. My footing was unsteady, and I walked carefully so as not to slip and fall while my mind chattered inside my head. What had just happened? What had I seen? Why was that vision so intense? I had honestly felt as if I were in the vision.

Immersed in thought, I stepped on a piece of smashed pumpkin and slipped. John pulled me by my elbow and kept me upright, but he didn't speak.

Once inside the car, seat buckles done up, I said, "John, I want to explain."

He lifted his hand in a sharp movement, as if to hit me, which made me slide down into my seat. "I don't want an excuse," he uttered. He lowered his hand and shook his head, sending little ice crystals flying everywhere. "I've heard so many over the years and, from you, I don't want one." He started the car; his tires squealed as he drove away from the curb.

"John, it's not what you think. I only had one sip."

For a brief moment, he took his gaze off the road. "It's never what I think," he said.

"But, John," I pleaded, "I have to explain."

"No, Indie," he screamed at me. "No explaining! Actions speak louder than words."

For a few blocks, I just gazed straight ahead out the window with tears pressing against my lids. I was stupid. Stupid. I hadn't stopped shaking yet, so I crossed my arms over my chest and slid further into the seat. My visions were wrecking my relationship. I would never, ever be normal. And now I couldn't even tell him anything, because he'd shut me out.

When we were parked in front of my house, we just sat in the car for a few moments.

Finally John said, "I'm sorry I yelled. You just don't understand. I've been taking care of my mother for years, and I don't want to have to take care of you, too."

"I don't want you to take care of me."

"My mother has never been there for me," he said. His voice cracked, and he sounded as if he were close to tears.

I put my hand on his arm. "I'm sorry to hear that, John. I'm not like your mother."

"Tonight you were."

"Are you going to break up with me?" I whispered.

Time passed. Maybe even a minute. Then he reached out to touch my hair, stroking it for a few seconds. "No," he said. His anger was gone, as were his tears.

He ran his finger up and down my cheek. "I'm glad you lost your witch hat. It didn't suit you."

Chapter Thirteen

"I can't. I'm going Christmas shopping tonight."

"When *can* you rehearse then?" Sarah had cornered me in the hallway. "Indie, I have to tell you, the girls are getting mad that you keep bailing. Can't you just leave John for one night? It's like you're obsessed with him. I never thought you'd be one of those girls who dumps her friends for a guy."

"I'm not shopping with him tonight," I said defensively.

"Well, just pick a day and time when you can make it, okay?" Sarah was definitely peeved. "We are still on for March with the animal shelter, and we only have two songs done."

"Okay," I said, "for sure, sometime in the week between Christmas and New Year's." John was going away for a few days during the holidays, so it would be the perfect time. He wouldn't have to know I was rehearsing.

Sarah held up her fist. "I'm holding you to that."

I fist-bumped her back, then we went in opposite directions. As I walked down the hall, I saw John leaning against the wall, watching me. I noticed his eyes and the redness surrounding them. Was he high? John liked to smoke dope now and again, and when I had told him I didn't like it, he just laughed at me and told me I was immature and innocent, but that was what he liked about me. But it did make his personality change, and not for the better.

When I approached him he asked, "What did Sarah want?"

I shrugged. "Nothing."

He fell into step beside me. "You want to go out tonight?"

I playfully slapped his arm. "I can't."

"Why not?" His eyes narrowed, and his tone was accusatory. "You're not planning on rehearsing with Sarah and *your lame band,* are you?"

"Why don't you like the band?" I blurted out. For months now, since we had revived the band, he had been criticizing it and telling me to quit. "I don't get it. We just have fun."

"Indie, those girls make you look dumb. And that's not something you need."

I could feel the tears behind my eyes. I wouldn't cry. I sucked in a deep breath and tried to let his comment slide. He was probably right, though. I mean, John was so intelligent and read such profoundly deep books. So many people would seem dumb to him.

I didn't want my afternoon wrecked, or my evening, so I bumped his shoulder and winked at him. "I can't see you tonight because I'm going Christmas *shopping.*"

"Ugh. It's so commercial," he replied.

"Ah, don't be a Scrooge." I rubbed my shoulder against his, and he didn't move away, which was good. Then he smiled down at me, playfully rubbed my head, and said, "Don't ever lose your innocence."

✤ ✤ ✤

Later that night, I strolled through the mall, carrying bags, wondering if I could get one more thing for someone. Christmas carols chimed through the speakers, sparkly lights shone everywhere, and the smell of cinnamon, ginger, and nutmeg lingered in the air. Last summer I had worked and saved enough money for Christmas just to see the expression on people's faces when I gave gifts, and it honestly had nothing to do with getting anything back. I bought for my family and friends and Sasha and Sheena and Cedar. Dad always thought I was crazy to buy for the pets, but I didn't care. When I got home, I would wrap the gifts—dog bones, little gem collars, rubber toys—and put them under the tree.

I stopped to look at a small fake silver Christmas tree that was displayed in a novelty storefront window. Beautiful ornaments of all colors and shapes dangled from its branches. Immediately, I was drawn to a pair of white feathery angel wings. I thought about the woman who had the heart attack, how she called me an angel. Thankfully, she'd never found me. I hoped she was alive and well and able to have a wonderful time at Christmas with her family after the scare of being rushed to the hospital. Warm feelings flooded me, like I was standing by a fire drinking hot chocolate after a day of tobogganing, and I knew she was okay. I smiled to myself, my reflection in the storefront window smiling back, happy that I had been able to help. When I realized what I was doing, I lowered my head.

My gaze returned to the wings. They were so pretty and free and pure, white like fresh snow, not the dirty, gross stuff that lined the roads after the snowplow had done its job. I glanced up and down the tree, at all the other colored ornaments, drawn to another one that was a smooth, clear, heart-shaped stone hanging from a leather strap. It looked masculine. So weird. As I stared at it, the stone seemed to pulsate, in and out, and I backed up a step. Sweat beaded on my forehead.

No, please.

I begged my mind to think about Christmas and presents. *Please. Don't.*

My begging didn't work, and all the visions I'd had when I first met John came crashing to the front of my brain: the shovel and smell of dirt, the man in the locket, the insane stuff surrounding Burke. I furiously shook my head.

No! I don't want them back.

The feathery wings gave me comfort so I turned my gaze back to them. They made me feel like John did, especially when I was wrapped in his arms. I rarely opened up to anyone, but with him I had let myself plunge down a tunnel. We spent every waking moment together.

He loved me.

At least I thought he did. He'd never said so, but we were together all the time. I hated the doubt. Would he love me if he knew that I had visions and saw things before they happened?

No one knew about the vision I'd had on Halloween. Not one single soul. It was a secret buried inside me. My visions were so weird. Some of them came true right away, and others took their time. I shuddered. Since Halloween, when I'd fallen and puked after seeing the weird stuff surrounding Burke, my visions *had* kind of stopped. And for that I was truly grateful. Had I been able to push them away? Maybe my mind was more powerful than I thought. Could I really keep that part of my life from John?

Chills like cold icicles ran up and down my spine. I crossed my arms. That vision about Burke had only happened because of Halloween. I was sure I had only seen it because I always had a crazy vulnerability around that time of year. That had to be it. As I stared at the light, fluffy wings, hanging so loosely and freely from the tree, I was glad it was Christmas and not Halloween. At Christmas I was happy.

What about the man in the locket, Indie? What about the shovel? What about the dirt? What about—

I put my hands to my ears and lowered my head. "Stop it," I whispered.

Because of the locket, I had not been back to John's house again. My reactions to his mother and seeing the cigar man inside the locket were not something I wanted to happen again. I had stopped searching for him, and he hadn't come to me again.

They're not over, Indie, said the soft voice of the kind man. He hadn't talked to me in a long time—I had thought he was gone from my life for good, too.

I straightened and looked through the glass and into the store, trying to see something, anything that would make my mind from thinking about any of this. Suddenly, Lacey popped into my view. I quickly turned, hoping to see her behind me, but all I saw were strangers hurrying with bags. I sighed. Now I was *really* seeing things that weren't true. She had yet to talk to me, and she was crazy in love with Burke still, and from what everyone told me, he still fooled around with Amber now and again. I'd also heard that Amber had moved on to a few other guys. A pain shot through my heart, and I put my hand to my chest. I could feel it beating through my winter jacket.

Who else was she hitting on?

I sucked in a deep breath and tucked my hair behind my ear. *Get back to Christmas, Indie.*

This was the first year in at least a dozen that I hadn't bought Lacey a gift. Although . . . I squatted down and pressed my face closer to the window.

Should I? I remembered what Sarah and Zoe had said about angels being the in thing but also being stupid. But I didn't feel as if I were buying something that was in; this ornament seemed so peaceful.

My feet moved, almost automatically, and I walked into the store and headed right over to the angel wings. I had to get her the wings. I just had to.

The feathered angel wings fluttered in front of me, and I touched them. So soft. So white. So pure. I pulled them off the tree and held them. What if she wouldn't accept them? Then I smiled. She didn't have to know they were from me.

Get them, Indie. She is going to need them. The man's voice again. Who was he?

I took the wings to the counter, and as I was paying for them, I spotted the jewelry under the glass countertop. I had already purchased a beautiful purple amethyst bracelet for Sarah and rose quartz necklaces for Zoe and Carly. But I still needed to get one more thing for my mother's stocking. Maybe she would like a necklace as well. The side of my mouth curled upward. I loved slipping little gifts into her stocking. She always looked over at me when she opened them, knowing they were from me.

As I looked below at the jewelry, I almost gasped out loud when I saw a red-velvet-covered board with a gold locket pinned on it, shining in front of me. I bent my head forward and looked at it carefully. That was the exact same locket as the one I'd seen in John's bathroom.

Oh, no! Why had this just appeared in front of me? For the first time in ages, I had thought about the locket, and now here it was. Talk about coincidence.

There is no such thing as a coincidence, Indie.

Without thinking about what I was doing I said, "Can I see that, please?"

The salesgirl used a small key to slide the glass case open, then she pulled out the board with the locket. My hands trembled as I reached forward, and I touched it before I decided to open it. The gold felt like . . . nothing. It wasn't hot, and it didn't burn my skin. With my fingernail I pried it open.

No photo. I put my hand to my chest.

Nothing was in the locket. Was I really expecting to see the man? Perhaps I was hoping to see him; then I would know that every locket like this had a picture of him and that it was all something I had imagined.

I quickly paid for the angel wings and left the store.

As I waited at the front door of the mall for my mom to pick me up, I tapped my foot. Snow fell from the sky, nice, big, fluffy flakes, and I decided I wanted to be outside.

I pushed open the big department store door, and once I was out in the winter wonderland, I looked up at the falling flakes, allowing them to land on my face. It was the perfect December night, with a perfectly blackened sky, beautiful soft snowflakes falling, and no wind. The world was silent, magical, and my mind stilled.

"Indie," I said to myself, "think of Christmas and John and nothing else." I just wanted to feel fluffy like the snowflakes, and I didn't want anything deep surrounding me.

I smiled. I could do this. I reached my hand into one of my shopping bags to feel the soft cotton of the simple navy V-neck sweater I had bought John. Would he like my gift? I had also bought him cologne and some shaving things and . . . I couldn't wait to give him his gifts.

I grinned as I wondered what I was going to get from John. He had said he hated Christmas, but I just knew he had gotten me *something*. Whereas I loved to give, he thought it excessive and ranted on and on about how Christmas was materialistic and over the top, and didn't I know there were starving people in Africa? Yes, I did know there were starving people around the world, but I still wanted to give to my family and friends. Warm, fuzzy feelings surrounded me as I thought of Brian and how he was going to love the vampire VHS series I had gotten for him. Brian loved anything to do with vampires.

I heard a car pull up, and when I saw it was my dad, I threw my packages in the backseat and hopped into the front.

"How was shopping?" he asked.

"Great!" I said. I glanced at my dad. "How come you're picking me up? Where's Mom?"

"She's busy." He winked at me.

For the rest of the drive, we talked trivial stuff, which I totally appreciated, as it took my mind off everything. Snow fell in soft flakes, landing on the windshield, and the wipers swished back and forth. Our drive was slow and easy, unlike the rush of Christmas. My dad made me feel normal. When a Beach Boys Christmas song came on, I started to sing along, and Dad laughed, turned up the radio, and joined in.

When we got home, Sheena and Sasha met me at the door, tails wagging, smacking against my parcels. As I patted them, I heard the voices from the kitchen, so I quickly slipped out of my wet shoes, hung up my coat and scarf, and went to the kitchen. Grandma was drinking tea at our kitchen table, and my mom was using a spatula to lift sugar cookies from an aluminum pan. A beautiful heat, and fresh-baked-cookie aroma, flowed through the kitchen.

Suddenly, I smelled roses. I glanced around the room. Had Grandma bought flowers? I couldn't see the vase anywhere. This was not the first time I'd smelled roses in our house.

"Indigo!" Grandma stood and hugged me.

"Grandma! When did you get here?" I hugged her back.

"Just a few minutes ago."

I sniffed the air. "Did you bring us roses?" I asked, looking around the room once again.

Mom turned from the stove and gazed at me over the rim of her reading glasses. "Why on earth would you ask that?"

I shrugged. "I smell roses." Then I sniffed again, like Sasha did when beef was cooking. "I still smell them."

"Indie, I just made shortbread and sugar cookies, but nothing that could possibly smell like roses. Butter perhaps, but not roses." She shook her head and turned back to the stove.

No one said anything for a moment. Then my grandmother smiled at me and clasped my hand in her worn but warm one. "My mother always wore rose perfume," she said softly.

My mom stopped moving, and I froze on the spot. The air took on an unruffled silence, and I instantly knew we were more than three in the room. I quietly said, "It's not the first time I've smelled roses in our house."

"You've never mentioned this to me," said my mom as she continued to put cookies on the waxed paper, her back to me.

Grandma pointed for me to sit. As I did what I was told, she went to the cupboard and pulled out a Christmas mug. When we were both sitting, she poured me a cup of tea. "Tell us about the roses," she said.

"Well, I don't know," I said, tapping the table with my fingers, trying to think back. "I guess I smelled them first after Great-grandma died."

Grandma put some milk in my tea and two heaping teaspoons of sugar, exactly how I liked it. "Continue," she urged.

I took a sip of tea, then I said, "Well, once when I walked into the front hallway after school, I smelled the roses and looked around, but I couldn't find any. Then another time, I thought I smelled them in the kitchen."

Grandma placed her hand on my forearm and whispered, "You are like her." Then she winked. "I bet she's with us right now."

My great-grandma had passed away three years ago. I felt lucky that I had seen her just before she died. We had traveled to California for a visit because she had just had a stroke, and my mom wanted to see her. I guess the thought was in everyone's mind that she didn't have much time left on the earth. When I saw her on that trip, Great-grandma couldn't talk, but she kept squeezing my hand and trying to speak, as if she wanted to tell me something. I couldn't stop looking at her and noticing that, even after her stroke, she was still beautiful: translucent skin, sparkling blue eyes, long gray hair pinned in a perfect bun. From Paris originally, she had this aristocratic quality that had always intrigued me, made me wonder about her life when she was little. My mom had told me that she had been a hatmaker.

She died a couple months after we got home.

My mom put a plate of hot cookies on the table, and Grandma picked one up and took a tiny bite. Then she put it on her plate. "When I was little," Grandma said, "people would come from all over town to pick up the hats my mother had spent hours and hours making. Velvet and pins and lace were a huge part of her hat-making room. I remember that I loved watching her work. As she adjusted the hats on the women's heads, they would ask her questions, and she would tell them things."

My body warmed just listening to Grandma tell her story. I loved the sound of her melodic voice. She continued talking, and from the faraway look in her eyes, I knew she felt as if she were a child again.

"I remember once, the woman was the owner of a store in town. I wore a little yellow sundress. Oh, how I loved that sundress. It was gingham with a white ribbon around the high bodice. My mother had bought me little white patent leather shoes to go with the dress and socks with yellow trim. I sat as quietly as I could in the corner, away from my mother working, just watching her adjust the pins and bows. The woman tilted her head one way, then another. Then she started to cry. I remember almost wanting to cry myself. My mother patted her shoulders and told the lady not to worry. Yes, her husband would lose the store, but my mother could see horses and cows and lots of land. They would move to the country and be very happy. The woman wiped her tears and nodded her head and said that they were looking at land. Then my mother said, 'Well, buy it.' Just like that—'Well, buy it.' Months later, the woman came back to the house with a little gift for my mother to say thank you. They had bought the land and were very happy."

Grandma paused for a minute to sip her tea. Neither my mom nor I said anything. My mother was now leaning up against the counter, motionless, with the spatula still in her hand.

Then Grandma continued. "Sometimes it took my mother a long time to fit the hat because she talked so much. But I also knew there was this code of silence among her customers because none of them would talk about what she said outside our house. And she told me that if I were to listen, then I had to keep what was said a secret. I never said a word on the swings at school. I understand now that this had to happen because her seeing things went against our religion."

Grandma looked my way, smiled, and patted my arm. "She always told me she saw pictures in her mind, like little snippets or photographs, and she used what she saw to talk to the people who came to see her. And she also saw angels, and they sometimes told her what to say. Inside the house, she was known as a seer. Outside the house, she was a hatmaker."

Again Grandma winked at me. "You are like her, my dear."

"If I am," I said quietly, "then I want to *really* be like her and keep all of this a secret."

Chapter Fourteen

On our last day of school before the Christmas holidays, I took the angel wings to school and discreetly taped them on Lacey's locker. Then I walked away and stood at the end of the hallway, watching as she approached her locker and furrowed her eyebrows. After glancing up and down the hallway, in obvious confusion, she fingered them and put them to her face and smiled.

I knew she thought they were from Burke. For some reason, that didn't bother me at all, as they were going to give her comfort, no matter who she thought they were from.

Comfort from what?

Although I felt lightened from being able to give someone something that might be soothing, I also had this heavy feeling surround me as if something were very wrong. I didn't like the feeling so I turned and headed down the hall and away from Lacey. With every step, the heaviness got lighter and lighter, until I was almost running.

✥ ✥ ✥

Christmas Eve. I sat in my bedroom, listening to Christmas music, bouncing up and down on my bed. I was so excited that John had agreed to come with me and my family to my grandparents' house on Christmas Day.

As I bounced, I talked to myself. "We're going to exchange gifts. And kiss under the mistletoe. And maybe I can get him to help me make a gingerbread house. Yeah. So fun."

I kept bouncing. Then I glanced over at my desk at the pile of presents I had wrapped for him. I couldn't wait to give him his gifts.

I jiggled my leg and tapped my fingers, wishing tomorrow would hurry up. I picked up my book of Jim Morrison's poetry and quotes and flipped through it. Maybe if I read something serious, I would calm down.

I stopped when I read, "There are things known, and there are things unknown, and in between are the Doors."

My movements did slow. What did I know? What did I not know?

Suddenly, I thought about John's dad. Had John ever spent a Christmas with him? Just yesterday I'd asked him about his father, and he'd clammed up and gotten moody with me. I hated that. Would he keep his dad in the unknown forever? I knew that I couldn't do that. I would have had to try to find *my* dad.

Could I keep my visions in the doors forever?

I drew in a sharp breath. I *hoped* my visions would stay hidden. Maybe that was how John felt about his dad. If anyone could understand that logic, it should be me. I flipped a page in the book, stopping to read another quote: "Love cannot save you from your own fate."

I snapped the book shut and put it back on my nightstand.

I didn't want to read anymore. I wanted to think about Christmas.

The day crept by, but soon it was evening. On Christmas Eve, as a family, we always went to a candlelight service at our church, St. Thomas Apostle. On the drive over, I stared out the car window at the snow-covered ground and the colorful outdoor lights strung across roofs and hanging on evergreen trees. Ever since I was little, Christmas Eve had been the most enchanting time of the entire holiday, and I honestly liked it better than Christmas morning, because I loved staring at the tree with all the presents underneath. It was like fresh snow before anyone walked through it.

Mom, Dad, Brian, and I silently entered the church, and I absorbed the reverence of the magically darkened room, lit only by candles. Blissful little flames flickered throughout the sanctuary, and I thought that perhaps this was what heaven would look like. I inhaled to take in every bit of solemn peace I could.

All too soon, it was over and we were back at home. "Brian and Indie," said my mother after we had hung up our coats, "I think it's time to open one present."

Brian nudged me, winked, and laughed. "I wonder what it is."

I laughed back. "Hmm. Could it have something to do with sleep?"

Jokingly, Brian tapped his face with his fingers, scrunching up his face as if he was thinking hard. Then he held up his hand. "I got it. It's pajamas!"

"Stop it, you two," said my mother, pushing us into the living room, where the Christmas tree stood.

Every year on Christmas Eve, Brian and I opened one present, and it was always pajamas. Then we had a pajama party and watched a movie, complete with treats that my mother put on the tiered silver tray that she used only at Christmas. This year, it was my turn to pick the movie and, of course, I chose *Labyrinth*.

"Nice choice," said Brian. Then he whispered, "Just so you know, it's not a Christmas movie."

I went to bed by midnight but awoke at 4:44 A.M. and sat up, wide awake. I always woke up at exactly the same time every Christmas morning—it was the one time I was not afraid of the dark. My movement disturbed Cedar, but I patted her gently and whispered, "Go back to sleep."

Barefoot, I tiptoed out of my room, by my parents' room, and into the living room, where our majestic Christmas tree stood. After I turned on the tree lights, I sat cross-legged on the floor and stared at the tree and all the shimmering, twinkling colored lights: blue, green, red, and yellow. Then there were the white ones that to me seemed to dance and wink.

I inhaled and exhaled. Over and over.

My breath slowed, and I could feel my blood calming inside me. For as long as I could remember, I had snuck down on Christmas morning to sit in front of the tree. Of course, when I was little, I would always wait in my room until Santa had arrived and left, and the cookies were gone, the milk glass emptied, and the sugar cubes licked by reindeer.

I inhaled again and slowly exhaled, my breathing loud but peaceful. I loved the serenity of the lights and the joy of brightly wrapped presents perfected with ribbon and bows, all ready to bring excitement to people. I picked up a present, shook it, then put it back under the tree.

I glanced up at the angel on top of the tree. We'd had the same angel since I was little, and she had white wings, a burgundy dress, and a little light inside that lit her halo and wings. I smiled. I knew that angels didn't look like that. Real angels were massive golden beings that vibrated energy—they glowed like a flickering light. Or at least that's what I had seen. I knew my body couldn't move that fast. Angels had this golden energy that surrounded them; it looked like huge wings circling their entire body. I got why people always drew them with wings or created ornaments that had wings.

To me angels were peaceful beings, and I always felt they could take me under their golden energy and protect me. Whenever they appeared, I was immediately bathed in a warmth and tranquility.

"Protect me," I whispered.

I shivered. Why had I said that? What did I need protection from? With John I had everything I wanted. All the warmth I had been feeling suddenly changed, and a chill surrounded me. I drew my legs in to my body, hugging them, resting my chin on my knees.

I glanced upward again.

"Protect me," I whispered again.

Then, quietly, through the serenity of the tree and the magic of Christmas, I heard the man's voice inside my head, and he said, Nathan.

Nathan?

You're like a butterfly, he had said on the bus.

Light and free to fly in the summer sun from bush to bush.

My body started to quake, and I felt as if I were trapped outside in a huge snowstorm, wearing nothing but my Christmas pajamas. I couldn't sit under the tree any longer. I was freezing. I got up and tiptoed down the hall, heading back to my bedroom and the warmth of my bed.

❖ ❖ ❖

When I heard the doorbell ring, I ran down the hall and flung open the door. A cold draft flew into the house, but I sure didn't feel it. All I felt was heat from John. Once he was in the door, I hugged him, and he hugged me back.

"Merry Christmas," I said, nuzzling my lips on his ear.

"Same to you," he replied.

Then I took his hand and guided him to the living room and our Christmas tree. Under the tree were the gifts that were already unwrapped from the morning and a few that were yet to be opened. I crouched down and pulled out a large rectangular box that was wrapped in gold paper and topped with a red bow. I grinned and held up my finger. "This is present number one."

"Present number one?" He arched his eyebrows. "I only bought you one thing."

I clapped my hands. "They're all little. Open it," I said eagerly.

The sound of paper tearing made me beam. As soon as he saw the sweater, he held it up. "I like it," he said.

"It will look so good on you. I loved the color, and blue will look good with your coloring."

He leaned over and kissed me, hard—a daring move, as my parents could walk in at any minute. Tingles ran the length of my body. Even after being together for months, his touch made me quiver.

The touch lasted all of about a second, and then he winked at me. "You want your gift?"

"Yes!" I clapped my hands together.

He handed me a little box, covered in silver paper, the wrapping job a bit messy and so obvious that he had done it himself. That made me smile even more. I held it in my hands for a moment, then I shook it, as I did with every present I received.

He laughed at me, shaking his head. "You're crazy. Just open it."

I tore off the paper to see a small, very distinct, blue Birks jewelry box. I gasped. Birks was real jewelry, not costume stuff like I had purchased for my friends. I held the box in my hands as if it were a treasure and stared at it for a few moments. We'd only been going out since September. Honestly, I'd been expecting a T-shirt or a book of some sort . . . or nothing at all, because of how John felt about the extravagance of the season.

Once my heart rate had settled, I carefully lifted the lid on the box. A beautiful butterfly pendant necklace, hanging from a silver chain, sat on a white satin backdrop. The turquoise and orange enamel on the wings of the butterfly dazzled. For a moment, I couldn't believe that he had bought me something so breathtaking.

"It's beautiful," I whispered.

"It reminded me of you," he stated softly. "So light and free and beautiful."

I fingered the chain, then held the necklace up and stared at the butterfly as it fluttered and almost danced in the lights from the Christmas tree, casting streams of color throughout the room.

Did he really think I was beautiful?

He had never said I was beautiful before. Ever. His words made my head spin. I was so used to him spouting off about his beliefs, never saying anything so personally meaningful. I stared at him standing in front of me, and my entire body felt as if it were basking in the direct heat of the sun on some tropical beach. Our eyes connected, and I held his gaze. He loved me. He had to. He'd never told me so, but this necklace proved that he did.

I wanted to be with him forever.

To say my heart fluttered would be trite. It thwacked, over and over, happily, the pounding sound strong in my ears, my head, and my entire body.

"Do you want your other gifts?" I asked.

"Let's put your necklace on first." In one smooth movement, he was behind me. He took the necklace from my hand, strung it around my neck, and tenderly pulled my hair off to the side. I could feel the tips of his fingers brushing against my skin as he did up the clasp, his breath on the nape of my neck.

I turned to look at him.

"It looks good," he said.

I put my hand to my throat to touch the necklace. "I love it," I said. Then I reached out to take his hand in mine. "Thank you," I said. I reached down and pulled out the little gifts I had purchased for him. "Here."

"Indie, I think the sweater would have been enough," he said. "You know how I feel about Christmas."

"Just open it. Christmas is about giving, and I want to give. To you."

✤ ✤ ✤

We left a few hours later to go to my grandparents' for Christmas dinner. John, Brian, and I piled into my dad's Oldsmobile Cutlass Supreme, a big car with a cushy, roomy backseat. Of course, being the smallest, and the only girl, I was squished in the middle. My grandparents lived in Maynard, a little town about an hour from Ottawa, in an old house that I loved. I wanted to show John the house, wanted him to meet my grandparents and enjoy our wonderful traditional turkey dinner.

As usual, my dad took the back road, Highway 31, until we hit what I called River Road, which traveled along the St. Lawrence Seaway. The roads were snowy and slick with ice, and my dad drove slowly, but I didn't mind; to me the world outside was beautiful, especially the sight of the seaway, frozen in parts but also majorly flowing in other parts. Chunks of ice floated with the moving water.

No one spoke in the car, as we were all enjoying the tranquility of a Christmas drive. I held John's hand under my coat so no one could see. I loved the feel of his warm skin, and he made me feel cocooned and protected from the cold outside.

We were all so quiet and serene that it was almost a shock when Brian shouted, "Look at that car!" He pointed out the window.

My dad slowed until we were almost crawling, and we all craned our necks to see a car that had obviously driven off the road and was sitting precariously on the riverbank. A massive pile of snow had, luckily, stopped it from toppling into the river.

The car looked abandoned, as if someone had just gotten out and left it there. So weird. Did the people run out of gas? Or did they hit ice and skid off the road? Once we were by the car, my father picked up his speed. I had just leaned back, snuggling close to John, when I heard the male voice in my head.

There's a woman in that car! He spoke loudly, instead of in his usual soft tone.

He was so loud he made me sit up and stare out the window. Without thinking, I said, "Dad, stop! There's a woman in that car."

Dad looked at me through his rearview mirror. "Did you really see someone?"

I hadn't seen anyone, but I had heard the voice, loud and clear. "Yes," I lied. "I for sure saw her."

"You're positive?" he asked.

"I didn't see anyone," said Brian. "And I saw the car first."

I sat forward and tapped my dad's shoulder. "I'm sure," I said. "Dad, you have to go back."

"Okay," he said, shrugging his shoulders.

Dad found a safe place to turn around as voices inside my head chattered.

What if you are wrong, Indie? You are crazy. There is no way you could see in the car. You are going to look soooo stupid if there is no one in the car. It's Christmas, and everyone just wants to get to Grandma and Grandpa's.

I held my breath the entire way back. If there was no one in the car, I was going to look like a complete fool in front of John. When we were by the car, my dad cut his engine, and then instinctively, like a whirlwind, we all whipped open our car doors and jumped out. My mom started running. I followed right on her heels, and John, Brian, and my dad were right behind us.

When we hit the car, I saw the woman, wearing a blue winter coat and a blue and gray scarf, slumped on the seat, knocked out completely. My mom flung open the car door and immediately put her fingers on the woman's neck, and I knew she was in emergency room nurse mode.

"She's alive! Call the ambulance," she yelled.

My dad made the call on his car phone, while John and I huddled around the woman's car, arms wrapped around each other, watching as Mom kept checking for a pulse and tried desperately to wake her up by talking to her and rubbing her skin. Brian found a blanket in the back of Dad's car and brought it over. Even with the blanket around the woman and my mom talking a steady stream to her, she didn't wake up. The voice? Who was he? I had no clue, but I was incredibly grateful that he'd told me about the woman. She could have died. He often said to trust him, and today I had.

Thank you. Thank you, I said to him through my thoughts.

You're learning to trust. This is a good thing, Indie.

I shivered under my coat. What was I trusting? Voices in my head? Visions? Snapshots of things that just appeared for no reason? No, this time there had been a reason. And a really good one.

I shivered uncontrollably. What if I had just kept quiet and not said anything? My shivers turned into trembling. John pulled me toward him, and I laid my head on his shoulder, liking the feeling of his strength and warmth and power. He wrapped his arms around me, and I knew he wanted to protect me.

Finally, the paramedics arrived, and the red and blue lights of the ambulance and the shrieking sound of a siren were a stark contrast to the joy of Christmas Day. The snow and ice, so beautiful to look at when you were safe from them, had taken on a different look. Now the winter scene was dangerous and foreboding. It could cause accidents. It could have killed this woman. John remained beside me with his arm around my shoulder. Silently, we watched the paramedics.

When the woman was on the stretcher, one of the paramedics said to my father, "It's a good thing you stopped. She would have died out here in this cold."

As the ambulance screeched out of sight, John stared at me. "Wow," he said, almost in shock. "You just saved someone's life." Then he hugged me. "Now, that's a Christmas gift. A real Christmas gift." He gently touched my cheek and gazed into my eyes. "You're amazing, Indie. I think you're the most amazing person I've ever met."

When we were back in the car and my dad was driving again, he said, "Indie, you have the eyes of a hawk."

"Hawk eyes," teased Brian. "That name suits you." Then he raised his eyebrows and shook his head. "I still don't know how you saw her. She was lying down. It would have been impossible."

I leaned against John, resting my head on his shoulder and didn't answer. Now I had yet another secret to keep.

Because . . . only I knew I didn't actually see her.

Chapter Fifteen

The Christmas week sped by. As promised, I met up with Sarah and the girls to rehearse, but only after John had left town. I didn't want to upset him by spending less time with him, so rehearsing when he was gone was perfect. He didn't have to know. We had gotten so close after what happened on Christmas that I honestly missed him as soon as he was gone. The rehearsal did help me forget, though.

"Let's do that Police song you like," said Sarah to me.

"'Every Breath You Take,'" said Zoe. "That's a good one. I know it, too. We've been practicing it without you."

"You guys have had rehearsals without me?" I asked.

"We have to, Indie," snapped Carly. "We're committed to playing in March with or without you. If you can't tear yourself away from John, the band will go on without you."

"I can," I said.

Carly rolled her eyes. "Yeah, well, whatever."

"Enough," said Zoe. "We're all together now, so let's rehearse."

"'Every Breath You Take,' from the top," said Sarah.

When it was my turn to sing, I closed my eyes and sang, every word reminding me of John. He was my breath. We were one. I couldn't help but feel the way I did. The girls didn't understand, but how could they? None of them had ever been in love.

❖ ❖ ❖

On New Year's Eve, I woke up with a terrible stomachache. Not because I was sick. John's uncle had just moved to Ottawa and was having a New Year's Eve party, and John had asked me to go. Of course, his mother was going to be there. I closed my eyes. I had seen his mother again, but not for any substantial length of time. I hoped I wouldn't have any more visions.

As I got dressed for the evening, I did my usual chitchat with myself behind my bedroom door. Brian had gone out already, so there was no one to barge in and tell me I was crazy.

"Please, let me handle this okay." I played with my hair, tying it in a knot on the top of my head. But I didn't like how it looked.

"I want everything to be perfect when the clock strikes midnight and John kisses me."

I tied my hair in a side ponytail like Sarah wore hers all the time. "I want this night to be magical."

I kept doing my hair and talking to myself. I must have done my hair at least ten times. Finally, I curled it and wore it down. After one last look in the mirror, I grabbed my purse off the end of my bed, making sure I had a full pack of cigarettes. Dressed in black pants (I hated how my body looked in jeans) and a pretty black and gray ruffled top that I had received for Christmas, I headed to the kitchen to say good-bye to my mother.

"You look nice," she said.

"Thanks."

"Is John driving you home?"

"Yeah. But don't expect me till after midnight. I want to be there when the clock strikes."

My mother was about to add something when the doorbell rang. "Happy New Year!" I kissed her on the cheek, grabbed my long winter dress coat and scarf from the closet, then bolted out of the room.

John's uncle lived only a few blocks away from their house. Cars lined the street in front of his house. Uncle Jonah had moved from Newfoundland at the beginning of December but knew tons of people from when he had lived in Ottawa years ago. The reason he moved back, I was told, was because he had a job. I knew it had something to do with John's mother.

When we got out of the car, I immediately knew something was up with the weather, but I had no idea what. A storm perhaps? The air had this heavy feeling. It had been so cold before Christmas and for a few days after, but now there was some warm front coming in from Texas, of all places. It was supposed to get unseasonably warm, and they were predicting freezing rain.

Warm I could handle. I stared at the white snowbanks lining the shoveled sidewalk. The snow was still pure, but warm weather would soon make a mess of it, creating slush and gross, dirty snow. At least it had been white and pretty for Christmas.

I wished John would hold my hand, but he didn't. Instead he lit up a cigarette.

"Sarah is going to come by later," I said, tucking my chin into my coat to get away from the cold. I rummaged through my purse for my cigarettes.

"Here," said John. "We can share this one." He handed me his. I inhaled and handed it back.

"I think some others are coming, too," he said.

"Like who?"

John shrugged. "Carly. Randy. Maybe Amber."

I frowned. "Amber? Why would she be invited?"

John casually shrugged. "Because she's fun." He butted out his cigarette on the cement wall near the stairs and then said, "Ready?"

I forced a smile. "Sure."

The tiny front hallway was littered with shoes and boots. I stepped over them and slipped out of my own, adding one more pair to the pile. John took my coat and hung it up in the front closet. Then he took my hand and led me through the hall.

Oldies music sounded from the kitchen, and I couldn't tell who it was, perhaps the Eagles.

My nerves twitched as I followed John into the kitchen, and I hoped that I wouldn't have any reactions to anything. Bowls of chips and pretzels sat on the counters, as did plates of cheese and crackers and pickles and olives. Lots of people in the room shouted our names. I saw his mother standing by the kitchen table with a tumbler in her hand. She smiled and waved at me, and I waved back. So far, so good.

From across the room, though, I could see she was wearing the locket. My throat clogged. Who was the man she held so close to her heart? Once I had tried to ask John about the man, but the words had stuck in my throat. Like, literally stuck. Something had held me back from asking the question. Perhaps it was because I didn't want him asking *me* questions.

Out of the corner of my eye, I glanced at John. His eyes had narrowed; he was shaking his head, and not in a good way. Then he left my side and walked over to his mother. I wasn't sure if I should follow or not.

Some nonverbal communication passed between them with John pointing to her glass and her shaking her head. I inhaled, then forced the air out, trying to keep the energy in the room from leaking into me.

Tune everything out, Indie. Just tune out. You need to have fun tonight.

After a few seconds, John came back to me and said, "Let's go downstairs."

"I should say hi to your mother."

"Okay."

Back in the kitchen, I weaved around bodies to get closer to his mother. "Mrs. Smith," I said, "I haven't seen you in a long time."

I stood far enough away from her that she wouldn't try to touch me. "Indie! It's so great to see you. You should come over more."

"Yeah." I nodded. "In the new year." I paused, then said, "It must be nice for you to have your brother back in Ottawa. I know John likes having his uncle around."

"It's good for John to have a male figure in his life." She put her hand to the necklace.

My pulse quickened. Gold gleamed in front of my face, momentarily blinding me. What was it about that locket? I clenched my hands together.

I don't want to know. I don't want to know.

"Do you have a picture in your locket?" I blurted out.

What had possessed me to say that?

I tried to step back, get away from the locket. Mrs. Smith dropped her hand from around her neck.

"It's just that I have a friend," I sputtered, "who has a locket, and she has a photo of her dog in it. But her locket was different. It was a heart." I knew I was babbling, but the words just came out. When Lacey was younger, she *did* have this costume jewelry locket, and she *did* keep a photo of her dog in it, so I wasn't lying.

Mrs. Smith rubbed the back of her neck. Then she tried to smile, but I could tell it was an effort. "Like your friend," she said, "I have someone I loved very much in my locket." She paused for a second. She attempted again to smile. "I'm glad to hear John is happy to have his uncle in Ottawa."

"Yeah." I was so glad she had changed the subject. I also tried to laugh to ease the tension I had created. "He likes to have him around to help him work on his car."

"I wish I could afford to get John a better car."

"Mrs. Smith," I started. Without thinking, I touched her arm. The pads of my fingers burned, so I drew my hand away, placing it on my hip. I took another little step back. "He's lucky to have a car. My parents won't get me one."

"Your parents won't get you what?" John butted in.

"A car!" I playfully jabbed his stomach with my elbow. I was relieved that he had joined us, because my entire conversation with his mother had been forced and awkward. And I felt the kitchen moving in on me like a throbbing heartbeat. I really needed to get away from the crowd.

As if reading my thoughts, John jerked his head toward the other side of the kitchen. "Let's go downstairs," he said. "Randy and Amber just arrived."

"Nice talking to you," I said to Mrs. Smith.

John put his hand on the small of my back and guided me toward the downstairs recreation room. Voices sounded from downstairs, as did music that I knew. When I got to the bottom of the stairs, there were at least a dozen kids from our school milling around, some of them playing pool or shooting darts, Amber included. I so hoped that Amber was hitting on someone like Randy tonight.

I gravitated over to Sarah and Carly. The talk revolved around Christmas break and midterm exams, and then the topic of grad came up.

"I'm going to get my dress soon," said Sarah. "I'm not sure whether to go long or short."

"I'm definitely going short," I said. "I don't want to wear a long dress."

"I think I want long," said Carly. "Le Château has some cute ones."

"Are you guys getting your dresses already? It's only January." I looked at the clock on the wall. "Well, it will be in less than two hours."

"Sure. Why not?" Sarah shrugged. "I may not have a date yet, but heck, I can still buy a dress, especially when all the New Year's dresses are half price."

"I thought I'd wait until spring," I said.

Sarah laughed at me. "Why? You just said you're going to wear a short dress, so just go get one. And you've got a date. I mean, you and John are, like, married for crap's sake, so you don't even have to worry about the stupid date thing. I've never seen a closer couple than you guys."

When I lowered my head to sneak a glance at John over by the pool table, I immediately noticed that he was standing awfully close to Amber. They looked as if they were flirting with each other, laughing and clinking beer bottles. My jaw clenched. When had he gotten himself a beer?

"You want to go outside for a smoke?" I said to Sarah.

I waved to John from across the room and held up my cigarette package. He held up his finger as if to say he would join us in a minute. Before we went outside, Sarah made sure she poured us each a drink from her private Coke bottle stash and I made sure I put it in a plastic cup. I would just have one. One wouldn't hurt.

Outside the darkened winter sky showed some large clear patches where stars twinkled. A full moon slipped out from a small cloud cover, and suddenly a grayish blue light lit the back yard. My mother always said that the emergency wards at the hospital were crazy when it was a full moon, which didn't surprise me because the full moon always made me feel weird, too. Often I would lose things or forget something. The temperature was hovering just below freezing, but the air had a damp feel to it. I couldn't wait for that warm front to move in. Sarah and I stood outside shivering, puffing. I hadn't eaten much dinner, so the alcohol Sarah had poured for me was starting to take effect. Her drinks were always so strong.

"Hey," I said to Sarah as I blew out smoke, "I have a question for you, and I want a serious answer."

"'Kay."

"Do you think Amber is putting the moves on John?"

Sarah burst out laughing and doubled over. "John fricking loves you, Indie. Why would he want Amber? You guys are, like, connected at the hip. You can't even make time for our band anymore because of him."

I flicked the ashes off my cigarette and stared out at the yard, which was bathed in a blue shadow. Then I stared up at the moon, round and full, illuminating the earth with a chilling and somber gray light.

We dropped the subject of John and Amber and chatted aimlessly about school and music.

My cigarette was almost done when Sarah said, "Holy crap, I almost forgot to tell you. Did you hear the awful news?"

"What?" I slunk deeper into my coat.

"That kid Nathan from our school died over Christmas."

Shivers ran up one side of my body and down the other. I stood frozen on the porch.

"You know the kid I'm talking about," said Sarah. "The one who always picked his nose."

This couldn't be true. A horrible feeling of sorrow sur-rounded my heart. Even when I was seven and my papa had died, I hadn't been overcome with this type of sadness. This sudden rash of emotions that had exploded in my body created unexpected tears that appeared to sit behind my eyes. I couldn't finish my cigarette—my hands were shaking too much—so I ground it out in the cigarette can. The door slammed, and John walked out onto the porch, hugging his body.

"It's freezing out here."

I turned to face John. "Nathan died."

"Nathan?" John furrowed his eyebrows then he looked at Sarah. "The little guy?" Palm down, he put out his hand to around Nathan's height.

"Yeah." Her teeth chattered as she talked. "I just heard today. So weird."

"How did he die?" John asked.

"No idea," said Sarah.

"He wanted to be a violinist," I said quietly. My knees buckled, and I could hardly stand up. Then the tears from behind my lids started rolling down my cheeks. "He didn't want to die."

John put his arm around me, and I rested my cheek on his chest. He kissed the top of my forehead. "Let's go back inside," he said. "It's too cold out here."

Inside the house, I couldn't stop crying. John and I went into the washroom, and he closed the door. "Indie," he said soothingly, "it's okay."

"It's just so sad." I shook my head over and over. I had heard the man's voice on Christmas Eve. He had tried to tell me something about this. But why? I couldn't have done any-thing to help. Now that voice just made this all worse. Could I have helped? Was that why I heard the voice on Christmas Eve? But I would have had no way of knowing where Nathan was to phone him and warn him.

What could I have done?

Maybe I hadn't heard the voice. Maybe it had been saying "woman," not "Nathan." Like the woman we found in the car by the side of the road.

Why was I given these stupid voices and visions, if I could do nothing about them?

The tears kept coming. And coming. I tried to wipe them away. I felt so stupid for crying so hard. But I couldn't stop myself, because I knew Nathan hadn't wanted to die. He just wanted the other kids to leave him alone so he could play his violin. He'd had something to show the world, and now he wasn't allowed to. He was dead. Dead.

John wrapped his arms around me and pulled me close to his chest, holding me, stroking my back. "Why don't you stay with me tonight?"

I snuggled against his chest.

His nose nuzzled my ear when he whispered, "You can sleep over."

"My mom won't let me do that." I lowered my head.

He lifted my chin and kissed me, so softly, so gently, and the salt from my tears blended with the sweet taste of his lips.

When we parted, he whispered, "I think you need me tonight. We'll sleep in separate rooms. My mom wouldn't allow anything else."

Then he released his hold on me and pulled a tissue out of the box that was sitting on the back of the toilet. I accepted it and wiped my eyes.

"Are we going to grad together?" I asked.

"Grad?" He touched my cheek. "Why would you bring that up now?"

I shrugged. "I don't know. Sarah and I were talking about it, I guess. Maybe I'm trying to take my mind off Nathan. He won't get to graduate."

John stroked my hair. "Of course we're going to grad together. We're going to be together for a long time. Maybe we can move to England next year and live together. I've always wanted to live in London."

"Are you serious?" I stared into his beautiful hazel eyes. "That would be amazing."

He kissed my forehead. "Of course I'm serious. Should we call your mom for tonight?"

"Okay," I nodded.

Once I'd washed my face, John and I went into the kitchen to make the phone call. "Mom," I squeaked out the words as I played with the telephone cord, "can I sleep at John's tonight?"

Silence on the other end. I waited.

"I don't think that's a good idea, Indie."

"Please. We're not going to sleep in the same room."

More silence. "Have you been drinking?"

"Not much."

"Are you crying?"

"A little. But, Mom—"

"I'm coming to pick you up right now."

"No! Mom. Don't."

When my mother arrived at the party, I wanted to vomit. No matter how I pleaded, she said I had to get in the car. She made me put on my shoes and my coat, and she opened the front door and made me go to the car. Why was she ruining everything? John just wanted to comfort me, hold me. We could have talked about Nathan all night.

I slouched in the front seat and refused to talk to her, and I most certainly didn't tell her about Nathan, because I was just so mad at her. If I had to suffer, she was going to suffer, too. She went on and on about how this was going to be something I thanked her for later, when I wasn't pregnant at 17.

When we got to our house, I slammed the car door and said, "Nothing would have happened."

I stalked into the house. When I was in the kitchen, I couldn't contain myself any longer. "How could you do this to me?" I yelled. "You embarrassed me in front of my friends and John. You ruined my night!"

Then I started sobbing. "I won't get to kiss John at midnight!"

I stormed to my room and threw myself on the bed. Mom knocked on my door a few times, and I told her to go away. I heard the television downstairs announcing midnight, music and revelers ringing in the New Year with kazoos. I cried so hard my shoulders shook.

I had missed my kiss because of my stupid overprotective mother. I sat up in my bed. Was he kissing Amber now?

A little while later, I heard a knock on my door again.

"Indie," my mom said from the hallway.

"Go away."

"I just talked to John's mother, and she said it would be okay for you to stay there in the spare room. She told me about that boy Nathan. I'm sorry, honey. I'm sure this is a shock for all you kids. I can drive you back to the party. John's mother said a lot of the kids are sleeping over to talk about this."

The ride back wasn't any more vocal than the ride home had been. I was still so mad that she had ruined my New Year's kiss. I wiped the tears from my cheeks, willing myself to stop crying. When we got back to the house, I opened the car door a crack. Cold air drifted into the vehicle. I hesitated for a second, then I turned to look at my mom. Her face was a mess of wrinkled worry lines.

"I'm not a child anymore," I said. "John is my life now."

"I said I was sorry, Indie."

"Mom, you have to let me go and live my life."

"I know. I just worry."

I reached over and touched her arm. "Don't worry about me anymore. I'm fine." I paused. "Mom, I love him. And he loves me back. He will protect me."

Then I got out of the car and walked toward the house without even a glance back.

Chapter Sixteen

School started the following Monday. As the meteorologists had predicted, the weather had changed and freezing rain was falling from an extremely gray sky. Every radio and television station was talking nonstop about the weather and how to drive with caution and watch your footing when walking and blah, blah, blah. I had listened to the news but only to find out if the city buses were still running, and unfortunately they were. No buses would have meant school was canceled. That was all I really cared about. But no go. We usually got one snow day a year, but with the buses still running, it wasn't going to be today.

With my backpack slung on my shoulder, I stepped outside and immediately slid on the sidewalk. Of course, I wasn't wearing shoes with any type of treads. I righted myself and stood for a few seconds to absorb the world around me. The air was still and serene, and there was no wind at all. The rain fell quietly from the sky, almost misty, and it felt soft. I knew I was standing on the ground, but I felt as if I were floating. I liked the feeling, because it was so surreal; it was like visiting a different planet. Ice was starting to coat tree branches and telephone poles. The world looked mystical and eerie.

Then a horn honked that shook me back to reality. I had to get to school.

As I walked slowly to the bus stop, each step an effort to stay standing, I continually looked around me. I knew I should have been looking at the ground to keep my footing, but I couldn't help staring at what was happening. Crystal-clear ice coated the branches of the trees and telephone poles, and they looked so stoic and magical. This was like being on a futuristic movie set.

I did notice that some of the smaller branches on the trees were already starting to bend toward the ground, which meant they could snap off. Cars drove slowly down the roads, tires spinning, and quite a few were already on the side of the road because of fender benders.

The bus was late, but that was to be expected. Once it arrived, it lumbered slowly along its route, the driver obviously nervous about the road conditions. People who got on immediately shook their heads to get rid of the ice that coated their hair. My mind traveled and my thoughts raced. Now, instead of thinking about how pretty the world looked, I thought about Nathan. He wouldn't be at school today. He wouldn't be at school ever again. I could see his face in my mind, and I wondered what had happened to him. Sometimes, the world was just hard and cold, like the ice.

By the time the bus had stopped by the school, I was in a panic. I had to find out what had happened to Nathan.

I went inside as fast as I could, but to avoid slipping again, I had to move a lot slower than I wanted to.

None of my friends really knew how Nathan died. All anyone could tell me was that he drowned. I needed details. I had to know the exact way in which he died. *Why* did he die?

"Excuse me," I said, when I entered the guidance office. I ran my finger through my hair to get rid of the ice.

The woman working reception glanced at me over the rim of her reading glasses. I didn't know her name because I rarely went into the office.

"I heard about Nathan Carroll," I said. "Can you tell me how he died?"

She continued to look at me as if I were some alien from outer space.

Normally in this kind of situation, I would back down and leave, worried that I was making a scene. Today, I didn't care.

"I'm—I *was* his friend. I need to know. It's important. Please."

The woman gave me a few little nods as if she somehow understood that it really was important for me to know the answer. "He was at a swimming pool at a resort in Mexico," she said, "and somehow ended up in the deep end. No one really knows how it happened, but he couldn't swim, so they figure he had some kind of accident and fell. The lifeguards tried to resuscitate him, but from what I heard, he was dead when they pulled him out."

I closed my eyes and grabbed on to the counter for support. I had felt the push. Twice. Twice I had felt it. And then we had talked about swimming and pools because he was going swimming and didn't want to. Should I have connected the two things? They ruled his death an accident so obviously nothing had been done intentionally. Maybe he was even pushed by a dog. Or he walked into someone because he wasn't looking. Or perhaps a group of kids had run by him and accidently knocked him over. I would never know. I should have warned him to be careful around water. Why hadn't I said something to him? I should have just said to be careful around pools. If I had said something, he might have been more observant.

I hated this! I hated knowing things and not knowing what to say and do.

I opened my eyes and put my hand to my forehead. "Is there going to be a funeral? I checked the newspapers and didn't find any information."

The receptionist shook her head. "The family kept it private. They didn't think he had many friends."

"Thank you," I whispered.

She eyed me with genuine concern. "Are you okay?"

"Yeah." My voice squeaked. "I'm fine."

The woman took off her glasses, and her mouth lifted upward in a small, simple smile. "I guess he did have a friend, after all. I'll make sure to tell his parents that someone asked about him."

My legs felt really mushy, like they couldn't hold me up, as I walked into the hallway. My hands shook, and all I wanted was a cigarette, something that would make me forget about everything. I didn't care if it was freezing rain outside or if I had a class.

With my head down, I rushed to the back door. When I was almost there, I heard John's voice and looked up. He was leaning against the wall, laughing with Amber. To see them standing so close made something bristle inside me. Amber must have sensed me staring, because she glanced my way, but only for a second before she patted John's arm and left. John waved to me as if what was going on with him and Amber was nothing.

Was I feeling paranoid about John talking to Amber because of Nathan? Was I being overly sensitive this morning?

With his lanky stride, John approached. "This weather is crazy," he said. "Were you going outside?"

"I need a quick cigarette before class." I shoved my hands in my jacket pockets. "Want to join me?"

"I can't." He pulled out a thick pile of papers and held them up. "Finished my essay on Cayce and want to hand it in first block." He grinned proudly. "I think this is the best work I've ever done. I got so into this guy. I could have written a book on him."

"About time you finished," I said. At least now we wouldn't have to talk about that fraud Cayce any more.

"He helped so many people," said John.

"Well, good luck with the paper," I said halfheartedly. I did not want to talk about this and how he had helped people.

But you saved the woman.

But Nathan is dead.

But you saved the woman.

But. Nathan. Died!

"I just kept writing, and it flowed." John continued talking as if I weren't standing in front of him. "I couldn't believe it. I think I'm going to get a good mark on this piece of work. Like, my best mark ever."

"Good," I mumbled.

"He was just so fascinating. The things he could do."

I didn't help Nathan. *Why didn't I help Nathan?*

"Hey, I forgot to tell you," John said with excitement. "I think I found someone like Cayce in the Ottawa area. He claims to be able to do the same thing. I might go to him to ask some questions. I think it would be a cool experience. Just to see how he does it."

"No one can see stuff that happens in the future!" I snapped.

John frowned and held up his hand. "Whoa. What's wrong with you? Amber thought it was cool."

"You talked to Amber about this?"

"Why not? Believe it or not, Indie, she wants to hear what I have to say and is open-minded. Unlike you."

"I'm—I'm sorry I snapped," I said quietly.

He leaned toward me. "Weather like this makes people crazy." He touched my cheek. "I gotta go," he said.

"And I need a cigarette." I turned on my heel and headed outside.

Once outside, I opted not to walk all the way to the smoking area and instead leaned against the wet brick and cupped my hands to spark my cigarette. My hands shook as I put the cigarette to my lips. The rain fell softly from the sky, but as soon as it made contact with a building, fence, tree, ground, or whatever it landed on, it froze. It was so ironic that something so beautiful and soft could end up so stiff and tough in just a second. Sometimes John was like that: one minute soft and rounded, then in a second, he could be hard and sharp.

The rain glistened and shone against a gray backdrop. I looked out across the field and could see that now the weight of the ice on the tree branches was causing them to bend. The sky was gray. And the rain just kept falling. But still there was no wind. I pulled the collar of my jacket up. At least being outside in this weather was helping me forget about Nathan. I didn't want to think about why I hadn't helped him, if I could have done anything at all.

Taking a drag on my cigarette, I sucked in the smoke, holding it as long as I could before I blew it out. I did that over and over, until I felt my body relax. I hated the fact that I liked smoking. I knew it was bad for me, yet I still did it.

A puff on a cigarette made me feel . . . what? Normal somehow? Yet another teenager who was trying to prove something? I was anything but normal.

Nathan. My heart hurt for him. I took another drag. And another. I was just so unsure about what I was supposed to do with my visions. I really just wished they would go away. They confused me and made me scared, because I had no idea how to handle them. I had told Lacey about the vision of Burke with Amber, and look what happened: she hated me. I hadn't told Nathan, and look what happened: he died.

You saved a woman, Indie.

"Why do you talk to me all the time?"

I'm here to help you. Guide you.

"I can't be guided. There is nowhere to go with all of this."

I glanced around to see if anyone was nearby. If kids at school heard me talking to myself, they would think I was certifiably nuts. But I was alone in a gray world with freezing rain falling from the sky.

You have a path you must follow. You see and hear for a reason.

"A path. Yeah, right. An icy road, maybe—one where I can slip and fall and look like an idiot." I took another huge drag from my cigarette, holding the smoke in my lungs until I thought they would burst.

Then it hit me. A huge jab.

Burke!

I straightened my spine. Something was going to happen to him. I had seen it on Halloween! I had to warn Lacey or say something to someone.

Nathan died.

Because I didn't say anything.

I couldn't live through another death like this one. I just couldn't.

My cigarette hung from my fingers, the ashes dropping, dropping. I just stood ramrod straight, unable to move. I stared out at the world, the rain, the ice, the gray. Why couldn't I move? My mind and body felt locked. Then I felt the heat on my fingers, the sting of fire. And I also felt the cold.

My hair was covered in ice, and I was shivering. There was nothing left of my cigarette; I had burned it to a stub. I had to get inside.

I ran back into the school, shaking my head, little shards of ice flying all over the floor.

✤ ✤ ✤

The freezing rain continued for the rest of the morning, and the sidewalks soon became one big sheet of ice. At noon the principal came over the loudspeaker, telling us that they were closing the school due to the ice storm. Hoots and hollers sounded from every classroom. When I arrived at my locker to get my coat, John was waiting for me, and I didn't see Lacey. Now I couldn't say anything about the Burke vision. With the weather, it was not the time. But what if he got in a car accident?

But I knew he wasn't going to have a car accident. That wasn't how it was going to be.

"Let's hang out at your place," said John, casually leaning against my locker.

"Sure." I smiled at him. Why was I always doubting him? He was always there for me. He smiled back, and all I wanted to do was fall into his arms. I wasn't mad at him anymore. I needed him. And right now I was the one who had him, not Amber. I should have been thankful.

John and I left the school together, and once outside, we discovered that the sidewalks and roads were sheer ice. The bus was late, but fortunately they were still running in the city.

John and I stood at the back of the bus. "Look at the trees," he exclaimed. "Some of the branches are almost touching the ground. They will snap in half if this continues."

I nodded and stared out the bus window. Ottawa was literally turning into one big sheet of ice. Finally, we got off the bus, but when we tried to walk we could hardly move because we were sliding so much. I had to grab on to John's arm to stay upright.

"Let me take your backpack," he said to me.

I handed it to him, and he took my hand. "Let's hold each other up," he said.

Although I knew the storm was wreaking havoc across the city and cars were skidding everywhere and trees were getting destroyed, I had to admit that I loved the feeling of walking with John in this science fiction world. By now, ice covered everything, making the trees, streetlights, telephone poles, and buildings glisten. The huge hydro poles covered in ice looked like monsters. The ice-coated cars parked along the road looked like huge bugs. I loved how John was holding me up. We had to walk so slowly that it took double the time to get to my house.

Once inside, we both laughed as we shook the ice from our heads. Then I called out for my parents and discovered that no one was home yet.

"I should call my mom," said John, "and tell her I'm here."

After John called his mom, I talked to my parents. They were both going to stay at work and finish the day. My dad was going to pick my mother up from work because she was afraid to drive. And Brian was out of town for the day with his job. John and I made some soup and grilled cheese sandwiches and ate in front of the television. A severe storm warning kept interrupting the programming.

Once we had finished lunch, we cuddled on the sofa downstairs, with the lights off, watching mindless television and reading the weather warning that continually ran along the bottom of the screen. Our bodies just felt so right together.

I turned to gaze up at him, and without saying a word, he kissed me. Passionately. My lips burned with the intensity. My skin ignited with his touch, and I pressed my body to his. He moaned and moved closer to me, wrapping his arms around me, his hands moving all across my body, his hard skin pressing into me. I had felt John this way before, but today . . . something was different. My body reacted like it never had before, and I wanted more from him. I'm not sure if it was the storm or the roller coaster of emotions following Nathan's death—or perhaps a combination—but I felt so vulnerable and open and needy. I wanted to be as close to him as I possibly could, to forget who I was and just be a part of him. I ran my hands up and down his back, touching his body with my fingertips. Then I touched his neck just to feel his skin against mine. He kissed me with fervor, on the lips, neck, and upper chest. And I allowed this. I wanted him to kiss me everywhere.

One thing led to another.

And another.

We lay together under a blanket, limbs intertwined. I was blissful and happy, and I felt so secure. He held me tightly, kissed me tenderly, and I molded into him. Warm sensations flowed through me. This was love. It had to be. There was no other word for it.

With every breath and every beat of his heart, I felt content. I laid my head on his bare chest and curled into a small ball beside him. I wanted him to protect me from the world, from the thin veil that I sometimes seemed to go through. With John, perhaps I could belong to the outside world and stay away from my visions and that other life of mine. What I felt with him was so powerful that it took away all my worried thoughts, visions, sensations. I wanted to stay where we were forever, in a darkened basement, during an ice storm, just him and me. Then I could forget about everything around me and who I really was. John had done something that no one yet had been able to: he had made me live in the moment and forget about the past and future.

The ice storm continued all afternoon and into the evening, and John had to sleep over, because there was no way he could get home. When I crawled into bed that night, I smiled happily, knowing that *he* was in my house, in my basement. I didn't need to cover my head with blankets.

❖ ❖ ❖

The freezing rain created chaos, continuing for more days than the weather reporters had originally thought. Three big storms—instead of the predicted one—hit the Ottawa area. The rain kept falling and freezing, and the weight of that beautiful ice destroyed so many things. Amazing trees, some of them huge maples, were split in half, their trunks looking like they'd been severed with a saw. Telephone wires hung so low they hit the ground, and telephone poles, instead of standing straight, leaned at angles as low as 45 degrees. Hydro poles crumpled and bent with the strain of the collected ice; they looked like broken toys. The power went out in many homes, including my grandparents' in the country, where we had just been for Christmas. My parents were freaked with worry until they found out that my grandparents had a generator that they could use for power. I had never been in any kind of storm like this before, and although it was a disaster, I liked how people pulled together to help one another. Schools set up shelters for those in the country who were without power. Neighbors stayed together to share generators. The storm became a national disaster, and the Canadian army was called in to clean up the mess that had been created.

There was another upside, too. Every day that the announcers came on the radio saying school was closed for yet another day meant one more day John and I could spend together. He slept in the basement for the next few nights, because trying to get home was next to impossible. We talked, we laughed, and we shared thoughts. We had no homework to do, no activities; Christmas was over, and neither of us worked. During the nights that he wasn't sleeping at my house, I was thinking about him. I couldn't stop my thoughts. John filled every single one—and they were all happy thoughts, because I was in love. I actually liked how the world seemed to stand still during the storm, because it gave me the time to be close to John without any distractions.

The ice storm consumed everyone's thoughts in Ottawa and surrounding area, even as far east as Montreal. But John consumed mine. Every once in a while, I wondered what life was going to be like after the storm finally subsided and we were back at school. Would Amber continue to hit on him? Because I knew that was what she was doing. Would Lacey continue to ignore me? Would my visions start again? Would John find out about me?

On Friday, we were still not back at school. John and I were home alone, curled up on the sofa downstairs. He rubbed a strand of my hair between his fingers. "It would be so great if school were canceled for the rest of the year. Then I could spend all my time with you."

"That would be so amazing," I said. "I wonder if we have to go back on Monday. I'm pretty sure we will."

"I bet we do. I heard the storm is supposed to stop this weekend." He paused. "But being like this, with you every day, has made me think. Next year," he said slowly, "let's move to England and live together."

"You're really serious about this, aren't you?" I turned to face him.

"I want to be with you next year," he said, touching my cheek. "Being together all week has made me realize I want to be with you forever."

Forever! Was I hearing right? It was all I wanted, too. I rested my head on his chest. England would be so romantic, and it was a place I'd always wanted to go.

"We could visit Scotland and Ireland, too," I said, excitement in my voice.

"I can't imagine life without you, Indie." John stroked my cheek.

"Me either," I said. I took his hand and kissed his finger. "I wouldn't want to be alive if you weren't in my life." I paused. Then I said, "Let's do it, John. Let's really do it. It would be so magical."

A twinge of something unpleasant ran through me, but I pushed it aside. Nothing or nobody could tell me that this wasn't the right thing to do. It was right. It had to be, because everything was right when you were in love.

He smiled at me. "Okay," he said, "we'll do it." He paused for a second and just stared at me, and the look in his eyes was so intense that I thought I would melt right in his arms. I felt as if I were being sucked into his body. My heart raced. My blood flowed. Something big was on the tip of his tongue.

I waited for him to speak. After a few seconds, he whispered, "I love you."

The shock of the words rippled through my body. I let the feeling flow, and it warmed me completely. Then I softly replied, "I love you, too."

Part Three

Chapter Seventeen

March 1998

I was running with John along a beach and then Lacey was running beside us. But she stopped and started choking, because the necklace was too tight. She clutched her chest and fell. John started to do CPR on her. Then Lacey became Burke, and John still did CPR, but Burke looked as if he weren't breathing. I just stood there doing nothing. Nothing. Nothing.

I woke up in a pool of sweat, my breath coming out in short gasps. I put my hands to my chest and tried to slow my breathing down. This was the sixth time I'd had that dream in a month. The last two had only been days apart.

I looked at the calendar sitting on my desk. Burke. It was all about Burke again. Week after week had passed, and every time I got close to talking to Lacey, I felt as if my tongue had been chopped off. I was so afraid of what would happen if people found out. If John found out.

He was *all* that mattered. I'd even quit the band to spend more time with him.

And as each day passed and nothing happened to Burke, I kept asking myself, why should I say anything? Nothing was happening. So what if I didn't say anything and nothing happened?

You have to tell Lacey, Indie.

"Shut up!" Who was he? The soft voice who came to me over and over again? And now I was being haunted by dreams, too. I wasn't sure how much more I could stand.

"I can't tell her," I said out loud to myself as I picked up an old teddy bear stuffy that I'd had for years on my bed and pressed it against my chest. "I just can't, okay? Nothing has happened, so maybe nothing *will* happen. I can't just wreck my life because something *might* happen."

I flopped back on my bed and stared at the ceiling.

You have to tell her NOW.

I immediately sat up again when I heard the word *now,* because this was the same man who had warned me about the woman in the car on Christmas Day.

"Who are you?" I whispered. My body started trembling.

NOW!

I jumped out of bed and threw on the jeans that were crumpled on the floor, my hands shaking as I tugged up the zipper. Then I put on a sweater, ran a brush through my hair, and headed to the washroom. I wasn't sure what I was doing or why I was moving the way I was, but I had to go. Without eating breakfast, I snatched my coat off the hook, and as I ran out the door, I yelled at my mom that I was going to school early. I heard her calling after me, but I didn't stop to listen to what she had to say.

Drab, dreary slush covered much of the sidewalk and soaked my feet through my sneakers as I ran. My nerves felt like they were on the outside of my body. Why was I doing this? My feet were moving, my body following, and I couldn't stop.

Stop. Stop. I tried to talk to my body, but it just kept moving. Since the dreams had started a month ago, all this had been building. And now here I was, on some mission that I didn't understand. In my head, I prepared a speech. It had to come out right. I could never live with myself if something happened to Burke and I'd said nothing.

The voice. He had yelled at me.

By now I was at my bus stop. I lowered my head and stared at my wet feet. My body wouldn't stop shaking. If I'd ignored the voice at Christmas, the woman would have died. He had been really urgent this time, too. He never talked to me like that unless it was important.

Or perhaps he was just tired of me stalling?

No. I didn't believe that for a second. In a daze I caught my bus.

I was at my locker, still going over my speech in my head while pulling out my books, when someone tapped me on the shoulder. I nearly had a heart attack.

"Scared you good." John stood behind me, his warm breath steaming my neck. The smell of fresh soap hit my nostrils.

I turned and looked up at him, staring into his eyes. Then he did something he'd never done before: he kissed me in the hallway. I kissed him back—like, really kissed him. When it was over, he immediately stepped back and looked up and down the hall.

"You hate PDA," I said.

He shrugged. "I had to do it," he said softly. "It's Monday, and I just had to kiss you."

"Meet me for lunch under the tree outside," I said.

He held up his thumb as he walked backward. Then he turned and headed to his class. I stayed at my locker. My heart pounded.

Forget about him, Indie. Concentrate on something else.

Where was Lacey? I stalled, pulling books out and putting them back until I saw her coming down the hall, late as usual. My heart picked up speed, raced like a ticking time bomb, and my legs felt like mush.

Indie, stay focused.

But you haven't talked to her in months.

Stay focused.

"Lacey," I said when she finally showed up at her locker.

She refused to look at me and instead spun the lock on the door. "That's my name," she answered.

On instinct, I reached out and touched her arm, like I would have done when we were friends. "I have to tell you something." I rushed my words.

She didn't answer.

"I had a vision." I knew I was speaking fast, but finally the words were there and I had to let them go. "I think Burke is in trouble." My words spewed from my mouth like an overflowing fountain. "It's cold and loud and bright, and he crashes into something and hurts himself."

Lacey gave me an incredulous look, then she burst out laughing. "Are you fricking kidding me? You're the weirdest person I know." Then she leaned forward, her eyes smoldering. "I kept the last one quiet, but this time, I'm telling *the entire school*." She pulled out her books and shut her locker door.

"By the way," she added, "I heard about Amber and John. Guess she wasn't going for Burke after all."

After she had stalked away, I just stood in the hall with my forehead pressed against my locker. After a few seconds, I straightened up and tried to take my books out for my first class, but my hands were trembling so much that I dropped them on the floor. When I picked them up, I saw Lacey's necklace and it was knotted again. I had put it back in there so long ago. I shoved it into my pocket.

Suddenly I felt drained of energy. I had been so charged just an hour earlier, running to catch the bus and now . . . I felt as if I could crawl into a hole and die. Why had I said anything? Was she right about Amber and John? It wasn't like she was going to help me now.

I looked up toward the ceiling. "How could you do this to me?" I whispered. "Why? How could you give me these visions? For what purpose?"

"Indie Russell. Time for class," said Mr. Leonard as he walked by me.

I spent my entire first class working out the knots of the necklace. By the time the bell rang, it was untangled.

In between my first and second classes, as I walked down the hall, I was so clouded and muddled in thoughts about everything that was going wrong that I didn't notice that I was close to Lacey and her pod of popular friends until it was too late to change directions. I lowered my head, hoping she wouldn't see me.

Just when I was almost by the group, I heard one of them shout, "Hey, fortune teller! Am I going to be a big star?"

They all started laughing. My face grew hot, and my body shook.

"Look into your crystal ball. Woooooo," another girl said, in a phony gypsy accent.

Just keep walking.

If I ran, I'd just encourage them.

When it was time for lunch, I was so relieved. Nothing more had been said to me. I headed outside to wait for John. The weather was crappy, cloudy, and gray, hovering just above freezing, so the snow was melting. I shivered under my light jacket. Why hadn't I worn my winter coat? I hated this time of year and wanted it to be spring, so I'd worn my spring coat just because. I wanted sun and warm air, not cold, dirty slush.

Time passed. I glanced at my watch and tapped my foot. With every passing minute, my heart sped faster and faster and my stomach twirled. Something was wrong.

I waited for 15 minutes. Then I scooped up my backpack, flung it over my shoulders, and ran into the school. I had to find him. I sped to John's locker. He wasn't there.

I ran to the smoking area. Not there either. My heart thudded. *Think, Indie, think.* I sucked in air as fast as I could to keep up with my gasping breath.

"John, where are you?" I whispered.

Come on, Indie, think.

The library!

I raced down the hall, skidding as I rounded corners. And I didn't slow, even when I got to the library. I barged in, looking, running through the aisles.

And then I saw him. He was at a table in the very back of the library. His legs were stretched out, and he was slouched in the chair, reading what looked like a paper of some sort.

I stopped. He looked exactly the way he had on the day, way back in September, when we were in the library together and had our first real conversation.

That day had been the beginning of us.

From the downward turn of his mouth, the dull look in his eyes, and the slumped body posture, I knew he'd heard. I'd told him repeatedly that I didn't believe in Edgar Cayce, in people who had visions, and I'd made it perfectly clear that I didn't agree with anything he thought about the spiritual dimension.

"John," I said quietly.

He looked up and just stared at me.

"I waited for you," I said. "Under the tree. Have you eaten lunch yet?"

"Let's see. Have I eaten lunch?" His words were deliberate and slow. "Maybe you could have one of your visions and find out. Did I have egg salad or tuna, Indie?"

I stood frozen, afraid to even move a finger or breathe.

John narrowed his eyes. "You do have visions, don't you, Indie?"

I swallowed.

"Are you going to answer me?"

"Yes," I said quietly.

Cynically, he raised his hands, palms up. "Yes, you're going to answer me, or yes, you have visions?"

"I sometimes have visions," I spoke slowly. "I've had them since I was young."

He contorted his face into a scowl and shook his head. "All this time, you've lied to me. Out and out lied." Then he mimicked me and said, "I don't know about Edgar Cayce. I think he's a quack. I don't believe people can have visions. No one can do that."

"I didn't want you to know." I choked out my words. "I didn't want you not to like me."

He frowned, his eyes almost slits. "And you think lying makes someone like you?"

"No."

"Relationships are about trust. Trust, Indie." He raised his voice, and I wanted to shrivel, curl into a small cocoon and forget the world around me. "I'm sorry."

"Sorry I found out? Or sorry you didn't tell me? Which is it, Indie?"

"Sorry I didn't tell you," I barely whispered.

"What *visions* have you had since we started going out?"

My throat clogged. The shovel, the locket—how was I going to tell him about those visions? They made no sense to me. Had the shovel just been a vision to tell me that my secrets couldn't stay buried? That they would be dug up? What about the man in the locket? I tried to speak, but no words would come out. I was lost. Nothing made sense. Energy depleted, I just stood in front of him, speechless.

He glared at me, then stood, holding up his hands. "Forget it! I don't want to know." He picked up his books and stuffed them in his backpack.

"Okay, I'll tell you," I said.

He rapidly shook his head and refused to make eye contact. "I said forget it." His words were clipped.

Then suddenly he picked up the paper that he had been reading when I first saw him. "See this?" He almost shoved the paper in my face. A big red A+ was written on the front. "This is my paper, Indie. Mr. White just gave it back to me. How ironic is that?"

"John, I said I'm sorry."

Suddenly, he started ripping the paper into shreds.

I reached out to try to stop him. "Don't," I cried, touching his arm.

He yanked his arm away from me. "You know, Indie, every time I tried to talk about anything in this paper, you just fed me another one of your lies." He kept tearing, letting the tiny pieces of paper fall to the library floor.

And he continued. "You know, what's really, really ironic about all of this is that I would have respected you. I would have honored your gift. But you couldn't respect *me* enough to even tell me. Do you think I'm such a horrible person that

I wouldn't have wanted to go out with you anymore? How could you think I was like that? That's what hurts the most. You didn't have any faith in me as a decent human being. You didn't want me to know because . . . what? I was going to laugh at you?"

"I wanted to tell you. I did. Honest."

"Indie, that's bullshit!"

John threw what was left of his paper on the floor. Then he came toward me and I tried to hug him, but he shoved me away. For a second, he glared at me before he stormed out of the library, leaving me alone with a big mess.

By now sobs racked my body, tears falling like March rain down my cheeks, the pain in my chest excruciating. I got down on my hands and knees, picking up the tiny pieces of paper and putting them in a big pile. After I had gathered up every piece of paper from the dirty carpet, I stuffed them in my backpack.

Then I quickly left the school and went home.

The bus ride seemed to go on forever, and I wished I had Nathan to keep me company.

Once home, I called to my mom but she wasn't home. I trudged up to my room and removed John's paper from my backpack, carefully putting it all in a shoebox alongside my crafts from elementary school. After storing the box in my closet, I curled into a tiny ball on my bed and pulled my comforter over my head.

I must have slept. I don't really know. All I know is that when my mom popped up to my room to ask me about school and dinner, I told her I'd be down.

I cleaned up in the bathroom and survived dinner. I don't know how I did it, but I did. It was as if I were on some sort of robotic mission to make like everything was okay when, very clearly, my life was a mess. I ate enough for my mom not to ask questions, then I excused myself, saying I had homework. Again, I curled up on my bed and slept.

Dreams crept into my psyche, and I woke up in the middle of the night, my pajama top soaked with sweat. I lay in the dark, curled under my covers, thinking about what had happened. I was never going to be normal. Ever. I hated myself. I wished I could cry again, but I couldn't. It was as if my tears had dried up and my heart had shriveled like a rotting apple.

The tears were gone. My anger was gone. And most of all, my joy was gone.

I was numb; I felt nothing.

I fell back to sleep.

In the morning, I got up as usual and got ready for school. Why not? I had to graduate, even though I might not get to go to grad. Or maybe I wouldn't graduate. I hadn't done my homework last night, and I hadn't studied for the test I had today. What difference did it make if I graduated? I wasn't going on to school. I wasn't going to England with John. I wasn't going to do anything with my life. And John wasn't going to be my date for the ceremony. He would probably go with Amber.

When I got to school, I talked to no one, listened to no one, just went directly to my locker. I stood in front of it for a few minutes, staring at the pieces of paper taped haphazardly all over it.

"Weirdo."

"Nutjob."

"Crazy lady!"

"Indie Russell was spawned from the devil."

"Witch! Cackle. Cackle."

And leaning against my locker was a broomstick with my Halloween witch's hat perched on top

For the first few minutes, after seeing the crap on my locker, I couldn't move. I just stood there, reading the words over and over.

Totally out of character for me, I completely lost it and started tearing at the paper. I ripped and I tore and I chucked the paper so it fell, littering the school's floor. I lost all my ability to think rationally, and something kept driving me forward. "I hate this! I hate this!"

I kept tearing.

When there was nothing left on my locker, my body felt like a tire losing air, hissing, until it was completely deflated. The rage was over. I had no more left in me. The calm that I'd had at breakfast returned, and I felt the void again. A small crowd had gathered around me to watch my performance.

"Hey, Indie," said a voice I didn't recognize. I turned to see a girl standing beside me. She wore all black and had dyed black and purple hair, piercings on her face, and tattoos running like serpents on her arms. "I wanted to give you this." She handed me a piece of paper. "We're part of the Extraterrestrial Club in the school and thought you might want to join our group."

I took the paper and ripped it up in front of the girl's face. Then I threw it at her.

"Geez," she said. "You always seemed so nice. When did you start being a bitch?"

Without even opening my locker, or picking the paper up off the floor, I walked away. I heard Sarah's voice in the distance calling my name, so I slowed down.

When she caught up, Sarah wrapped her arms around me. "You're still the nicest person I know," she whispered. "This will all blow over. If you want to talk, give me a call. I'm still here for you, no matter what."

I looked into Sarah's eyes. I couldn't believe she was being so nice to me. "Thanks," I whispered. "I know I haven't exactly been a great friend lately." I paused for a second. "Do you think he has something going with Amber?"

Sarah shook her head. "Nah. Nothing serious. They're just really good friends." She paused for a split second before she spoke again. "But he doesn't treat you right, Indie."

I felt a sharp jab to my stomach, and it began doing somersaults, making me want to throw up.

"I'm gonna go home," I muttered. "I don't want to be here."

Sarah nodded. "I understand. I'll call you later."

No one was home at my house, because everyone had left for work. Instead of going to my room, I went to the washroom, shut the door, and locked it. I looked at myself in the mirror and could see nothing but a blank pink wall behind me. I couldn't see my face; it was as if I were nonexistent. But that's what I wanted to be. I didn't want to live without John.

What about living together in England? Sharing a life together? Being together forever?

I thought I was going to collapse, so I sat on the edge of the tub. The pink room vibrated and throbbed, in and out, in and out. *Boom. Boom.* Pink and more pink. That's all I could see. Why was it pink? It should have been red, blood red.

I opened the medicine cabinet. My dad's pills lined the shelves. I picked up a bottle and looked at it. If I took the entire bottle in one dose, that would do. I turned the bottle around in my fingers and read the prescription.

Take one pill three times daily with meals. Yes, I would take the whole bottle. I would go to sleep, and that would be that. John would never miss me. No. I shook my head, clutching the bottle to my chest. My dad needed these pills. I couldn't do that to him. I put them back and closed the medicine cabinet door.

This time when I looked in the mirror, I saw my papa behind me.

"This isn't right, Indie."

"I'm coming to see you, Papa."

"No, Indie. It's not your time."

"It wasn't Nathan's time either, and he died. I want to die!"

A razor sat on the counter, and I picked it up. Would my blood match the pink pulsing walls? I would have to stick my arm in the tub so the blood wouldn't get all over the bath mat.

I hated myself.

Hated who I was.

Hated my visions.

Hated seeing dead people.

And hated hurting people I loved. Why did John have to find out? Now he hated me like I hated myself.

I put the razor down. Too much blood. My mom would have to clean up the mess. Wash the bath mat. Scrub the tub. Clean the floor. I grabbed a full bottle of aspirin, unlocked the bathroom door, and made my way down the hall.

The sun shone high in the sky, and the air had warmed and taken away some of the slush. Little rivers of water trickled into drains. I had no idea what time it was. I felt emotionless.

I walked to the bus stop and caught a bus, finding a seat at the back by myself. I clutched the aspirin bottle in the pocket of my jacket. If I jumped off the bridge, I would drown. Then my parents wouldn't blame themselves for being bad parents, for not seeing that something was wrong. I didn't want them to feel bad. They loved me, always had. They only wanted what was best for me. I wanted them to think I drowned, like Nathan drowned. I wanted everyone to think it was some sort of accident.

John. What would he think?

He wouldn't care.

He would go on without me and perhaps end up with Amber and take their friendship to another level. Something jabbed me deep inside, made me ache, my heart throb.

I looked at the trees and their lack of leaves. In a few months, the buds would come, then the leaves and the butterflies. I put my hand to my necklace.

No, don't think about John.

Lacey's face popped into my mind. She hated me too and wouldn't care. And Sarah would also forget about me over time. Zoe and Carly had already forgotten about me after I quit the band. Up ahead I saw my stop, so I pulled the cord. Then I walked off the bus and toward the middle of Billings Bridge. The Rideau River flowed below it, and I stared at the swirling water for a few moments, watching its continuous run and the little blobs of ice bobbing along, bouncing into tree limbs, bouncing off again. At this time of year, the water moved quickly and was cold and deep. This was the best season for what I wanted to do.

"Go home, Indie. It is not your time yet." Again my papa spoke to me.

"I'm tired of this, Papa. So tired. Because of who I am, I lost the one person I truly love. What does that say about me? My whole life will be one person after another leaving me because I'm weird."

Your grandfather is correct, said my gentle male voice.

"Shut up! Do you hear me? Just shut up and get out of my life. I hate you."

I am here to help you.

"But you don't help! You just make everything worse," I said into the wind.

If you purposely try to die, you go right back to where you were. You will have to do this again, Indie. You don't have a choice. You won't pass go, you will go to a similar situation, and in that moment, you will lose your free will. Your time has not arrived yet.

"Yeah, right. And I'm supposed to understand any of that?" I muttered. "And what is free will?" Here I was in the middle of the day, on a bridge, having a conversation with a voice from inside my head. No wonder John broke up with me. Who would blame him?

Free will is choice.

"You won't do what you were meant to on the earth, my little sweetie pie." said my papa.

"Don't, Papa. Don't try to talk me out of this."

"You need to go home, Indie."

"Why?"

"Your family is there. They love you," said Papa.

And you haven't fulfilled your life's purpose.

As I watched the water, my mind slowed like a toy running out of batteries. I only had enough juice to think about my family. Holidays would be a sad time for them. Thanksgiving. Would my parents cook a turkey anyway? How would Brian react to my death? We were always fighting, but we loved each other, and we were close in a funny and amazing way. He thought I was crazy and didn't believe in my visions, but for some reason, that didn't matter. He didn't judge me. And Christmas. I loved Christmas. Loved giving gifts to people. After a few years, would they even notice I was gone?

They would get over it. The world would get over it. After years had slipped by, no one would remember Indigo Russell, or if they did, it would be someone looking at my grave and saying, "She was the weird girl who died when she was a high school senior. Offed herself on Billings Bridge." Then they would say, "Didn't she date John Smith for a while?" And someone would reply, "Yeah, but he ended up with Amber McKinnon." No one would care, just like they didn't care about Nathan.

"Hey, look out!"

I opened my eyes to see a guy in a wheelchair flying toward me. I stepped back to get out of his way, but when he got to me, instead of zooming by, he lurched to a stop.

"Ya hanging? Perfect day, eh?" He grinned. "I'm so glad spring is going to be here soon. The snow sucks when you're in a chair. Sorry if I scared you."

"It's okay," I said. Right away I noticed that his legs were strapped into his chair; he was paralyzed from the waist down. I wondered if he had been born disabled or if something had happened to him.

He tilted his head and eyed me. "Are you okay?"

I stuck my hands into my pockets. "I'm fine."

He nodded. "Life is good, y'know. We live in a great part of the world with no war or any crap like that. You get what you get. But no matter what, you have to enjoy the day."

Then he put his hands on his wheelchair. "Well, I got to go and—"

"Enjoy the day." I finished his sentence.

He gave me a thumbs-up, then continued to the other side of the bridge.

"This was your wake-up call, Indie. Go home, please." Papa spoke loud and clear.

I squinted at the sun. I couldn't jump now. Not after what that guy had said.

As I walked across the bridge to my bus stop, I whispered, "You arranged that, didn't you, Papa?"

Chapter Eighteen

As Sarah had assured me, within days I was no longer the topic of conversation at school. A week later, I was forgotten by everyone, including John.

Halfway through the day on Friday, I was at my locker, trying to figure out what books I needed for my next class and wondering if I should even go to class, when I smelled soap and cigarettes. My heart picked up speed. I was alone in the hall. *Would he talk to me?*

I slowly turned. He was looking straight at me, but then he jerked his head so he was facing forward and walked right by.

Something about his look scared me. His eyes were bloodshot and his pupils wide. There had been a rumor floating around that John had been doing drugs all week and that he'd been getting into harder stuff. I felt sick about this and wished I could talk to him.

I slammed my locker shut without taking out a book. With my hands shoved into my pockets, I rushed outside to the smoking area. Was this pain in my chest, the continual throbbing, going to follow me forever?

Sarah, Zoe, and Carly were smoking and talking excitedly about something. As soon as I approached them, they stopped their animated conversation. Were they talking about me?

"Hi," I said. I pulled out my cigarettes.

"Hey," said Sarah back.

Shifty-eyed, they glanced at one another.

"What's going on?" I patted my pockets, checking for a lighter. Right away, Sarah gave me her cigarette. I took it and lit mine, inhaling deeply to get it sparked.

"Not much," said Zoe. "We're just . . ." Zoe stopped mid-sentence and a weird silence hovered over us.

"Just what?" I inhaled as if I didn't care what they were talking about, but really I wanted to know. Were they talking about John and Amber?

"We were talking about the band," said Sarah.

"And our upcoming gig," said Carly.

"Oh," I replied.

Carly did a little dance with her arms. "I'm so stoked and can't wait for our big debut."

What date was it today? I tried to think. Friday, March 6. They were playing next Saturday, on March 14. The fund-raiser was being held at a community hall, and it was an afternoon event. In January, I'd quit in order to spend more time with John. And that's all I'd wanted at the time, thinking it was sweet of him to want me all to himself. But now the girls had excitement flashing in their eyes, and I had nothing.

Again silence.

I puffed on my cigarette and looked out into the distance. I had given up a lot of things for John. But it had been my decision, too. And our breakup was a result of my lying.

"You want to come and do a song with us?" Sarah asked.

"You think that's a good idea?" Carly responded before I could. Then she stared at me. "You basically dumped us for a guy. I wouldn't give up my friends for a guy. Ever." She blew out a perfect smoke ring.

And then, as if I weren't even present, Zoe said, "She could do 'Every Breath You Take.' We all know that one, and it was so good when we rehearsed it."

"I gotta get to class," I said. I quickly stubbed out my cigarette and rushed out of the smoking area. I ran into the school with my head down. Then I heard his voice, laughing like he didn't have a care in the world. And I heard her voice.

Amber.

I kept my head down and walked as fast as I could, but I guess curiosity got the best of me. I glanced up briefly to see John leaning casually against a locker and Amber standing right beside him with her talons in his belt loops. Vomit lodged in my throat.

I ran to the washroom, flung open the door, and ran to the stall. I had barely shut the door when I threw up. I sat on the toilet and wiped my mouth with toilet paper. That was the worst, most hurtful thing he could have done to me. Amber. He had hooked up with her for the *entire school* to see right after we broke up!

I cleaned myself up and went back to my locker. It was almost time for lunch, and I really wasn't hungry. I saw Lacey coming down the hall. Again I felt sick.

I just couldn't face Lacey today. I yanked out my entire backpack. I wouldn't return to my locker.

As I was rushing down the hall with my head down, I felt a tug on my arm. I turned around to see Sarah.

"Stop for a sec, okay?"

Once I was standing still in front of her, she said, "We were serious about you playing the one song with us." Her voice was almost soothing. "Carly doesn't mean to be rude. You know she's just super independent and would never let a guy control her. That's just how she is. It would be fun to have you join us. You were part of our band until—" Sarah stopped.

I tried to smile.

"All that crap," she said, smiling. She put her hand on my arm.

"Thanks." I could hardly get the word out of my mouth. If I spoke, I might cry, and I didn't want to do that in the hall.

"Hey," she said, with brightness in her voice, "I've got tickets to the Sixty-Seven's game tonight. You want to come? It'll be fun."

When I didn't answer right away, Sarah playfully frowned at me. "You need to get out. I'm picking you up at six thirty."

"Picking me up?"

Sarah's eyes widened. "You're so far behind. My parents gave me an old clunker car. You're going to love it!"

Sarah was right; I did love her car. It was a canary yellow Pontiac Sunbird, and she had feathers and beads hanging from the rearview mirror and some sort of colorful blankets on the seats, covering up the rusty springs.

With AC/DC's "Thunderstruck" blaring through her speakers, she sped away from the curb. "Should be a good game tonight," she said. "Burke's team is fighting for first spot." She pounded her steering wheel in time with the music.

"How does Amber get all the guys?" I asked, slouching in my seat and sticking my hands deep in my jacket pockets.

Sarah took her eyes off the road for a second to glance at me. "For what it's worth, I don't think John cheated on you with her when you two were together, but he's a shit for hooking up with her, like, ASAP."

"He didn't even wait a week."

"He wants to hurt you." Sarah drove for a few seconds before she turned the volume down. "I've been meaning to ask you this for a few months now."

"What?"

"Why did you dump the band? You were so into it. And we rocked!"

"John wanted to spend time with me."

"This might not be the right time for me to say this, but I'm going to say it anyway. *That's* controlling." Sarah turned the music up again, and I leaned back in my seat and stared at the frayed ceiling. It wasn't just him. I had given up the band, too, to be with him.

The first thing I did when we entered the arena lobby was to scan the crowd for John. I know, so sad, but so true. I did not want to run into him, especially if he was with Amber . . . but if he was alone, perhaps we could talk? Our first date had been at a hockey game, so there was a good chance he'd be here. Sarah and I made our way to our seats just as the Zamboni took its last loop around the ice surface and headed off. Within minutes, the lights were lowered and the refs sailed onto the ice, completing a few laps under the moving strobe lights. Then the music blared, and the announcer came over the loudspeakers to tell the crowd that the players were hitting the ice. Everyone stood up and cheered.

I watched as Burke skillfully skated onto the ice, circling around the back of the net, then out to the blue line and around again. The other night at dinner, my dad had informed me that Burke's name had recently appeared on a list as one of the top NHL draft picks. Rumor had it that Burke had had some really successful meetings with the managers of the Pittsburgh Penguins team. I remembered my drive with him and how I had seen the jersey. I really wished *that* team hadn't been the one to show interest; if it were another team, it would prove that not all the things I saw came true.

When the game started and everyone was once again seated, I spotted Lacey, looking gorgeous, sitting in the same seat as the time when I was at the game with John. I guess, in a way, I was happy for Lacey and Burke—but selfishly I wished Amber were with Burke now and not John.

I still had the silver necklace, and it wasn't tangled. If only I could give it back to Lacey. I ached inside.

Sarah leaned into me and, as if she had read my mind, said, "I can't believe Lacey still won't talk to you. It's been, like, months."

She's going to talk to you tonight.

Why I heard those words in my head, I had no idea. "She's still with Burke," I said.

Sarah rolled her eyes. "And I have no frigging idea why. I know he's hot and good at hockey, but he cheats on her all the time. I heard he was with Chelsea at a party. And Lacey is so beautiful; she could have any guy she wanted."

At first I hadn't understood Lacey and her attachment to Burke, but looking back on my relationship with John, I did. She loved him.

I glanced at Lacey again, and suddenly a sharp pain hit me hard in the chest. Her heart was really heavy, and she was in agony, just like I was. Outside she looked gorgeous, with her dark hair curled to perfection and her red coat the exact right shade for her skin and her makeup flawless, but inside she was raw and hurting. Were they going to break up, too? What was going on with her?

"She deserves someone better," I said to Sarah.

"So do you," replied Sarah without taking her eyes off the ice. "Great hit!" She jumped to her feet and started cheering.

A player from the opposite team got smashed against the boards, and the glass rattled, sending waves of noise through the arena. The fans freaked out, and the ones sitting close to the glass started pounding on it. I thought it was going to break; it shook so hard. Cheers echoed throughout the arena, bouncing off the concrete walls.

"Man, I love those hits." Sarah punched her hand. "Best part of hockey. Well, that and the fights."

The smash against the boards had freed the puck and Burke raced toward it, his legs moving in long strides, his body hunched over. His skate blades scratched and crunched the ice. Being a fast skater, Burke reached the puck first, picked it up on his stick, and drove toward the net.

Suddenly I felt weird, really loose in my joints, and my limbs felt wobbly and the arena noises—bodies hitting the boards and sticks slapping the ice—pumped through my brain like loud metal music. The smell of greasy hot dogs and popcorn and beer burned my nostrils, and the fluorescent lights from the scoreboard jumbotron blinded me. Bright red numbers flashed, and I felt my stomach heave.

I had done this before. Felt this before.

I heard Lacey's voice—she was yelling, telling Burke to "skate," and I swiveled my head toward the high-pitched sound. Of course, Lacey was intently watching Burke . . . but she wasn't yelling. Loud noises banged against the wall of my skull, and I turned back to the game.

Bang. Bang. Bang.

I held my hands to my head. This was way too familiar. Suddenly, my throat became parched. I needed water. My face flushed. Beads of sweat erupted on my forehead. I felt as though I had been struck with a really bad flu. I wanted to pass out. Blood. I smelled blood.

I looked at the ice again. Then I saw the defenseman for the other team. He was skating hard, too, picking up speed with every one of his long strides, his skates digging into the ice, making scraping sounds. He was heading right toward Burke, who still had the puck and was concentrating only on the net and the goalie. The other player wanted the puck, too; he wanted to take it away from him in whatever way he could, including a bashing cross-check or a trip. Burke was too obsessed with driving to the net to see the guy coming at him or, maybe, to care—his thoughts were only on scoring. Burke thought he was invincible, could beat anyone, because he was the best.

Suddenly the vision from Halloween flashed into my frontal lobe. The defense from the other team was coming at Burke and was going to accidentally smash into him, and Burke was going to crumble.

Brain. Brain. I heard the words loud and clear, and then I felt the hard jab, as if a knife had pierced the middle of my forehead.

They were close to the net. The goalie crouched, placing his stick on the ice. Burke was going to get hit and ram into the post and hit his head, rattle his brain. My head throbbed, the pain blinding.

I had to stop this. I stood up and cupped my hands. "Burke! Look out!"

For a nanosecond, Burke looked in my direction, and I knew he had heard me. Or had I imagined it? How could he, with all the noise? But he heard me, I knew it . . . didn't he? I held my breath.

Burke looked to his side and shifted his weight slightly, just as he collided with the other player. The sound of two bodies crunching together reverberated through the building. My stomach careened, and I felt a sharp pain in my shoulder, as if it had been pulled out of its socket. My headache disappeared.

Burke catapulted through the air, flipping, twisting, and landing with a thud. Then he slid toward the goalie, headfirst, passing the metal goalpost by less than an inch.

The action stunned the crowd. Out of control, Burke knocked the goalie clear off his feet, sending the net flying as well. As the goalie landed on his back, Burke glided right into his sharp skate blade, neck first.

The arena hushed. There was an eerie quiet as everyone watched in shock.

Blood started squirting from Burke's neck, landing on the white ice, creating a huge red spot. The spot started small and grew as the blood kept spurting. A player from Burke's team immediately fell to his knees and put his hand on Burke's neck. The rest of the players yelled for help. The door to Burke's team bench swung open, and his team trainer sprinted out onto the ice, sliding in his running shoes but never losing his stride as he went full speed toward Burke. He got down on his knees beside Burke and pressed a towel into Burke's throat while he talked in his ear. Burke lay still.

The towel turned red. People winced and ohhed and ahhed and scrunched their faces as if they were the ones in pain. A woman sitting behind us heaved, sounding like she was going to vomit, the gurgling sound nasty in her throat. Security guards ran down the steps to help a woman who had fainted. Parents shielded their children's eyes from the sight on the ice. Security guards and police were suddenly everywhere.

The players on the ice stood in shock, many resting their chins on their sticks and looking to the ground, not wanting to see the blood on the ice. Some would take the chance and glance over but would immediately look away, holding their gloved hands to their mouths.

Burke lay motionless on the ice. Murmurs started.

"He's hurt bad."

"Burke didn't see the guy."

"Oh, gawd. This is awful. I can't look."

"I hate seeing this kind of thing happen."

Sarah turned to stare at me. "Indie," she whispered, "how did you . . ." She trailed off. "Burke heard you yell at him. How could he have heard? That's not possible."

I pressed my hands to my forehead. "I don't know," I said. "I don't know how it happens."

"He's losing a ton of blood," said Sarah.

I glanced at Lacey, who was now down by the glass, looking at Burke, her hands covering her mouth, her eyes wide.

As if she felt my eyes on her, she turned and spotted me in the crowd. She looked so scared—and remorseful, like she was just figuring out that my vision about Burke had come true. Suddenly, the world in front of me stretched, and I felt as if I were moving through a motion picture; nothing was real.

The paramedics arrived and, in a flurry, brought the stretcher onto the ice, working like well-oiled machines. They talked to Burke and continued to apply pressure to his neck as they lifted him on the stretcher. As they rushed him away, the crowd cheered, and the players tapped their sticks on the ice. The refs huddled in a group to try to figure out what the consequences should be, or if there would be any. It wasn't really anyone's fault. The ice would have to be scraped, the blood removed before the game could continue. I shuddered, cold encasing me as if I were standing in the middle of a deep freeze. I crossed my arms over my chest. The loss of blood was making Burke cold. Again, Lacey glanced my way, and we connected through some sort of electrical energy. Her oversized pupils showed shock and unbelievable fear.

Then her pain hit my heart, and I struggled to breathe. The world around me swirled, and I wanted to move. And fast.

"We have to go to the hospital," I said to Sarah, rushing my words. "And we need to take Lacey with us." Before Sarah could answer, I had pushed by the knees and bodies of everyone in my row and was running down the concrete stairs. I grabbed Lacey's arm. "Come on," I said. "Let's go to the hospital."

Lacey and I ran up the stairs, picking up Sarah on the way. The three of us dodged bodies, not once saying excuse me. When we were finally in the parking lot, we broke into a sprint, and we didn't stop until we got to her car.

Huffing and puffing, we jumped in. I sat in the front with Sarah, my heart beating out of my skin, and Lacey sat in the backseat. Sarah fired up the engine and sped away.

"That's what you saw, isn't it? On Halloween?" Sarah could hardly breathe.

I nodded. I turned and looked at Lacey. "Stay positive. We have to think he will be all right."

Sarah passed cars and sped through yellow lights to get to Ottawa General Hospital. After a horrible sideways parking job, the three of us ran through the hospital emergency doors. Sarah stopped and doubled over to catch her breath. Lacey frantically searched the halls for any sign of where Burke was.

The antiseptic smell hit my nostrils, and I had to breathe deeply to ease the nausea that bubbled in my stomach. Jitters took over my body, as if I had just drunk copious amounts of Coke. Adrenaline pumped through my body. My mind bounced, distracted, and I had to push myself to focus. I had to help Lacey.

By now, she was over by the administration desk, talking to the lady working. The woman was reading her computer. Lacey had her head between her hands, and her shoulders were convulsing. In an instant, my body slowed down. I walked toward her.

"Lacey," I said softly.

She looked up, her face a waterway of tears. "I didn't listen to you."

"That doesn't matter right now." I looked at the woman. "Where is he?"

"Intensive care unit."

"Can she see him?" I asked the woman.

"Sorry, not right now."

"Do you know if he's okay?"

"Are you family?"

"I'm his girlfriend," whispered Lacey.

"I'm sorry. I can only give out information to direct family members."

I took Lacey's arm and walked her over to some chairs. "But I *should have* listened," she mumbled. Her eyes were vacant, hollow. From across the hall, Sarah gave me the thumbs-up, then pointed down the hall and mimicked smoking.

"It's okay." I touched Lacey's arm. "What good would it have done? He still would have played."

"But maybe he would have kept his head up. Or maybe he would have been more aware. Or maybe he would have just sensed something."

We sat down. "You need to focus on Burke and hang on to hope that he will get through this. You have to send him love."

She tilted her head. "I do love him, you know," she said almost wistfully. "No matter what, I love him. I can't help it." She touched my arm. "And, Indie, I know he loves me back. If he makes it to the NHL, he wants me to go with him." She paused to pick a piece of lint off her beautiful red winter jacket. "I'm not sure I want to, though."

I put my arm around her shoulders. "Believe me, I do understand your love for Burke. No matter what, you have to think positive thoughts," I said.

Suddenly, she turned and looked at me, her pupils huge. "Can you see something? Can you see if he lives?" She shook my arm. "Indie, can you see?"

Sweat poured from my forehead, and I took off my jean jacket. I wished I weren't so hot and clammy. Maybe if I closed my eyes.

I shut my eyes tightly and tried to concentrate on seeing something. But nothing appeared. No pictures. Nothing. I tried to conjure up any little fragment that would give me a clue whether Burke would live, but all I got was a blank piece of paper and nothing more.

I kept trying to see something, but nothing appeared in front of me. I remembered the vision about the black and gold jersey I had seen last fall. Maybe I had seen it and couldn't tell him because he had to go through this first. Maybe he wasn't supposed to play for the team, but do something else for them instead. Had I missed something? Maybe this was to come true, but in a different way. Were my visions sometimes just sequences? Riddles?

I really didn't understand so much of what I saw and heard and felt. Sometimes things were clear and happened exactly as they came to me. And other times, like this, or like with Nathan, it was as if I had been given a puzzle to figure out.

I took a deep breath and opened my eyes. Lacey was staring intently at me, breath drawn, desperately searching my face for a sign that I had good news.

Although I wanted to lie and tell her I'd seen Burke alive, I slowly shook my head. Lies didn't get a person anywhere. I'd learned that the hard way. "I can't see anything," I said. "I'm so sorry."

"Do you think that means something? If you can't see anything, maybe he's not going to live." Her voice bordered on hysterical. "What does it mean when you can't see something? Indie, what does that mean?"

"I don't know. I don't think I have any answers. I think Burke's future is all with Burke. It's all up to him right now. It's his choice whether he lives or not."

She grabbed my arm. "I don't want him to die. Earlier today, I told him to die and go to hell. It wasn't supposed to mean anything. Now I wish I could take my words back."

I gathered her in my arms, and her body immediately went limp. I honestly thought if I let her go, she'd turn into a puddle on the floor. I held her tightly for a few seconds. "You didn't mean to say that to him. I know you didn't."

She started to sob, and I let her cry. After a few minutes, she pulled back and wiped her face with the cuff of her coat. "But I did say those words." She shook her head. "I was just so sick and tired of him always cheating on me. I know he was with Amber before." She lifted her head and tilted it back so she was staring at the hospital ceiling, then she blew out a rush of air. After a few seconds, she looked at me. "You were right about Amber. And I knew it when you told me, but I didn't want to admit it. And I know she's not the only one. I want Burke to love *me* and only be with *me*."

"That's the way it should be."

"I don't know what to do. I love him so much, but I know he doesn't treat me right."

"We deserve better," I said.

She tilted her head and gave me a puzzled look. "Are you talking about John, too? I made that up about Amber and him to hurt you. He didn't cheat on you with her."

"Yeah, but he . . . does other things. He's not always nice to me."

"What does he do?"

I sucked in a big breath. "I dunno. He always tells me I'm stupid to be in the band. He tells me I'm a lousy singer. Stuff like that."

And he bruised my arm, too. I can't tell anyone that.

"You're a great singer." Lacey made a face. "And I bet your band is awesome." She paused. Then she wrapped her arms around her body as her eyes welled with tears. "Indie, I'm so sorry I didn't believe you."

"Lacey." Lacey's mom interrupted us, her voice breathy as if she'd been hurrying. We both looked up at the sound of her voice.

"I heard about Burke," she said. She sat on Lacey's other side.

"Mom." Lacey collapsed into her mother's arms.

"His parents are in the lobby." Mrs. Hughes helped Lacey stand. "I think he's going to be okay."

As we walked down the hospital hall, I tried to put on my jean jacket, but it got tangled behind my back. I struggled with the arms, and while I was trying not to look spastic, I walked into a chair. The clang of the chair falling to the hard tiled floor echoed off the wall.

Mrs. Hughes turned.

The last thing I wanted was someone checking to see if *I* was okay. I immediately held up my hand and said, "I'm fine." But I didn't feel fine. I was edgy and out of sorts, vibrating at some unusual frequency. Why was I feeling like this?

When we got to the lobby, I saw a distraught couple and right away figured out they were Burke's parents. They rushed toward Lacey, and Mrs. Brown hugged her tightly.

"Have you heard anything?" Lacey's words came out in a broken whisper.

"He's in surgery."

I wanted to hear more about Burke's prognosis, but someone tapped my shoulder. A low, recognizable voice said, "Indie."

I slowly turned.

"I just heard the news." John spoke quietly. "I knew you'd be here."

I stared at him, noticing his oversized pupils and the little red lines seeping into the white of his eyes. "You didn't have to come for me," I replied.

He touched my cheek, and I was instantly comforted. I tilted my head toward his fingertips.

"I wanted to," he said softly. "I knew you'd need someone to talk to."

Just seeing John standing in front of me made my eyes well with tears. I hadn't cried yet, not a drop. He put his arm around me, and I rested my head on his shoulder, liking the familiar feel of his strong body. I needed something familiar to ground me.

"You want to sit down somewhere?" he whispered.

"Sure," I whispered back.

We found a quiet bench and sat. We didn't say anything for a minute or so. So much was swirling through my mind that I needed to give it time to slow down and get in sync with my body. Why had he shown up? John reached for my hand, and I allowed the gesture because I still loved the feel of his skin against mine. It had electrified me from the first day we had connected, and it still had the same effect.

"Do you think he's going to be okay?" he finally asked. "I wasn't at the game."

I shrugged. "I dunno. Lacey asked me if I could see anything, and I couldn't."

"You tried?"

"Yeah. But nothing worked."

"How do you usually see things?"

I sighed and turned to look him square in the eyes. "My mind goes blank, and I feel as if I'm looking through a telescopic lens into a fishbowl. It's so crazy."

He squeezed my fingers. "It's not."

"She asked me to see something for her about Burke, and I couldn't get past the blankness."

"Maybe you're not supposed to see anything."

I sat back, pulled my hand from his, and slouched in the chair. Suddenly, my heart started beating at a speed that made me almost gasp. Was I feeling Burke's heart? "He's going to live," I blurted out. "I can feel his heart." I lowered my head and stared at my white-knuckled fingers, which were laced together.

"Indie," he said softly, lifting my chin with his finger and maneuvering my face until we were staring into each other's eyes. "I'm sorry I got so mad at you in the library."

"And I'm sorry I didn't tell you," I whispered.

He pressed his forehead against mine. The steam from his breath circled my face, and I stopped shivering.

"So many times I've wanted to pick up the phone just to talk." He stroked my hair. "Even for little things." He paused. "And especially"—he leaned back and ran his hand through his own hair—"when I found an old photo of my dad. You were the only one I wanted to show it to." He continued the repetitive movement of running his hand through his hair. I really wanted to put my hand over his and tell him to stop.

"You can show me now if you have it with you," I said instead. "Lacey is with Burke's family."

John leaned over onto his side and fished his wallet out of his back pocket.

"I just found it in this old box of stuff my mom had thrown in the trash." He opened his wallet and dug deep in one of the slots where cards usually went. "She still doesn't know I picked it out. I didn't mean to look in the box, but I dropped my keys in the bin outside, and when I reached in, I found the box, and something made me look in it." His words came out in one big rush.

I didn't want to see the photo because suddenly I knew exactly who I was going to see. My hand shook as he passed it to me. When I looked at it, my heart screeched to a complete stop.

I was right. And I had no idea what to do to help him.

Chapter Nineteen

"I've decided I'm going to find my dad," said John, running his hands along his thighs. "I have to. I can't stand not knowing where he is."

I couldn't speak. I didn't know how to respond. Anything I said would hurt John, and I had this weird feeling he wouldn't believe me anyway, like Lacey hadn't believed me about Burke. Maybe this was one I wasn't supposed to tell. Again, confusion bounced through my brain.

"It's time," he said. "I need to search for him. I need to do this for my mom and me."

Help me, I begged.

John's father was the man in the locket. The man with the cigar.

Was I the only one who knew he was dead?

I couldn't deal with this right now. This was all too much for me to handle. "John." I touched his arm. "Let's talk about this later. I really feel as if we should go find Lacey right now. I want to see if Burke is okay. But I do want to talk about it with you, okay?" I hoped he wouldn't notice the tremor in my voice.

John put the photo back in his wallet. "You're right," he said.

Crisis brought people out in numbers. The waiting room and halls were full of Burke's numerous, and I mean *numerous,* friends. His entire hockey team was there. They must have come after the game. No one was talking about the score, who had won the game; that news was insignificant tonight. I blew out the stale air I had been holding in my body. I wondered about death and what happened in the afterlife. John's dad was dead. Why had his mother told John he was alive? Burke was going to live; he'd escaped something horrible. Or at least I thought he had.

Trust your intuition, Indie, and what comes to you. If you do, you can help people.

Had I helped? I had called out to Burke. Perhaps I had made a difference. But then maybe not. If he died, I wouldn't have helped at all. Why did some people live and others die?

Suddenly, I felt sick to my stomach. My head seemed to spin in circles. Why did everything have to happen at once? John's dad and Burke all in one day; I couldn't deal with all of this.

I saw Sarah with a few of our school friends, and she waved to me. Even from a distance, I could see the puzzled look on her face, and I knew it was because I was with John. I was just about to go over to her when Lacey walked toward me. I left John's side and immediately went to her.

"Any news?" I asked, taking her hands in mine.

"He's in surgery. That's all they'll tell us."

"You want a tea?" I put my arms around her. "Peppermint?"

Lacey gave me a quirky but sad half smile. "I haven't had peppermint tea since you and I stopped talking." She sighed. "I'm so sorry, Indie."

"Stop," I said gently. "Don't talk about that anymore."

"You gave me the angel wings, didn't you?"

I smiled.

"Thank you."

"You need peppermint tea," I said. By now, John had come up to us. I turned to him. "I'll get you a coffee while I'm there." I felt Sarah's eyes still on me, so I glanced across the room to where she was standing. I waved, then I pretended that I was drinking. She mouthed back, "Double, double."

As I walked down the long hallway toward the hospital cafeteria, my jitters returned and my body felt unearthly, spacey. The cafeteria was quiet, and I went directly to the tea and coffee. I filled two takeout cups with hot water and picked up two packets of peppermint tea. As I was pouring the coffee, I thought about that morning at school, weeks ago, when I'd had a cup with John—how when we had touched, I'd felt such incredible sparks. I still felt those same sparks every time he got close to me, and I couldn't figure out why. He did something to me physically, drew me in somehow. Would we get back together?

Things had changed. I wasn't sure if we were right anymore.

Juggling the four cups, I walked to the counter to pay.

"Do you have a cardboard tray?" I asked.

The girl, who wore a net over her hair but was digging dirt from under her fingernails mumbled, "Yeah. Sure do."

Once I paid, I took the steaming drinks over to add some cream and sugar.

After I dropped the tea bag into the steamy water, I inhaled the peppermint smell. Suddenly, my nostrils burned, and I swear, if the hot drinks hadn't been sitting on a countertop, I would have dropped them on the floor. Cigar smoke wafted around me.

I didn't want to turn, so I kept my back to the smell.

Maybe if I stayed still, he would go away. But the cigar smell got stronger and stronger, overpowering the peppermint smell. Finally, I could hardly breathe; I coughed to try and clear my throat.

Then I heard a gurgling noise, as if someone were choking. I quickly turned to see him standing behind me.

But what I saw made me gasp. Not a word came out of my mouth. I just stared at the paring knife stuck in his throat. Blood spurted from the knife wound, soaking the front of his white T-shirt. His cigar lay smoldering on the floor.

Suddenly my mind went blank, and my vision narrowed. Through my telescopic lens, I saw *a paring knife and an apple.*

Then I was back in the cafeteria. The man grabbed his throat with his hand, the blood soaking his fingers, making him look like he was wearing red gloves.

"I know who you are," I whispered.

He tilted his head, and I detected sadness. The obvious pain in his eyes made my own limbs heavy. I felt like I were stuck in mud and couldn't move my feet. It made no sense. Had this man hurt her?

"Tell her I'm sorry," he gasped.

"For what?"

I quickly glanced around to see if anyone heard me talking. I was the only one in the cafeteria, and the cashier was sitting on her stool at the register, flipping the pages of a magazine. She didn't look up.

I turned back to see blood oozing from his throat, dripping down his neck. The sucking sound it made as it escaped was horrible, just horrible.

I must have moaned or groaned or something, because the cashier piped up and said, "Hey, lady, you okay over there?" She peered over the top of her magazine.

"I'm fine."

"Suuuuure you are." She rolled her eyes and went back to her magazine.

I had to get away from this spirit standing in front of me. I wondered if I could walk right through him. But that would mean going through the knife and blood, and I just couldn't. I sucked in a deep breath and stepped to the side. But he stepped to the side, too, blocking me from moving. So I stepped to the other side, but again he mirrored my movement and made sure he was in front of me.

"What do you want?" I was getting frustrated. "Get out of my way."

"She buried me in a hole she dug with a shovel. I hurt her, so she hurt me."

"Don't tell me any more!" The sound of my voice echoing off the walls made me look over at the cashier. She had a phone in her hand.

"Got another one escaped from the psych floor," she said, staring at me. "Come and get her before she messes the joint. Cleaner's gone for break, and I don't want to do no mopping."

Crap.

"Tell her I'm sorry," he said again. Then he disappeared.

I put my head down and left the cafeteria, walking as quickly as I could down the hallway without spilling the drinks. When I came closer to the waiting room, I stopped to lean against the wall and catch my breath.

A paring knife and an apple.

I slid down the wall.

My mom does that, John had said. *She often has a knife by her bedside.*

No! I opened my eyes and stared at the concrete blocks on the other side of the wall. Then I put my hands over my ears. "Lalalala." I rocked on my heels.

I had seen a shovel. And smelled dirt.

My body was almost convulsing; I was so overwhelmed. This was way too much to absorb.

Then I thought about Lacey and Burke and everyone in the waiting room. John included.

"Act normal, Indie. Today, just be there for your friend."

I stood, picked up the tray of drinks, and walked back to the waiting room. As I rounded the corner, I saw John still sitting with Lacey. I tried to breathe. My entire body shook and shivered, but not like it had earlier when I was jittery. This was the shakes of a person who had stood out in the snow with nothing on for much, much too long. How was I going to tell him his father was dead?

And that . . . his mother . . . had . . . killed him.

Did I know that for sure? Or was I just jumping to conclusions?

I walked back into the lobby with the drink tray and immediately went over to Lacey and John. I waved to Sarah, and she also walked over to our little group. Before taking her coffee, Sarah gave Lacey a big hug.

"I heard he is going to be okay," she said to Lacey.

"Did I miss something while I was gone?" I asked. How long had it been? I touched the side of the cardboard cups—they were still hot.

"They managed to stitch up his neck before he lost too much blood. He's already in recovery." Lacey sighed—a good, relieved sigh. "The doctors came out and said it could have been so much worse, and it's like a miracle that he's okay." She took her tea from the cardboard container. "They also said he has a torn shoulder from the fall, but that's minor. He'll probably be out for the rest of the season, but they don't think his career is over completely." She sipped her tea and looked at me. "Thanks, Indie. If he hadn't looked up just before the hit, the doctors say it could have been much worse."

Sarah gave me a little jab in the ribs.

"How will that affect his draft?" John asked, also taking his coffee.

"Pittsburgh," I blurted out. "They'll still draft him."

Lacey smiled at me and shook her head. "I've missed you, Indie."

"Me too."

Sarah sipped her coffee and made a face. "I hate crappy coffee." She glanced at her watch, then jingled her keys. "I got to head out soon," she said. "It's after midnight. You need a ride, Indie?"

I was about to say yes when John piped up and said, "I'll give her a ride."

Sarah widened her eyes and stared at me as if to say, *don't.* But I touched her arm and said, "It's okay, Sarah. I can go with John."

Before Sarah walked away, though, she turned to me and said loudly, "See you at rehearsal." Of course, her comment was more for John than it was for me.

I turned to John and said, "I'm ready when you are."

I gave Lacey a big hug before leaving. It felt great to be friends again.

As John and I walked toward his car, I glanced at him out of the corner of my eye. He seemed so jittery. Inside the hospital he had been the John I knew, but now I sensed some tension, and it made me nervous. I was still totally freaked out about his father, and I had no idea what to do with the information. I didn't want to be the one to tell him that his father was dead. I couldn't. Perhaps he would figure it out on his own, now that he was seriously searching for him. John still had some sort of huge hold on me, and I could feel myself being drawn to him again—it wasn't good. I couldn't figure it out, but it was there. Was it need? Want? What? John and I drove for a few blocks before either of us said anything. John spoke first. "I'm glad Burke is okay."

"Yeah," I said.

"He is going to be a star," continued John. "He definitely has a pro career in his future. And the guy's got great grades. Plus . . . he has the best-looking girl in the school, and he can have every other hot girl any time he wants."

My back went rigid, and I turned my head to stare out the window. Was he talking about Amber? Was he trying to hurt me on purpose? Why would he say something like that, today of all days? I mean, saying that about Lacey was okay with me. She was my friend, and she *was* the prettiest girl in the school. But Amber? My skin itched, and I gnashed my teeth together. Did he not think I was pretty, too? He'd only ever once said anything about my looks, and that was at Christmas. I opened the car window to let in some air. It flowed through my hair and around my body.

Why was I worried about something like how John feels about my looks just after such a crazy night?

Forget about it, Indie. Just forget.

John continued talking, obviously not noticing my silence or my hurt. "The guy got really lucky. He could've been paralyzed."

I helped him. I fiddled with the clasp on my purse. Life was worth living if I could help people.

"I met a guy in a wheelchair one day at Billings Bridge, and he seemed really happy," I said. "Maybe Burke would have worked in hockey in a different way, just not as a player. Or maybe he would have made a total recovery with some new research." I knew I was babbling, but I couldn't help myself.

John glanced at me, from the side of his eyes. "I was wondering," he mused, almost hemming and hawing. He paused for a beat. Then he quickly said, "If you still wanted to go to grad with me?"

My heart hummed, my blood bubbled, and my nerves tingled just like when I had first met him.

"Yes," I replied without hesitation. "I'd like that."

"Me too," he said. Then he took his gaze off the road for a second to look at me. Our eyes connected. He smiled at me, and my body thawed and felt warm and fuzzy. Then he looked back at the road but put his hand on my knee.

His touch sent shivers flying through my entire body. What was it about him that made me react so strongly? Why could he control me with such a small gesture? But then something else crept through my body like a slithering sneaky snake. I could feel his hand vibrating on my thigh. He seemed distant, jittery, overly talkative . . . and his eyes were always bloodshot. Deep down, I knew he was high; I just didn't want to admit it.

He took his hand off my thigh and casually rested it on the back of my seat, behind my neck. I felt the pad of his fingertip circling the skin on my neck, like a brush of warm air.

So much to say, but how to say it? I needed to tell him about his father and his mother. It was as if a pile of words were lodged behind a dam in my throat. I stared straight ahead. How was I going to tell him?

You have to learn when to talk and when not to talk. Some people have to figure things out for themselves. My gentle man's voice spoke to me. *You can't save people, but you can help.*

Were these words of wisdom? *I don't know what to do,* I thought.

Patience. When the time is right, you will tell him.

Tonight I had stood up and yelled at Burke, and perhaps by doing that, I had saved his life.

But I hadn't saved Nathan.

Because you didn't know how.

"You want to hang out tomorrow?" John interrupted my thoughts.

"I can't," I said. I paused for a second before I said, "I have a rehearsal with the band. They're going to let me do one song with them."

"Are you serious?" His tone was accusing again, the old John.

I turned and looked at his profile. "Yeah," I said firmly, as if his question was stupid.

He took his eyes off the road long enough for me to see the frown on his face. "So lame, Indie. Rise above that crap," he said, shaking his head.

"You've never even heard us."

"Well, don't ask me to come to your stupid performance if that's what you call it."

"I won't."

He tapped his hand on his steering wheel in obvious agitation. Then suddenly, he cranked the steering wheel and pulled the car over, skidding on the gravel on the side of the road. He grabbed my upper arm and squeezed it until I could feel his fingers digging into my skin. "I don't want you in that band."

I yanked my arm away from him. "Don't. That hurts."

He sank into his seat. "I'm sorry," he whispered. He hung his head. "It's just this thing with my dad is eating me up inside."

I wanted to hug him, tell him everything was going to be okay, that I would help him through the stuff with his dad. Instead, I said very calmly, "It's not an excuse, John."

He glanced at me and in a hushed tone said, "I didn't hurt you, Indie. I barely touched you."

"I want to go home."

The car lurched forward as John pulled away from the curb, going well over the speed limit. I gripped the door handle and stared straight ahead. Why had I agreed to ride with him? He pulled into my driveway, and when I went to get out of the car, he tenderly put his hand on mine. I turned and stared directly in his eyes.

"I'm sorry, Indie," he said. "Would you help me find my dad?"

"John, I don't know how to tell you this, but I think your dad is gone." The words came out of my mouth before I realized what I had said. If the truth be known, at that moment in time, I would have done anything to take them back. The pain etched on John's face was unbearable, more than I could handle. I looked down at my hands, letting my hair fall in front of my face. My heart beat through my skin, and it ached. His pain seeped into every pore in my body.

"Dead?" he asked.

I nodded.

John smacked his hands against the car steering wheel over and over and over. He cursed and yelled. I just watched quietly. Finally, after more than a minute of him ranting, I put my hand on his. His body stilled, and he curled over the steering wheel, sobs racking his body. "I'm like him," he said. "I hurt you tonight, just like he hurt my mom."

I didn't speak. I didn't want to tell him it was okay, because it wasn't. I moved beside him and put my arm around his shoulders and rested my cheek against his arm. I let him cry until he had no more tears to cry. Then he turned and took me in his arms and hugged me. I hugged him back. When we pulled apart, he lifted my chin and looked me in the eyes. "How did he die?" he whispered.

Without thinking of my words, I replied, "That's something you should ask your mom."

Chapter Twenty

Roses bloomed, and their sweet smell lingered in the air. Nathan splashed around in a huge lake, wearing a bright red life jacket. "Look at me, Indie," he yelled. "I can swim." A lady in a red coat skated across the lake, and it turned to ice, and as she skated, Nathan played his violin, the high notes ringing. He was now standing on the ice but still wearing his life jacket. "You'll be great at your concert," he said. The lady made a perfect hockey stop, and suddenly she became Burke in a black and gold Pittsburgh Penguins jersey. "Thanks, Indie. You saved my life." He flashed his perfect smile, and as he skated away, he turned into a woman wearing a blue winter coat and a gray and blue scarf, walking, holding a child's hand. Nathan still played his violin.

❖ ❖ ❖

My alarm buzzed. I reached over and turned it off, glancing at the time. I had an hour to get ready. I sat up and shook my head. What a weird dream. So muddled and full of characters. Feeling my movement, Cedar sat up, licked her paw, and glared at me.

"Sorry," I said.

Nathan had come to me to tell me he was going to be with me in spirit. That was so Nathan. He remembered about the concert.

"Thanks, Nathan," I said.

"I told you I'd come," he replied.

With only an hour to get ready and drive to the animal shelter, I had to forget about my dream. Today was the big debut of the Bad Girls, and I had to shower, do my hair, and rehearse my song. I was going early to set up with the girls then I would watch while they did four songs. I was playing the final song.

"Dad and I are coming to watch," said Mom at breakfast. "Do you need a ride?"

"Nope." I swigged some orange juice and put my glass in the dishwasher. "Lacey is going to drive me."

"I'm so glad you girls are friends again."

I smiled. "Me too." I kissed my mother's cheek just as I heard Lacey honking. Then I picked up my guitar case and headed outside.

As soon as I got in the car, I noticed that Lacey had her silver necklace on. I had given it back, untangled, and she had readily accepted. I think she'd worn it every day since. We didn't talk until she had backed out of the driveway and was driving forward. Lacey hated backing up. When we were on road she asked, "Is John coming today?"

I laughed. "Doubtful."

"You guys break up for good? I saw you talking at school."

I nodded. "Yup. We're done. What about you and Burke?"

"Yeah, we're done, too. I wasn't going to break up with him until he was better, but I just got accepted to Queens, and I've been recruited to play volleyball there, too."

"That's awesome," I said. "What did Burke say?"

"He wasn't too happy and thought I'd be better off being his 'hockey girlfriend.' I think we both need a clean break. A fresh start. Maybe one day we'll get back together. Who knows? You think John and you will ever get back on track?"

"He's got a lot to work on, and so do I. Tell me more about Queens."

"I'm pretty stoked. We're going for a school visit next week. I'm so excited. What are your plans for next year?" she asked.

For a few seconds, I glanced out the window, at the trees whizzing by me. They were kind of like my life; everything just whizzing by without any direction in mind. Soon the trees would have leaves, and the lilacs would bloom, and the colorful tulips would brighten the world. And what would I do?

I glanced at Lacey and shrugged. "I have no idea. Get a job, live in the Glebe. Travel. Or . . ." I turned the radio up and made my hand into a pretend microphone and sang along with the pop song that was blasting through the speakers. Lacey started laughing, and I continued singing. When the song ended, seconds later, I said, "I could always star in a rock band."

"Whatever you do, you'll be awesome," said Lacey. "Don't give up on who you are," she said. Then she held up her hand. "Promise."

I gently slapped her hand. "Promise."

But could I *really* promise that? I had no idea how to be who I was. Could I use my visions to actually help people every day? So far everything I'd done had been a fluke.

"I'm excited to hear you sing," said Lacey, interrupting my thoughts.

My stomach did a somersault. "I'm so nervous," I said.

"You'll be great," said Lacey.

More than a hundred people showed up to the fund-raiser, and I sat at the back listening to the girls play. They sounded awesome—like, really awesome. Somehow, they had raised enough money to buy an incredibly good microphone, and Sarah's raspy rock voice shook the place. All the songs were upbeat and more or less kid-friendly. There were silent auction items set up on tables, and people milled about, looking at everything while listening to the music. Little kids danced in front of the stage, and it was so cute to watch.

I was watching the band so intently that I didn't hear the woman beside me until she said, "Buddy, no."

I looked down to see the cutest little dog, jumping in front of me, tongue hanging out, tail wagging. The woman pulled on his leash. "Sorry," she said. "I just got him from the shelter yesterday."

I looked at the dog and smiled. He was definitely the same dog I'd seen that day in Denny's. I immediately got down on one knee and gave the dog a big hug. "I know who you are, and you are soooo cute." He licked my cheek, and I grinned. His eyes weren't sad anymore; he had a home.

The woman walked away, Buddy straining on the leash, panting, happy to be alive, just as Sarah finished singing the fourth song. When the last chord was played, she motioned for me to come up on the small stage with them.

"Break a leg," whispered Lacey.

Butterflies swarmed my stomach. Then I remembered Nathan telling me I was like a butterfly, free to fly. I approached the stage and slipped my guitar over my shoulder, letting it hang comfortably in front of me. When I looked out, I saw my mom and dad, Brian and Lacey. No John.

We played the intro, then I stepped up to the microphone and started singing. The words flowed out of my mouth. At first I did what I always did with this song—I sang to John. But about halfway through, I suddenly realized the words weren't for him anymore. They were for me. I was the breath.

I needed to breathe for me, not for him.

I was put on the earth and given breath for a reason. I had the ability to make a difference, even if I didn't know what that difference was yet.

Soon, said my soothing man's voice. *Soon you will find out.*

About the Authors

Tara Taylor is an internationally known intuitive counselor, spiritual teacher, and motivational speaker. She has been featured in newspapers and on radio and television, and has helped many people through her workshops, seminars, and public speaking. Tara counsels people of all ages and guides professional intuitives and children with clairvoyant gifts, as well as friends and family who need help understanding these special children. She is president and CEO of Whitelight Wellness, as well as Sacred Space, a wellness center located in western Canada, and co-founder of the Just Say Yes seminars. Tara attended St. Paul's University, studying world religions, theology, and pastoral counseling. She is also an Integrated Energy Therapy® Master/Instructor, and a Usui/Tibetan Reiki master. Tara is one of the contributing authors to the Amazon bestseller *Manifest Success: The Ultimate Guide to Creating the Life of Your Dreams.*

Visit: www.tarataylor.ca and www.throughindigoseyes.com

Lorna Schultz Nicholson has been a television co-host and reporter, radio host and reporter, community theater actor, fitness coordinator, and rowing coach. Now she is a full-time writer who has published both fiction and nonfiction. Her list includes children's picture books, middle grade readers, young adult fiction, and nonfiction sports books for all ages. She has written more than 20 award-winning books, including *Roughing* (Lorimer, 2004) and *Northern Star* (Lorimer, 2006). Her books have been nominated for the Red Cedar Award, the Golden Eagle Award, and the Diamond Willow Award. Her nonfiction 2010 Olympic book, *Home Ice* (Fenn, 2009), was on the *Globe and Mail* bestseller list for many months and was a top-selling sports book during the 2010 Olympics in Vancouver. Lorna divides her time between Calgary and Penticton, where she and her husband share their homes with their crazy golden retriever, Snowball, and whiny bichon–shih tzu, Molly.

Visit: www.lornaschultznicholson.com and www.through indigoseyes.com.

Acknowledgments

From Tara

First, I want to thank the Divine and all the souls, living and crossed over, that have come in and out of my life: each one of you is a blessing and a great teacher. I also want to express my gratitude to my clients over the years; you have allowed me to live my passion to help serve in this world. My appreciation goes out to Hay House, the design team and the fabulous editorial team. A special thank you to Sally Mason for your hard work and for sharing your love for the Great White North, Laura Koch for your warm welcome when I arrived in New York, and my gratitude and much love to Patty Gift for being the wonderful light that you are.

I am extremely grateful to my wonderful parents, whom I love with every part of my being; you have taught me to be strong no matter what comes our way in life, to forgive always, and that love conquers all. Thank you to my big brother, who has always tried to protect and support me; Pat Armstrong, my earth angel who took me under her wing, I love you big; and my dear friend Peggy McColl, whom I love and adore, and who inspires me on a daily basis. Thank you, Peg, for believing in me and for all of your hard work. My love and gratitude go to Angie, Erin, Natty, Jen, Megan, Wild D, Lee Ann, Krystal, Shauna, and Emily for your support over the years.

To the love of my life, Jeff, thank you for all of the support, your unconditional love, and keeping me grounded when I need it the most. And a special thank-you to Tom and Bev for raising such a wonderful son and for the encouragement you have given me.

My mentor, Cindy, not a day goes by that you do not make your presence known to me and still help me grow and work on strengthening my intuition from the other side. You always gave me the kick in the pants when I needed it, and you still do. I love you, my friend.

As I come to the ending of acknowledgments, I well up with tears of gratitude for my co-author, Lorna. It feels like yesterday when you opened your arms, heart, and home to me. It felt like we had known each other forever (many lifetimes, that's for sure). You, Bob, and your wonderful children, Mandi, MJ, and Grant, have made Calgary home for me when I was alone in a new city. I am forever grateful for those moments of love and laughter with you and the kids as you made me feel like a part of your family; shortly afterward we found out that the Divine had quite the plan for us. I am honored to work with such an amazing and talented writer and best of all work alongside a best friend. I could not think of anyone else I would rather share this whole experience with besides you. You are truly one of the most beautiful souls I have ever met. I love you beyond words, my friend. My heart and loyalty always!

Finally, to all of the readers, my prayer is that this series inspires you to explore and embrace your own intuition.

From Lorna

My first thanks, and my biggest thanks, is to Tara Taylor. Tara graciously opened the door to her past and allowed me in. Without any hesitation, she told me story after story and provided me with numerous old photos that helped me pluck away at the keyboard to create Indigo. Tara was always available to talk, but she also knew when I needed to lock myself in a room to write. Sometimes it would take days, even weeks, before I resurfaced, and Tara was always patient. Tara is a gifted intuitive who is committed to helping others understand their own intuitions. She is lovely and generous and kind. I'm extremely honored that she chose me to write the novel based on her life. Even if it means (and this is the truth) that I'm now talking to dead people! How crazy is that?

I am grateful for the Hay House editorial team: Patty Gift, Sally Mason, and Laura Koch. Their enthusiasm for this project was genuine and so refreshing. Their brilliant insight and professionalism definitely made for a better book. And a big thanks to the Hay House design team for creating such a marketable package. I would also like to thank Peggy McColl for her help in getting the deal signed.

What would a writer be without a writers group? Patty, Jackie, Kath, Andrea, and Joan are the best group of women a girl could ask for. Even though we now live all over Canada and the U.S., we are still connected because we share that writer's soul. I appreciate these women for their expertise on the art of writing, their advice about the publishing business, but most of all their friendship and silly laughter.

And I must, must thank my family. Big sister, Brenda, although you didn't actually work on this novel with me, you read some of my early works, when my dream was still a dream, and you were never thanked properly. Your encouragement still means a lot to me. My daughters, Mandi and Marijean, who read and critiqued the novel in its infant stages and provided me with invaluable teenage lingo and tips. And to my son, Grant, who lived with me during the creative process. I do tend to serve a lot of leftovers when in creation mode.

Sorry, bud. And to my husband of almost 24 years, Bob, (yes, he gets the same leftovers), I owe huge gratitude. He gives me the space I need to write, sometimes rubs my shoulders, sometimes brings me coffee, and never grumbles when I jump out of bed at 3:00 in the morning because I suddenly have an idea that I announce to him before I run to my computer.

And to you, lovely reader, thank you for reading the words I write.

Questions and Answers

Through Indigo's Eyes, while a work of fiction, is loosely based on the life of intuitive Tara Taylor. To further clarify some of the situations in the book, the writer of the novel has asked Tara Taylor to answer questions about the character of Indie.

Lorna. Indie hears and sees things. And she also feels things. What does all this mean?

Tara. There are four different ways to work with your intuitive gifts or, as I call them, abilities. I like the word *abilities* better, as to me *gifted* is a catchphrase and means special. I am human just like you are, but I was born a bit different, as we all are, which makes every individual special. As an intuitive, I was born with the ability to see and hear. Everyone is born with at least one of the abilities. Over the years, I have worked hard at developing my other abilities so that I can be a professional intuitive. In the book, Indie does work with all four abilities, and we purposely had her do this so you have examples of each of these. But she is more apt to see and hear.

Just to clarify for you, here are the different abilities that you can be born with:

Clairvoyance—This is the intuition that allows you to "see" messages, either by physically seeing or through snapshots or mental pictures. Sometimes a person who does see visions is also known as a "seer." Edgar Cayce in the book was a seer. My great-grandmother, whom Indie talks about, was also a seer. And I'm a seer. In the book, there are many examples of how Indie sees things, as this is her strongest ability. Sometimes she sees scenes and sometimes just images. For example, Indie has a vision of Burke and Amber, and then at a completely different time, she sees just a red heart. One vision is quite specific, whereas the other is just an image that she has to decode. Part of my job as an intuitive is to allow all visions to come into my mind, then try to figure out how they are applicable.

Clairaudience—This is the intuition that allows one to "hear" a message or an answer. In the book, Indie hears the word *Curtis* and knows something has happened to her cousin. She also hears the thumping of the heart when the woman is having a heart attack. And she hears the voice telling her that there was a lady in the car. There are many situations in the book where Indie hears.

Clairsentience—This is the intuition that allows one to "feel" an answer. With this one, you can feel what another person is going through to help you be intuitive. Indie often feels a sharp pain in her chest or heart when someone around her is in emotional pain. This doesn't mean they physically have a bad heart, but perhaps that they have a hurting heart. She also has a pain with the woman who has a heart attack but it is accompanied by the thumping of the heart. The locket is hot and burns Indie's skin when she picks it up, giving her intuition that something is wrong regarding the locket and John's mother, who owns it. And she feels the seat being kicked when she is sitting with Nathan, and that is a feeling that he is going to be pushed. Again, there are many situations in the book where Indie feels.

Claircognizance—This is the intuition that allows you to have that "knowingness." This could mean that you know something is going to happen, even though you don't have proof. Indie knows John has something or is going to have something with Amber, even though she has no proof. She also knows Lacey is going to be upset and blame her, and that is why she doesn't want to tell her anything. This is probably the ability Indie possesses that is the least developed in the book.

Okay, so to further explain all of this, I want you to think of a volume dial with frequency. On that dial, I was born at a ten, and anyone who has one of the intuitive abilities will be born at a five. The only reason I was born with more than one is because I tend to be hypersensitive. That is what Dr. Z picked up on in the book.

Just for fun, read through these categories and then for the next few days or weeks, pay attention to what you do and how you speak about things. This can give you a clue as to which ability comes most natually to you. For example, when I'm trying to make a point with someone, I tend to always say, "Do you see what I mean?" I use the word *see* to make my point, because I am clairvoyant. Someone else may have a similar experience and say, "Do you hear what I'm saying?" because they have clairaudience. Or someone else may say, "Do you have any feelings regarding this issue?" because they are clairsentient. And for the last one, you might be the one who says, "Do you know what I mean?" Of course this indicates that you might have claircognizance.

L. Why are Indie's visions stronger when she touches things?

T. When I was young, I wasn't really comfortable enough to trust what I was seeing. So by touching something, I would engage another ability so the information would be stronger. As you become more in tune with your ability and work with it, you learn to trust what is coming to you without questioning. I didn't trust when I was Indie's age, so I needed to use more than one ability at a time. My mentor (you will learn about her in the second book) taught me how to best use my abilities and how to work with each individual ability and how to use them one at a time, depending on the situation.

L. What is the pulsing feeling Indie gets in her brow before some of her visions?

T. The pulsing is what is called the third eye. It's when an intuitive sees something. The Eastern world talks about the third eye as a chakra, and this chakra allows an intuitive like me to see and predict future events or to go back into the past. When this pulsing happens, I feel as if someone is pressing a finger in between my eyebrows. If you want to understand the feeling, take your thumb and push on the space between your eyebrows. For me it is a heavy feeling that makes my head pulse. When this happens, something opens up and I often see snapshots or movies in my head. I like to say that the third eye is the gateway to clearly seeing events.

L. Why did Indie get ulcers when she was little?

T. Indie wasn't born with the ability of clairsentience. So, as a kid, I would see and hear like Indie, but because clairsentience wasn't my first ability, I didn't know how to use it. I absorbed so much energy that it added up in my body and couldn't be released. My body had to do something with the energy and it came out in sickness. Pent-up emotions can cause a body to be sick. Illnesses such as colds, flus, strep throat, even shingles or anything that is reccurring, are often caused by unreleased emotions. For me, it was ulcers. Also, because I was so shy and withdrawn, this caused me to let energy stay inside my body. I didn't understand that I was supposed to let it go. I had funny feelings, but I didn't recognize these feelings, so I basically made myself sick by holding the feelings inside.

Over the years I have learned to protect myself. For example, in the morning when I'm in the shower, I let the water run over me, and I close my eyes and allow myself to see a swirl of white light. To give you a mental picture of this, I often see this white light as soft-serve ice cream. I always choose something pleasant! I love the way soft-serve vanilla ice cream twists around from the bottom of the cone to the top to make that perfect swirl. I let that white swirl circle my body, starting at the top of my head and ending at the bottom of my feet. Once I am covered, I say to myself, "I now surround myself with white light." And I actually visualize this white swirl covering my body and bathing me in white light. Another mental picture I sometimes use is a white bubble. I go through the same process of having it completely cover me and again I say, "I now surround myself with white light."

You will need to figure out what kind of white light works for you. We all need this white light because people are either givers or takers of energy, and it is important to be balanced so we're not taking on their stuff and giving. Protection helps us stay balanced and healthy. I find that when I do this in the shower every morning, I feel protected. But—and this is important—this protection usually only lasts one day, so I do have to protect myself every morning.

L. How do Indie and Edgar Cayce relate?

T. They're both seers—or what they called an intuitive in Cayce's day was a visionary/channeler.

Also both Cayce and Indie were *born* as seers; they didn't have a near-death experience that created their intuitive abilities. Some people develop their abilities after such a life-changing experience. In the movie *Hereafter*, with Matt Damon, he has a near-death experience and, honestly, there is a lot of truth behind that movie. I loved it! Someone did their homework. But to go back to Edgar Cayce and Indie, they were born with the abilities.

L. Indie talks to her spirit guide throughout the book. Who is this person?

T. Stay tuned for the next book. Okay, I will give you a little info. We all have a divine team. Think of it this way: we have our own private entourage who looks out for us, even when we're in the shower. LOL. We are never alone. I don't want to scare you, because these energies are around you to help you achieve what you are on earth to do. Your spirit guide is the leader of the pack. In the second book, you will find out a lot more about Indie's spirit guide, who is also my spirit guide.

L. Indie wants to die but is told she must follow her life's purpose. Why is that?

T. We're all here for a reason, and there is no such thing as a coincidence. During our time on earth, our soul needs to grow, and that's why we are here. Some people refuse to let their soul grow because of fear and fixed belief. What you're meant to do on the earth is your life purpose, and it can be anything, from being a good friend or daughter to being a doctor. Suicide is never the right option, because most people don't realize that when we take our own life, it's almost as if we are ending a contract early, and we still have to finish the contract. It's like handing in an essay that is half done. When we hurt ourselves like that, we may go directly through the light and to the afterlife, but we aren't allowed to stay there for very long. We are sent right back to earth and into the same situation with different parents and perhaps a different city, but that soul will experience the same issue, only that next time it might be worse. So once again, I will tell you, suicide is not an option ever, and if you ever think of doing it, get support, reach out to others and your divine team, as they will help you. Like Indie, I've been there. Do not think you are alone. I am a living example of "it will all work out." Believe me, there is always a light at the end of the tunnel.

L. Indie talks about "vibrating at a different frequency than most people." What does she mean by this?

T. When we talk about vibrating at a higher level, it just means that Indie's (and my) consciousness is more in tune with the other side. We're all energy, and if we plugged in just one body, it would light up an entire city. We are static and electricity. That is what makes us vibrate. We're like a heartbeat, and we are constantly moving.

L. Why is Indie able to sleep for 17 hours straight?

T. Because she's a teenager. LOL. But there are other reasons. Indie is so drained energetically and emotionally that she sometimes goes into a comatose state and just sleeps for hours. I was like that as a teenager. Plus, Indie is not protecting her energy and is allowing it to be depleted, and sleeping allows our bodies to reenergize.

L. Why does Indie smoke?

T. First things first, smoking is not good for you and hurts the body so DON'T SMOKE. Indie smokes, and yes, I smoked when I was Indie's age, because smoking gave me a chance to meet people and I thought it would make me feel normal, but it just made me feel worse. This goes back to not being protected. With no protection, I felt the need to add something to my body to make me feel numb and make me stop feeling everybody's emotions. Toxins make your body feel numb.

L. Why does Halloween have such a strong effect on Indie? And Christmas? They are totally different reactions.

T. In this world, we get excited for celebrations, and energies are really high or low during festivities. Intuitives are sensitive to this energy. Christmas is about giving, so it raises vibrations, and this gets Indie super excited because she loves to give, so it fuels her energy. Halloween focuses on fear, scary costumes, etc., and this drops her energy to fear level, so she is confused. She likes Halloween because it is fun, but what she doesn't like about it is that people are focused on things that frighten them. She is only low energy on Halloween Eve because the curtain between here and the other side becomes thinner. On this night, people have more experiences with the other side. Sometimes people take that and spin it to be fearful. Now, that I'm older and wiser (ha ha), it's not like a horror movie for me, because again, I know how to protect myself and know there is nothing to be afraid of.

Becoming Indigo

Chapter One

July 1998

The sound of water running woke me up.

Tangled, sweaty hair was stuck to my face, so I pushed it away. Who'd left the tap running? This was crazy. I needed sleep—big time. Light from the outside streetlight shone through the open window, and I covered my eyes for a second. We definitely needed a curtain on that window, but more than that, we needed air-conditioning or a fan. I pulled my T-shirt away from my body, hoping that would cool me off a bit.

What time was it, anyway?

The red lights on my clock radio said 4:30 A.M. I groaned; I had to work at nine. I rolled out of bed and stepped over shirts and pants and high-heeled shoes to get to the kitchen. Water was flowing full blast from the tap, and it sounded like it was splashing against the metal sink and onto the kitchen counters. In the dark, I stumbled to the sink and quickly shut the tap off. Then I stood there for a second before I decided I needed to turn the cold water back on because I was so parched that I had a drink. I took the one clean glass from the cupboard, filled it up, and gulped the water down. Then I put the glass in the sink with the other, now wet, dirty dishes. Sarah was supposed to do them—it was her turn—but she must have forgotten or gotten too busy. Between the three of us, they did manage to get done at least a few times a week.

I would do them in the morning before I left for my crappy job. Just thinking of another day at work almost made me puke. I leaned my butt against the kitchen counter and stood for a few minutes listening to the white noise: the refrigerator humming, the kitchen clock ticking, the gentle buzzing of night life. The sounds all blended and made me feel as if I were listening to a soft ballad. White noise had a calming effect on me. Too bad an air-conditioner couldn't be added to the band. It would fit right in. I pulled at my nightshirt again, to get it off my skin and cool me down.

Then I heard a door slam.

I jumped at the sound. My heart picked up its pace, and all my senses kicked into high gear. Was it the front door? Was someone coming into our apartment?

I had to stay quiet. I sucked in a deep breath, held the air in my lungs, and stood ramrod straight.

We had all gone to bed around midnight, so I knew Sarah and Natalie were asleep. Unless they had gone out for a smoke . . . but . . . in the middle of the night? And they wouldn't slam the door coming back in, and there certainly was no wind to push it shut. I grabbed a frying pan from the sink and tuned my hearing toward where I thought the sound had come from, which was the front door.

But I only heard white noise. No creaking. No footsteps. No anything. Just white noise and my own breath, which was now coming out in staggered rasps because I had held it in for too long. I lowered the arm holding the pan, letting my shoulders sag and consciously slowing my breathing, allowing it to return to normal.

I stayed in the kitchen for a few more minutes, leaning against the counter, waiting, listening for another slam, and when I was absolutely positive that I had imagined the noise, I knew I had to go back to bed. With the frying pan still in my hand, I tiptoed across the linoleum floor.

No matter how much things had changed since high school, I still felt like I had some weird disorder. I really wasn't normal. Was I being told something? Was I being warned? Did we need to buy a deadbolt for our door? Was that what this was all about?

Or was I just imagining everything?

This is not your imagination. His voice spoke in my head; he always came to soothe me and reassure me that these abilities I had to see and hear and feel were okay.

"Really?" I whispered. "Then why am I hearing noises?"

Once I had scanned the hallway and found it empty, I padded down the hall and back to my bedroom. "It was nothing. Nothing at all," I whispered to myself.

The noises had to be all in my head, because there was obviously no one in the apartment but the three of us. After placing the frying pan on the floor beside my bed, I quietly lay down on my back and stared wide-eyed into space. I tried to suck in some air, but it was so stagnant that I felt I was being suffocated with a pillow over my face. Again, I pinched my T-shirt away from my body, flapping it back and forth. The sticky, humid air hung around the apartment like an unwanted guest. When a heat wave hit Ottawa in the summer months, the air seeped with moisture, air conditioners ran full tilt, and everyone across the entire city complained. Newspaper headlines shouted it out in big bold black letters, NO LETUP IN SIGHT!

The television news coverage talked nonstop about how hot it was and where the warm front was coming from and how the moisture was building. Then they would tell old people to stay inside and parents to not let their little ones out. Find indoor activities, they would recommend. Pools and recreation centers were jammed to capacity, as were the lake beaches in the Ottawa Valley, because people didn't listen to the news reporters when there was a beach in sight. Businesspeople literally ran from their cars to the shelter of their air-conditioned buildings.

As I lay on my sheet, I wished I could jump in a lake or a fountain or take shelter in a deep freeze somewhere. Or at least be in an air-conditioned apartment. But no, I had to be in a hot, stuffy room, awake in the middle of the night, with too many thoughts blasting through my brain.

I would *have to* buy a deadbolt tomorrow.

With that thought solved, my mind started bouncing, thinking about other things, like my life. What the heck was I going to do? This thought seemed to appear all the time, and it made me uncomfortable. Sure, I'd moved out of my parents' house and was living in an old, run-down apartment in the Glebe, and it was fun because it was summer.

But . . . then what?

I couldn't—I wouldn't—stay at my job for any longer than I had to. I hated it more than I had hated anything in my life. For now, it paid the rent, but that was all it was good for. I needed to find another job, and I needed to figure out what I wanted to do. So many kids my age knew exactly what university or college to go to. After my split with John, that unrealistic dream of living in England (yes, it was *totally* unrealistic, I realized now) was gone, and I had nothing. Nothing. I hadn't applied to any universities because I had no idea what courses to enroll in.

John. My chest still constricted when I thought of what we'd had and how close we'd been, or how close I thought we'd been. I hadn't dated anyone since him, and I figured it was better to live a carefree single summer life, or at least that's what Sarah had convinced me to do. Our apartment motto was "Girls Just Want to Have Fun."

You have unfinished business with him.

"I know," I whispered.

Yeah. And you never told him how his father died. And you know how it happened.

"Stop," I whispered to myself. I squeezed my eyes shut to block out the mean voice that spoke to me.

Forget John, forget what you saw. He will find out some other way. And forget the voices.

I needed sleep.

If a girl wanted to have fun, she had to have money, so she had to work, which meant she needed to sleep.

Slam!

My eyes popped open, and I stared at the stucco ceiling that was supposed to be white but was really stained yellow. I didn't move a muscle. I just lay there, arms by my sides, listening.

Through the white noise, I thought I could hear the faint sound of someone singing a mournful lullaby.

Sadness seeped through my veins. My head pounded, right at the temples. I wanted a pain reliever to make the throbbing stop. But I couldn't move. Not even to put my hand down to reach for the frying pan. But I did know it was there. I did.

The old brick apartment building we lived in was constructed in the early 1900s and was probably once some rich family's residence. The landlord had converted it into apartments, adding kitchens to a few rooms. We were up on the third floor, and there were three other tenants. I knew the place came with noises, but this sounded different, like nothing I had heard before. It wasn't footsteps from the middle-aged Southern woman who practiced her clogging in the morning because she worked at night as a nurse, or the screeching sound of the man playing his accordion during the week because he was a banker by day and in a polka band on the weekend, or the blaring television of the elderly man across the hall who wore a hearing aid. No, this was definitely different. The mournful sound made my throat catch, and I gasped.

A wash of cold air circled my body, and my skin erupted in goose bumps, which was totally nuts. You didn't shiver in a heat wave unless you were dehydrated and ill. I didn't cross my arms over my chest because I didn't dare move.

The wailing stopped.

Slam, slam, slam, slam . . .

My entire body tensed. I felt as if I were being watched by someone. I touched the frying pan on the floor.

Was I being watched? I grabbed my top sheet, which I had thrown onto the floor, and wrapped it around me. The cotton stuck to my skin.

Then the slamming just stopped.

And I could hear insects buzzing outside.

Hot air once again bathed my skin, and I felt clammy and gooey and gross and disgusting. My hair stuck to my cheeks. My T-shirt stuck to my body. My skin stuck to the sheets.

Clutching my top sheet in my fists, I rolled over and closed my eyes.

✤ ✤ ✤

"Who left the tap on last night?" I asked when I entered the kitchen a few hours later, feeling like a bag of trash.

Natalie took one look at me and started laughing. Then she took a clean mug from the drying rack and filled it with coffee. "Lahrd Jesus, as my grandma would say. You need this 'ere cuppa."

I took the steaming mug of coffee and wrapped my hands around it. "Thanks."

Natalie was Sarah's friend from Newfoundland. Why I was surrounded by Newfoundlanders, I wasn't sure, but Natalie was nothing like John. Bright, bubbly, and caring, she took everything in stride, never judged, and never talked like she knew everything. And she had the cutest accent, which made Sarah and me howl in laughter, especially when she mimicked her grandmother.

All in all, she had been a well-packaged gift, complete with a ribbon and bow. Natalie had arrived in Ottawa at the perfect time. When Sarah and I made the definite decision to move out from under our parents' roofs, we scoured newspapers daily and finally found an apartment in the Glebe, but we needed another roommate to help pay the bills. At first I was a bit unsure about the apartment, because it was an old building and every time I walked into it, my body got hot and felt a bit weird. But it was cheap, and the utilities and cable were included. But Sarah convinced me it was the best we could do and was a "rocking good deal" if we had three people. Minimum-wage jobs sucked and created limitations on what kind of apartment we could afford.

Sarah and I felt we'd hit the lotto when Natalie showed up and jumped in headfirst, paying her first and last months' rent no problem. It took her all of one afternoon to find a job.

"What are you talking about the tap for?" Sarah looked worse than I did. Her red hair had turned into a mass of curls in the humidity, and the sweat glistening on her face just made her freckles blotch together. Of course, the beer she had drunk last night probably didn't help how she looked and felt. And, really, with Sarah, a lot could be chalked up to the fact that she was *not* a morning person.

Unlike Natalie, who was an anytime-of-the-day person. Her dark, almost black, short hair looked like she had styled it when really she had just slept on it. I honestly would have cut my hair exactly the same way if it would have looked like that. But mine would be everywhere and a disaster, and hers just suited her high cheekbones and sculpted face. Built like a wafer, with a backbone like a ruler, Natalie stood at around five foot nine, which in my world was really tall. I think she might have been the most striking girl I'd ever met, with her round dark eyes, full lips, thin eyebrows, and pale skin. Childhood storybooks, the fairy-tale ones, always had a queen, and to me Natalie looked like some kind of stately queen—but one of the nice ones, not the mean one from *Snow White.* As thin and majestic as she was, she had this huge laugh that came from the bottom of her stomach, and generosity and kindness oozed from her pores.

"Someone left the tap on," I said. "I had to get up in the middle of the night and turn it off." I sipped my coffee.

"Wasn't me," barked Sarah. "Holy crap." She picked up a newspaper and waved it in front of her face.

"I'll pick up a fan at Zellers today after work," I said.

"Maybe I left it on," said Natalie, shrugging her bony shoulders. "I don't think so. But maybe." She paused. "But this 'ere building is so old there could be plumbing problems."

"It doesn't matter," I said. "It's off now." I paused but only for a second. "I was thinking of buying some sort of deadbolt, too."

"Why?" Sarah scrunched up her face when she looked at me. "The stairs are so creaky it's not like anyone could come upstairs without us hearing. And if we hear them, we call the cops, then bang them over the head with something."

"A frying pan," I said. I thought about the frying pan that was still in my room.

"That would work," replied Sarah. "I've got a baseball bat in my room just in case."

I mimicked whacking someone to lighten the conversation, even though my brain was bursting inside just thinking about Sarah's creaking comment. I had only heard slamming. Sarah was right—if someone came up the stairs, there would be creaking.

Natalie laughed at my antics.

Sarah laughed, too, but suddenly she just stopped, eyed me, and pointed. "Are you nervous about something?

"Nah," I replied, trying to sound flippant.

Sarah narrowed her eyes until they were slits. "Do you know something we don't?" Then she turned to Natalie. "You probably don't know this, but Indie has this weird thing going on. She can actually see things before they happen. It is *soooo cool* . . . but also kind of creepy."

"Wow," said Natalie. She looked at me with wide eyes. "I had no idea. That does sound . . . interesting." She stared at me, full of curiosity, like I was someone she had never met before, someone who had three heads or came from some distant planet. This was not a conversation I wanted to have right now because, really, I just wanted to crawl in a hole.

Sarah stood up and slung her arm around me. "She was going to find out sooner or later. Aren't you glad it's out?"

"I got to get ready for work," I said quickly.

"Are you like the gal on *Sabrina, the Teenage Witch*?" Natalie's eyes were bulging out of her head.

"Girl, you are too funny," Sarah said to Natalie. "If that's the case, we need a big fat black cat. Hey, let's go to the Royal Oak tonight. It's Saturday night—it will be hopping for sure."

"I'd be up for that," I answered. Thankfully, Sarah changed conversations like she changed clothes.

"Sounds good to me, too," said Natalie. "I'm finished with work at six."

"I hate my job!" Sarah tossed her coffee down the sink. "I don't want to go to work today. I want to go to Britannia Bay and float in cold water all day."

"Trade yah," I said.

Sarah and Natalie both looked at each other, then they looked at me, shook their heads, and in unison said, "No. Way."

✤ ✤ ✤

I caught the bus and, although normally I hated the constant lurching, this morning I was grateful for the air-conditioning. The driver had it on full blast. I stared out the window at the sky, trying to find the sun, but the thick haze wasn't allowing it to shine to its fullest, at least not yet. It would have to rain soon. Soon, that's what the news kept saying, perhaps by the weekend. Suddenly, I saw in big letters, written in the sky, the word *Monday*.

Okay, I thought. *It is going to rain on Monday.* Of course, because Monday was a day off for me. At least I would have Sunday to go to the beach and lounge in the water to get out of the heat.

The bus lumbered to a stop, and as soon I stepped off, I went from being cool to being zapped of energy by wet air. I trudged across the street to the Victoria Park Suites, a run-down motel that had kitchenettes in every room. It was two floors, and guests entered the rooms from the outside. Some guests stayed for a night, and then there were the ones who seemed to linger on and on, like the smell of rotting banana peels.

Or fish.

A bell on the front door rang and announced my arrival. Esther and Juanita were already in the front lobby and had their papers with the numbers of the rooms they were to clean in their hands. They both said hi, all smiles, and I immediately knew that I had drawn the crap duties. Standing in the office, I felt like the stinky fish out of water. In her early 40s, Esther had one tooth knocked out and wrinkles that looked like knife cuts. And she was bone thin; I swear, it looked like skin and nothing else covered her bones. Then there was Juanita, who had to be in her 60s and was probably overweight by 50 pounds. She always got the lower suites to clean because she couldn't climb the stairs. Just the three of us cleaned rooms, and we rotated our days off. This week I had Sunday and Monday off—not nearly enough days.

Miles Mason, the owner of the suites, and the nastiest man I think I'd ever known, leered at me over his reading glasses. The hairs on my arms and the back of my neck stood at attention. He stared me up and down, and I wished I had on long pants and a huge baggy hoodie—but who could wear that kind of clothing on such a hot day? My short shorts and T-shirt clung to my body, because I was already sweating profusely. Was my clothing too tight? Could he see through my shirt? I crossed my arms over my chest.

"Blondie, here's your list of rooms" he said.

I hated how he pronounced the nickname he'd given me. He always raised his eyebrows and made a big deal of pronouncing the *bl-* in the word. It took every ounce of energy I had to walk forward and take the sheet from his grubby hands. They looked like meat hooks. Dirt festered under his nails. Sweat glistened on his forehead. His slicked-back black hair looked slimy and greasy and in desperate need of a shampoo. My stomach heaved. My skin tightened. Everything about him oozed evil. I took the list from his hands, barely holding it by the corners, and stared at it. Even the paper that he had just touched smelled of fried food, bacon in particular.

Of course, I had room 112.

On the bottom level, at the very back, 112 was a room occupied by "Mrs. Fish Face." We housekeepers had nicknamed her that. She'd been here for weeks—she didn't seem to want to leave—and cooked fish every single day. Without saying a word, I headed outside into the heat.

We all retrieved our cleaning carts from the storage room outside and filled them with towels, little soaps, and cleaning supplies.

"I'm not sure I'll make 'er today," said Juanita, wiping her face with one of the clean towels. I so hoped she wasn't going to fold it back up and put it in one of the rooms. Sweat dripped off her double chin like a pouring fountain. Or like the tap last night. My stomach lurched again. I had to forget about the tap. Natalie had left it on. End of story.

"You're a young thing." She squinted until her eyes were slits surrounded by puffy fat. "You should be a kind little girl and offer to do the rooms for an ole lady like me who needs money 'cause her husband left her high and dry without a red cent."

"Never yah mind," snapped Esther. "Get a move on." Esther waved her hand in my direction. "She got Mrs. Fish Face. That's like cleaning ten rooms in one."

"Ladies," sang Miles from the front door, "rooms need to be cleaned today, not tomorrow." Then he raised his eyebrows. "Blondie, I forgot to tell you, I like those shorts." He winked at me.

If there had been any food in my stomach I would have thrown it up all over the ground. Both Esther and Juanita looked at me. Then Esther whispered, "You better watch your ass, pretty little girl. 'Cause he wants it. And he's been known to take what's not his."

I sucked in a deep breath and pushed my cart forward. I felt really, really sick. *I need the money, I need the money.* I repeated the words over and over in my head.

As I unlocked the door to my first room, the man's voice spoke to me. *Gut feelings are important. It's called following your intuition.* His voice was soft and gentle, and it calmed me down, but I still had no idea who he was. Lately, he hadn't been around much, because I'd been way too occupied. But now he'd come to me twice in less than 24 hours.

Sometimes I didn't understand what he wanted to tell me, but today I understood exactly what he was saying. Miles Mason made me sick, and I needed to never, ever be alone in a room with him.

It's your own fault he leers at you. Look what you're wearing.

I knocked on the door of the first room on my list, and when no one answered or snapped at me to come back later or get lost, I opened it. When I walked in, I let out a good round of expletives under my breath. Some people were such slobs. Chinese takeout containers, potato chip bags, and cigarette-filled soda cans lay scattered all over the furniture and floor, and wet towels were draped over chairs and lying in clumps on the floor. No use procrastinating. I snapped on my rubber gloves and got to work stripping the bed, throwing out garbage, scrubbing the toilet, and vacuuming up chips and pretzels. As I yanked the vacuum across the carpet, I kept saying, "I need a new job. I need a new job."

When I was finished, I put the little soap in the bathroom and took a quick look around. Satisfied that Miles wouldn't scream at me for missing something, I stepped outside. The hot air blasted me, and I had a hard time even breathing. I picked up my paper and crossed off the room I was just in. I wiped the sweat off my face and started to push my cart.

Suddenly, everything started spinning. I held on hard to the handle of my cart and stared straight ahead. I knew enough to just let it go and not fight it. Since I was little, I had had visions. Last year, I had finally figured out that if I stopped fighting them and really focused on what came to me, I could help people.

My mind twirled and spun, then stopped, and I saw white. A blank piece of paper. I breathed in and out. In and out. I saw . . . the words *liver and onions*. Juanita's chubby face floated into the picture; she was talking to a little boy. Everything was pretty grainy, but the child looked to be around four, maybe five.

The picture dissolved, and I was once again standing in the oppressive heat, gripping the handle of my cart. That made no sense. Was I supposed to warn Juanita about eating liver and onions? So gross. Grandma Russell liked to order liver and onions at our favorite family restaurant, which was just outside Ottawa, near their home in Maynard. Every time it arrived at the table, I excused myself and went to the bathroom just for a little breather. When I returned I just tried to ignore the smell by not looking at her plate. But Grandma loved it, just like a lot of old people did.

I wiped my face with my arm and started pushing my cart in the direction of the next room I had to clean—Mrs. Fish Face's room. I groaned. Suddenly, I felt eyes boring into me. I turned, and Miles was staring at my backside.

"The woman in one-twelve says she needs her dishes done," he said. Then he gave me a smile that made me take a step back. I desperately wanted to run away, yelling, "I quit."

Money. I need money.

I knocked on the door to room 112. The smell of cooked fish seeped through it, and I put my hand to my face, covering my nose and mouth. When no one answered, I sucked in a deep breath, put my key in the lock, and flung the door open. If I was going to do this, I just had to do it.

I propped the front door of the room open to give me some air, albeit stiflingly hot air. I knew if I wanted to get this room clean without throwing up, I would have to work like a maniac, fast and furious. First I scrubbed the dishes with so much dish soap the bubbles spilled over the edge of the sink. I kept squirting the bottle to add more to get rid of the smell. Every few minutes, I would run to the door and stick my head out just to get any kind of fresh air.

Finally, I had the dishes done and kitchen cleaned, which made the entire room smell a little better, not so much like fried fish. I leaned against the refrigerator for a second. How could one person use so many dishes in just one day? Yesterday Esther had this room, so she'd probably pretended that she had forgotten about them.

When the room was completely finished, I looked at my watch. This room alone had taken me an hour. Usually I could get a room done in 30 minutes, but this one had pushed my limits, so I was going to have to work later than usual. I exhaled, loudly, knowing that tomorrow the room would stink again, but then I smiled, because it was my day off.

I stepped outside and was blinded by the sun, which had by now, mid-morning, burned off the haze. I was about to move to my next room when I saw Juanita and Esther across the courtyard standing by the big metal ashtray. Esther waved to me. Five minutes was all I could manage.

"So?" Esther raised her eyebrows up and down when I approached. "How was Mrs. Fish Face's room?"

"Gross," I replied. I shoved my hands in the back pockets of my shorts and tried not to watch them smoke. I was trying to quit, and it was so much harder than I'd thought it would be. Right now, I desperately wanted a cigarette.

"Mrs. Fish Face needs to move on," said Esther. "Who the hell can eat fish every fuckin' night?"

Juanita's breath was coming out in rasps, and she wiped the sweat off her face, over and over. Esther sucked on her cigarette. I didn't want to look like I was staring at Juanita, so I snuck a glance, immediately noticing how yellow the whites of her eyes looked and her skin, too. I felt a sharp jab to the side of my body. Something was wrong with her.

"Juanita, you feeling okay?" I asked.

"I'm old," she wheezed, stubbing out her cigarette. "I never feel okay. But my grandson is comin' today for a visit. He makes life worth living." She waved her hand in front of her face, then she coughed and spit something into her handkerchief.

I turned my head and tried not to gag.

"How many grandkids yah got again?" Esther blew out smoke rings, totally ignoring Juanita's gross coughing fit and her chatter about her health woes.

"Jerrod's my one and only. And his mama said she ain't having no more." Juanita coughed again.

I tapped my fingers on my thighs, shifted my stance, and tried to listen. I didn't really know much about either of these women. Was the little boy in my vision her grandson? Probably. Why had I seen liver and onions and her grandson?

After a few more minutes, I said, "I'm behind. I got to go."

"Yeah, break is over, I guess." Juanita coughed one more time, then waddled toward her cart. As I watched her, I again felt the sharp, knifelike jab to my side. This time I almost doubled over. Then, as soon as it had arrived, it left and I felt fine. I started to head back to my cart, but I couldn't help turning around to stare at Juanita. Her yellow skin shone in the powerful sun that had fought through the haze and won.

Yes, I was behind in my work, but I knew I had to help her. She didn't look well at all.

I walked back to Juanita. "Let me do some of your rooms so you can spend more time with your grandson."

She pinched my cheeks. "I knew you was some kind of angel."

We hope you enjoyed this Hay House Visions book.
If you'd like to receive our online catalog featuring additional
information on Hay House books and products, or if
you'd like to find out more about the
Hay Foundation, please contact:

VISIONS

Hay House, Inc., P.O. Box 5100, Carlsbad, CA 92018-5100
(760) 431-7695 or (800) 654-5126
(760) 431-6948 (fax) or (800) 650-5115 (fax)
www.hayhouse.com® • **www.hayfoundation.org**

❖ ❖ ❖

Published and distributed in Australia by: Hay House Australia Pty.
Ltd., 18/36 Ralph St., Alexandria NSW 2015 • *Phone:* 612-9669-4299
Fax: 612-9669-4144 • www.hayhouse.com.au

Published and distributed in the United Kingdom by: Hay House UK,
Ltd., 292B Kensal Rd., London W10 5BE • *Phone:* 44-20-8962-1230
Fax: 44-20-8962-1239 • www.hayhouse.co.uk

Published and distributed in the Republic of South Africa by: Hay
House SA (Pty), Ltd., P.O. Box 990, Witkoppen 2068
Phone/Fax: 27-11-467-8904 • www.hayhouse.co.za

Published in India by: Hay House Publishers India, Muskaan Complex,
Plot No. 3, B-2, Vasant Kunj, New Delhi 110 070
Phone: 91-11-4176-1620 • *Fax:* 91-11-4176-1630 • www.hayhouse.co.in

Distributed in Canada by: Raincoast, 9050 Shaughnessy St.,
Vancouver, B.C. V6P 6E5
Phone: (604) 323-7100 • *Fax:* (604) 323-2600 • www.raincoast.com

❖ ❖ ❖

<u>**Take Your Soul on a Vacation**</u>

Visit **www.HealYourLife.com®**
to regroup, recharge, and reconnect with your own magnificence.
Featuring blogs, mind-body-spirit news, and life-changing wisdom
from Louise Hay and friends.

Visit **www.HealYourLife.com** today!